Reviews of
SELDOM AS THEY SEEM

"Richard Alan Hall reminds me a great deal of Richard Hooker, the author of M*A*S*H. How interesting that they both were in the medical professions. How interesting that they both found ways to bring humor and love to some of life's most serious challenges. **Seldom As They Seem** will have you laughing out loud and, a chapter later, will bring tears to your eyes. Both **Remarkable** and **Seldom As They Seem** are winners. They help us to find the best in ourselves in beautifully profound ways."

— *Pat Mazor, Author*
Lubbock, Texas

"**Seldom As They Seem** kept me so intrigued with the characters and wanting to know more about them and what was about to happen next! It is a real page turner. Richard writes with great detail and sometimes when I did need to put the book down, I would nearly feel like I was walking away from something really happening, almost like I was part of the story."

— *Amy J. Thoreson,*
Author, Cedar, Michigan

"Once again, love triumphs over hate in this eagerly anticipated addition to Richard Alan Hall's Big Bay series. Nothing is as it seems when the 'usual suspects' are exposed to threats, kidnapping, murder and state secrets. A fast-paced thriller with lots of twists and turns, **Seldom As They Seem** keeps us guessing about all final outcomes but one: true friends are always faithful."

— *Jim Rink,*
Editor of American Wine Society Journal

"If you liked **Remarkable** and enjoyed getting to know the inhabitants of Big Bay and the frequenters of Poor Joe's Bar...you are going to love **Seldom As They Seem.** I can't think of a more fitting title for the sequel to Richard Alan Hall's first novel. Just when you think you have the story put together he gives you an unexpected twist. These twists and turns take you through the highs and lows of life in Big Bay and beyond. With the detail given, you feel as though you are right there with Stanley, his friends AND enemies. Each chapter thickens the plot and the last chapter leaves you asking, 'What could possibly happen next?' I cannot wait to see where Captain O'Malley takes us in the third book!"

— *Heather Fortin,*
MidMichigan Innovation Center

"It's with pleasure that I recommend **Seldom As They Seem**, the new novel by Richard Alan Hall! Appreciators of Key West, and its rich mystique and historic locales; from Mallory Square to the Southernmost Point to the Truman White House, will be transported into a world of crime, intrigue and romance. And then, from Cayo Coco to Big Bay, the story twists and turns, guided by the able pen of Mr. Hall. Special agents? Got 'em. Political dictators? Yes. Love? Check.

"**Seldom as They Seem**, will inspire you to root for characters like Doug, Miriam and James...oh, and Fidel Castro. Who?! Why? You'll have to read it yourself in **Seldom As They Seem**. "

— *Colleen Janson Wares,*
Talk Show Host

Seldom As They Seem

second in the **Big Bay Series**

Richard Alan Hall

Richard Alan Hall

rahBOOKs
keep it under your hat publisher

Printed in the United States of America

To contact the author, email: rahall49684@gmail.com

Visit the author's Facebook page at: Richard Alan Hall-Author

To order additional copies, call
Big Bay world headquarters @ 800-587-2147

rahBOOKs
keep it under your hat publisher

"The truth is seldom accurate."

— *Christal Wilcox Frost*

"When every dream seems broken, our Eternal Daddy reaches really close and says, 'Trust Me, things are seldom as they seem.'"

— Richard Alan Hall

To Debra Jean Hall, who inspires me every day.

Acknowledgements

Thank you to artist Janet Mortensen-Chown for creating **Seldom As They Seem**'s cover.

Thank you to my editor Lisa Mottola Hudon. She did the hard work.

Thank you to Jill Beauchamp for her invaluable assistance. She made this a better book.

Most of all, I thank my wife, Debra Jean Hall. She inspires me.

And thanks always to our Eternal Daddy.

Table of Contents

Seldom As They Seem
PROLOGUE

Two scenes from **REMARKABLE** stick in my mind as I begin this next adventure: the first is when Timothy and Stanley are saying goodbye while they sit in Poor Joe's bar, facing the Goebel mirror behind the counter. Timothy says, "I'm going to miss the guys that live here Stanley. I'll sure miss Doug, Morris, Jonathon and Wendell, Pete and Wayne. They've experienced some absolute horror in their lives and not a one of them will ever whine about it."

"The guys love you, Timothy. They know you understand…you've been there too…. Each one for very personal reasons needed the comfort of this old building and each other. They are amazing human beings," Stanley said with admiration in his voice. "They made their choices and don't judge others for theirs."

The second scene is in the final chapter of **REMARKABLE**. Stanley and Danielle were walking on the beach towards their hotel on Cayo Coco, Cuba. While watching the sunset, they had met Dr. A.W. Blue who had the reputation of a man of low morals in his hometown of Big Bay. A conversation on the beach with the doctor revealed another side to the popular story. As Stanley and Danielle enter the hotel lobby, Danielle turned to Stanley and said, "Isn't it something; things are seldom as they seem."

Chapter One

Face Down In the Dirt

In the glow of a clear 40-watt incandescent bulb, Wendell made several attempts at inserting a skeleton key into the rusty lock, finally locking the back door to Poor Joe's. Muttering to himself about the 'damn lock,' he turned towards the parking lot. A dark complexioned man with high cheekbones and sneering lips struck him on the forehead above the right eye with a rusty metal pipe. Bright blood spurted through the soft light and splattered on the white clapboard exterior of the old bar. Wendell slumped, unconscious, facedown in the dirt. Three men dressed in dark Armani suits stood over him for a few seconds, discussing something in Spanish. The men picked up the limp veteran and tossed him in the trunk of a black Lincoln Continental. They drove slowly down Union Street and turned left on Wayne Street, traveling up the hill, past the big elm tree and Benjamin's Seafood Restaurant, and towards a cabin deep in the woods.

Doug and his German Shepherd named Malcolm exited the bar using the front door at sunrise the following morning, Doug to smoke a cigar, while Malcolm relieved himself. Malcolm sprinted towards his favorite peeing locations behind the building. Doug lit a cigar and followed. They were the first to see the arc of blood sprayed on the back wall.

A prickling sensation spread over his body, and Doug froze for several seconds. He reached into his jacket pocket and tightly grasped a Smith and Wesson Thirty-Eight Special. Slowly, he surveyed the parking lot through adrenaline dilated pupils. Malcolm ran back and forth, sniffing in the tall dead grass on either side of the back door, and then picked up a set of keys, holding them in his mouth by a short leather strap.

Oh shit... it's Wendell! Doug thought. He reached down and took the keys from Malcolm.

Dora had arrived to start cooking breakfast while Doug was walking Malcolm. The aroma of coffee coming from the old Bodum coffee maker had the bar smelling sweet. Doug, followed by Malcolm, charged through the front door and stopped. Dora looked up from the large frying pan she had just filled with western hash browns and studied Doug's face, his jaw clinched and a burning in his eyes she had not seen since the night the "HELL'S SPAWN" biker gang from New York City had crashed Norma's retirement party.

"What's wrong Doug?" she queried with a hint of alarm in her voice.

Doug stared back at her. Dora saw tears appear in his brown eyes.

"They got Wendell last night when he was closing. Somebody got Wendell."

Dora had never seen even a hint of tears in this battle-hardened man's eyes.

"What...who?!" she asked.

"I don't know." And he held up the set of keys that Malcolm had retrieved.

"There's blood all over the back wall and on the ground by the back door. Dora I'm going to find them and I'm going to kill the bastards!" Doug said with certainty.

Dora watched Doug climb the stairs leading to the apartments above the bar to wake up Wayne, Morris, Pete, Ralph, and the new fellow, Ric. Her hands trembled as she reached under the counter for their coffee mugs.

Dora carried a tray with six mugs of black coffee to the southwest corner table. The men huddled around, staring at the bloody keys.

A ripping grief and anger built around the table. The unshaven men with matted hair stared at the keys and each other. This shock, compounded by the recent loss of their closest friend, Timothy, to Nashville, and the absence of Stanley who was on his honeymoon in Key West, seemed overwhelming.

"We need to call the cops, I guess," Ralph stated.

"I suppose, but that new guy is no Charlie Johnson," Pete commented, referring to the beloved Big Bay Chief of Police who had been shot to death by a junkie named Ronnie.

"I'll call Chief Strait," Dora volunteered from the kitchen area. "You guys need to call Timothy."

Chapter Two

Teenage Pheromones

The rank of "The Usual Suspects," was back to six. The hole created when Jonathon left for the west coast with Rose was now filled by Ric, who rented Jonathon's old room upstairs in Poor Joe's Bar.

He had just shown up on a hot, dusty summer afternoon, riding a green military issue 1945 Harley with a suicide clutch. After complimenting Dora for her clam chowder, and drinking several Schlitz beers with Wendell, Pete, and Ralph until after midnight, he was invited to "move in." Since he had no other plans, he did.

The memory of his childhood is a blur of hard work without much fun on his father's truck farm in Avon, Ohio. Growing up, he spent many hours in the very same fields his great-grandfather, the son of a Civil War Veteran, worked, hoeing potatoes and root vegetables. In the evenings after chores were completed, he would take a kerosene lantern to his favorite place in the woods under a giant sycamore tree, next to French Creek, and escape with novels. He especially enjoyed reading Ernest Hemingway and John Steinbeck. *The Old Man and the Sea* was his favorite, followed by *Cannery Row*.

Age 14 was his favorite year. His father purchased a John Deere LA tractor to cultivate the row crops. He received a 4/10 shotgun for his birthday. At the end of that summer, after paying for his school clothes and a new pair of shoes, he purchased a Schwinn bike.

Ric fell in love with a 16-year-old Baptist girl at age 18. His strict Catholic parents forbade the relationship, as did her parents who believed Catholicism to be an evil cult. During supper one evening, her mother chastised with disgust, in front of her two younger sisters, "What are you thinking, taking up with a Catholic boy?"

They met under his favorite reading tree late one night, and clung together, trembling. In the light of the old kerosene lantern, they made love for the first time, breathing rapidly and exploring each other with anticipation. Early the next morning, Ric left the farmhouse, patted his dog Rainey on the head, and walked through the woods until he hit Stoney Ridge Road. He walked several blocks north to St. Mary of the Immaculate Conception Church, and entered through a side door, which he knew would be unlocked. In the dark, he lit a candle at the side altar, and gazed up at the large gothic statue of Jesus holding a child. Ric prayed for forgiveness, and for a blessing.

Then Ric walked out of the church. In front of Buck Hardware Store, he climbed up the metal steps into a Greyhound bus headed for Columbus. That afternoon he walked without hesitation through the front door of the Marine recruiting center. A week later Ric was a United States Marine.

A strong, athletic farm boy without any quit in him, Ric did well in basic training. He especially excelled at the firing range, scoring even higher than his instructors, and he was singled out for sniper training.

The first Gulf War, later to be named Desert Storm, was looming. The United States and England headed the development of a multinational military force. Ric was assigned to a British Special Forces Unit, and a Special Ops Advance Unit with the job of disabling Scud missile launchers before the invasion.

At 1000 yards with his Remington M40 sniper rifle, Ric could hit a basketball. His special ops unit had infiltrated Baghdad, and from high-rise windows or rooftops, Ric picked off Republican Guard troops who were operating the motorized Scud launchers. One by one, he would see their heads explode in his scope.

Lying in the dust on his belly, Ric peered down from the roof of a

Baghdad office building with the hot sun at his back. Methodically, he adjusted the riflescope on an officer shouting at soldiers one block away. There were children running around the launch vehicle looking up at the poised missile. Ric gently squeezed the trigger at the same instant the officer lurched forward, shaking his fist at the troops. Through his scope, Ric watched the right side of a teenage girl's forehead blow away, with pieces of her skull and bloody brains splattered on the sand colored door of the launch vehicle.

Now every night Ric is awakened by the nightmare of seeing that young girl's head explode in slow motion and the shower of red. Every night he turns the light on and reads a few chapters of something by Hemingway, and wonders what the Baptist girl is doing.

With the light still on, each night he closes his eyes and remembers the wonder of that last evening with Michelle, and how he trembled. When she unbuttoned his shirt, it had been hard to breathe, and when she pushed him down on the patchwork quilt his grandmother had made for him, his heart pounded harder than when the bull had chased him in the stockyard. The warmth of her body floods his mind, the gentle fragrance of her perfume, and the look in her beautiful blue eyes when she looked down at him. Then Ric falls asleep for the remainder of the night, with the light on.

"I believe if I felt that way, I would seek that lady out, young man," Wendell commented to Ric late one night, munching on free salty popcorn, drinking Wild Turkey on the rocks, and talking about love. "Yes, sir, I would look her up."

"I love her too much," Ric replied, "to burden her with my messed-up self."

Chapter Three

The New Chief

"**I** think we are looking for a late 80's Lincoln Continental or Cadillac Fleetwood," Chief of Police Larry Strait commented to a young patrolman and the assembled inhabitants from Poor Joe's. Carefully, he measured the depth and width of tire tracks in the parking lot mud, and consulted a book lying on the ground.

Lawrence (Larry) Strait had been hired to be the Chief of Police by the Big Bay city council three months after the murder of Chief Charley Johnson in front of Lisa's Meat Market by the junkie, Ronnie.

A short-tempered man with an adolescent's sense of adventure, Larry had received numerous lessons in humility while serving in Vietnam under an Air Force Brigadier General who liked him. On one occasion after partying with several local village girls who accidently slept over, the Brigadier General offered to reduce Captain Strait to 2nd Lieutenant. When the Captain responded by saying, "You're just mad cuz you didn't get an invite," the Brigadier General did just that, for one week, and assigned him to drive the General's Jeep around the Da Nang air base, and to keep the Jeep polished to a high sheen at all times. When his rank was reinstated, Larry was a well-behaved Captain for the rest of the war, for the most part.

Following the war, Larry Strait became a New York City Police Officer. He eventually worked his way up to Deputy Inspector before being hired as Chief of Police for Big Bay. His wife Dawn had grown up in the small town of Ontonagon in the upper peninsula of Michigan and had attended Northern Michigan University in Marquette where she majored in psychology. She was thrilled to be leaving The Big Apple after fifteen years.

"Yeah…right," sneered Pete.

"Seriously, Pete, these are 205/70-15 tires on a heavy car," Chief Strait muttered.

"And that's the tire size used by Cadillac and Lincoln in the late 80's," he continued.

The Chief stood up with mud on both knees, handing the open book to Pete.

"I'll be damned. Look, fellas, the Chief is right!" Pete exclaimed, and there was no longer sarcasm in his voice.

Doug sat on the back steps of Poor Joe's watching, with Malcolm at his side looking up at him. After Chief Strait shared his findings, Doug entered the bar through the back door and walked down the creaky hallway past the men's room to the pay telephone.

"Timothy, this is Doug. I'm sorry to bother you…" and with a hesitant voice choking, he continued, "Wendell is missing. Someone attacked him by the back door after he closed." Doug could say no more.

"When?" Timothy demanded.

"Last night. Malcolm and I found blood splattered all over the back wall and on the ground by the back door. And Malcolm found bloody keys in the grass."

"Who the hell is Malcolm?"

"My dog; got him after you sold the bar and moved."

Doug could hear Timothy taking deep breaths.

"The new Chief of Police measured the tire tracks and says they took him away in a Continental or Fleetwood."

"Doug, get to the airport. Make sure there is no Lear jet at the hangar."

"Why?"

"Doug, listen to me very closely. Remember when Dr. Nazar and his three brothers were in town raising all sorts of hell, demanding that Stanley be fired after that incident in the ER?"

"Will remember those scumbags till my dying day."

"Well…when my friend Vincent sent five men from St. Paul, Wendell went with them to Nazar's condo and somehow convinced the Egyptians to leave town immediately. I never wanted to know the details. I'm afraid they may be back."

"Shit!"

"I'll talk to Carla and fly up tomorrow. Let me know if you hear anything."

"I will."

Timothy sat in his living room, stunned. The Lieutenant who had saved his life by catching a grenade with his bare hand during the evacuation of the Embassy in Saigon was missing and perhaps dead. The same heavy feelings that he experienced after losing Thi Kim in Saigon, and after Chief of Police Johnson's death, pressed against his soul. Timothy felt a nauseous fear in his stomach for his friend, and he felt like crying. He picked up the telephone and asked the information operator for the number to The Pier House Resort in Key West.

Chapter Four
Can't Blame A Girl For Asking

"You can't blame a girl for asking," Karen said with a smile. Stanley and Danielle had driven back up A1A to Fisherman's Hospital in Marathon to thank the Director of Nursing in person for her job offer.

"It's just that we love living in Big Bay, Karen; otherwise we'd be here in a heartbeat," Danielle said.

"It would be exciting working here," Stanley chimed in, "and who knows, it could happen someday, but right now we need to be in Big Bay."

"Even when she was so sick with that damn ovarian cancer and in your Hospice Unit, our friend Darleen actually tried to convince me to move up there; that's how much she liked it," Karen said.

Karen reached over and picked up Danielle's left hand.

"You guys get married?" she continued, looking at the gold band studded with three diamonds on Danielle's ring finger. "I don't remember seeing this; it's beautiful!"

"Yes, we're married!" Danielle exclaimed. Stanley and Danielle excitedly told the Director of Nursing the story of traveling to Cayo Coco, Cuba with Captain Quinn O'Malley, and later having the captain marry them while in international waters.

"You met Quinn, huh? He is quite a man," Karen said with a big smile on her face. "Your story does not surprise me in the slightest. I'll bet you met him in the Green Parrot."

"Exactly right!" Stanley exclaimed. "You must know him well."

"One could say that," Karen said with a wink. "Thank you for coming back and telling me in person. I hope someday you'll change your minds. You guys have my best wishes…all three of you."

She patted Danielle's swollen belly.

* * *

The sun had set by the time Stanley and Danielle arrived back at The Pier House on the north end of Key West's Duval Street.

A smiling desk clerk by the name of Holly greeted them.

"Good evening, Mr. and Mrs. McMillen. I have a note for you." She handed them a small envelope with a Pier House seal on the back.

"I wonder how long it will take me to get used to hearing Mrs. McMillen," Danielle laughed. "What's in the note?"

"It's a telephone number for Timothy. He wants me to call him ASAP."

Stanley picked up the bedside phone and dialed the number.

"Timothy speaking."

"Hi, Timothy, this is Stan; what's up?"

"Doug called me. Wendell is missing; they found blood all over by the back door and his bloody keys in the grass. God damnit, Stan, we've gotta do something, buddy. We gotta find him." And his voice choked.

Danielle stood by the sliding glass doors that led to the balcony and watched her husband's complexion turn ashen.

"We'll be home as soon as Danielle can change our tickets. What the hell's going on?"

"I think the Egyptians are back, evening up the score, Stan. That's my guess."

"Oh shit. Doug is going to be on a vendetta. Wendell is his best friend."

"I know. See you soon my friend."

Stanley put the phone down and looked up at Danielle.

"What's happened?" she asked, and there was fear in her trembling voice.

"Wendell's been abducted. Someone attacked him behind Poor Joe's. Doug called Timothy; said there's blood all over the place. Oh man, this is awful. Love that man, honey. He's always been there for his friends-- always."

"I'll change our tickets in the morning. That story is legend... how you and Wendell saved a nurse's life," Danielle continued, "when she was attacked by a drunk in the old Coronary Care Unit."

"I hope we can help him," Stanley whispered. He stared through the sliding glass doors at the swimming pool. Images swirled through his mind, angered and bewildered.

Danielle held him tightly. He could feel their baby kicking between them.

Chapter Five
It's Who You Know

"**I** 'm half inclined to go to divinity school. Marrying you two was fun," Captain Quinn O'Malley said with a smile. A beautiful young bartender handed him a fresh tall-pour of Mount Gay Rum, with a wink.

The three friends sat at the bistro table next to the Southard Street entrance to the Green Parrot. It was the same table where the three had met for the first time almost a month earlier.

"That would go well with your law degree from Habana University," Danielle chuckled.

"You guys heard that rumor, huh?"

"Yup, you and Fidel Castro, best buds in college, is the word over at Schooner Wharf," Stanley added.

"There's more to Fidel than the world thinks it knows," Captain O'Malley said. He smiled and winked at Danielle.

"Probably true for most of us, Quinn," Danielle added.

Stanley took a long drink from his tall glass of Mount Gay, cleared his throat and said, "We have to leave early, first flight in the morning."

"I thought you guys were here all month."

"We have an emergency, Captain," Danielle replied.

Stanley took a deep breath. He wasn't sure if he could talk without breaking down. "A very good friend of ours has been abducted, Quinn. He was closing Poor Joe's Bar and somebody kidnapped him. The guys found blood all over the back entrance. We've got to go home and see if we can help. He's a good friend." His voice refused to continue, briefly.

"Any speculations?"

"A few years ago there was a confrontation with an Egyptian doctor and his brothers. They left in a hurry one night on their Lear jet. My buddy Timothy told me last evening that Wendell was instrumental in their departure, and thinks they may be back to settle the score. He did that for me; it was me they wanted fired."

Danielle now had tears in her eyes.

"They won't stop with Wendell; they'll be after you and Timothy too, Stan."

Stanley's head slumped a little. He had hoped this fact would not occur to his wife.

Captain Quinn O'Malley sat facing his friends, the couple who had trusted him, and to his great surprise and delight, had asked him to marry them. He stared at them over his hands, fingers interlocked and folded, snapping his front tooth using his thumbnails.

"I can help," he said quietly. "I can help here. You say they fly around in a Lear?"

"That's what they were using when they flew from Egypt for their last visit," Stanley said with a question on his face.

"I have acquaintances in high places. I'm going to help you with this problem Stanley. This is just between us friends, understand?"

"Yes, Captain," Stanley and Danielle, replied in unison.

"And you guys pick up the tab," the captain grinned, shook Stanley's hand, hugged Danielle tightly, patted her on the butt, and left the bar, heading south.

The flight from Key West to Atlanta, and then home was uneventful, except for the squeezing nausea in Stanley's stomach. Danielle held his hand the entire way.

Timothy and Chief Strait were sitting on bar stools facing The Usual Suspects when Stanley walked in the front door of Poor Joe's. Malcolm growled; he had not met Stanley, and Doug patted his dog on the head.

"Hi Stan!" everyone said at once.

"Chief Strait was just telling us about a phone call he got from some guy. Said he was acquainted with our situation."

"Really!"

"As mysterious as it seems, somehow this fellow knew we have a problem here. I haven't called anyone," the chief stated with a shrug. "Asked him who he was, and he chuckled, said 'a friend.'"

"I noticed a Coast Guard Chopper flying a search pattern over the city and up on the bluffs last evening. Thought the boys were just practicing. Now I get this phone call stating there is a black Lincoln Continental parked in the woods next to a hunting cabin ten miles west of Benjamin's Fish House. And that's not all; this fella told me that the FAA has a record of a Lear jet landing at Boston's Logan International five days ago... flew from Benito Juarez International in Mexico City. He gave me a number to call if I needed help."

Shivers went up and down Stanley's spine, and he tried to look nonplused.

Doug stood up from the table. "That's my best friend in that cabin." He walked up the stairs to get his twelve gauge.

"I'll call the State Police for help," continued Chief Strait, "but time is of the essence. We have one problem right up front; the helicopter pilot reported the cabin sits in an opening with at least a hundred yard clearing in all directions."

"That's not far at all," came a voice from the southwest table where Ric was sitting alone. "Hundred yards is nothing if I had my M40."

Chief Strait stared at Ric for several seconds before saying, "I heard all about your skills in Iraq, young man; you made quite a reputation for yourself. Thank you for your service."

"Thank you, Chief."

The chief continued, "There is an old saying we had in the Air Force. 'There is no substitute for flight time.' There are men in this room who have battle tested flight time that would be invaluable in this situation we are about to face. If any of you would like to help, I will swear you in as auxiliary police right now. And Ric, I have a Remington M40 in the gun safe at the office."

Doug stood up, holding his twelve gauge. Timothy jumped off the bar stool and stood next to Doug. Ric stood up from the southwest table and walked over, joining them.

"Chief, I want an ambulance out there; I'm going to be ready in that ambulance when you guys rescue Wendell."

"Good idea, Stan."

Chapter Six
Operation Salamander

Hardwood smoke coming from the cabin's fieldstone chimney smelled sweet, like maple cured bacon frying, in the freezing night air. The darkness around the cabin was broken by sodium lights commonly used on farms, hanging on poles at the entrance to the cabin and next to the outhouse thirty yards from the cabin.

Hiding behind trees in the woods surrounding the cabin were law enforcement officers, including the State Police, Big Bay Police officers, as well as the newly sworn-in police auxiliary.

"I'm not sure having these civilians here is such a good idea, Chief," the State Police Lieutenant commented to Chief Strait.

Chief Strait stopped walking. "Two things, young man: first, if I hadn't asked for their help, they would have already been here; second, neither you nor I have anyone working for us with the skills these men have. You'll see, young fella."

Chief Strait and the State Police Lieutenant joined Timothy, Doug and Ric, standing in the shadow of a large maple tree, staring at the cabin.

"I'm not sure we can get close without being detected," the Lieutenant said, peering through night-vision binoculars at the cabin.

"In another hour I can do it," Timothy replied calmly. "I can do it as soon as that fireplace smoke settles at ground level and mixes with the night fog. I'll crawl under it, right to the cabin and have a look through that window."

About 1 a.m. the State Police Lieutenant put his portable radio to his mouth and said, "Stay alert; here we go."

Timothy, dressed in camouflage from head to toe, climbed over a fallen beech tree and slowly moved towards the cabin. His face had black greasy makeup covering it. Timothy crawled towards the cabin under the hanging fog and smoke, through the tall thistles and ferns, moving like a salamander.

"Must have been in Special Forces," the State Police Lieutenant muttered.

"Yup, Vietnam. You just be happy he's on our side, Lieutenant," Chief Strait replied.

Doug fidgeted with his shotgun and watched from behind the trees.

Ric positioned himself against a log and peered through a night scope into the smoky fog, taking aim at the cabin door.

Timothy crawled very slowly without stopping. In his right hand was Doug's Thirty-Eight Special. In a leg pocket was a single stun grenade. His grease-covered face now had dead leaves sticking to it. In the shadows, his face hit a groundhog mound. He smiled.

Within moments he was at the cabin, next to the lone window. He slowly stood up and looked through the filthy glass and then turned in the direction of Doug and gave a thumbs up. He held up three fingers.

Budweiser Beer bottles littered the wooden floor. A small Formica kitchen table held broasted chicken containers and cold cereal boxes. Bunk beds were pushed against the opposite wall. A man, lying in the bottom bunk, propped up with pillows, watched as his cohorts interrogated Wendell. He had high cheekbones and thin lips that sneered when he spoke.

"Maybe we just push you out of a helicopter...one hundred feet," the man with sneering lips said from the bottom bunk. His black eyes reminded Wendell of a snake.

Wendell sat on an old wooden chair in the middle of the room. Duct tape held his arms tightly to his sides and was wrapped around him, keeping him secured in the chair.

Timothy took a deep breath, his fists clenched, and he felt the pulse pounding in his neck. His body tensed, and for a flash, both eyes filled with tears as he stared at the puddle of urine under the chair, mixed with coagulated blood. A three-inch gash above Wendell's right eye gaped open, showing exposed skull. Thin brownish-yellow exudate drained down over his right eye, which was swollen shut.

Two men with dark complexions were interrogating Wendell who had a forced grin on his bloody, swollen face.

As Timothy watched, the two men took turns screaming at Wendell while the other hit him in the face with a fist.

"WHERE IS TIMOTHY?" the shorter of the two screamed just inches from Wendell's face, and then he pulled back. The taller man hit him in the face again.

...And then young Wendell was with his family, walking past his Grandfather's casket, looking at the old man in repose. Wendell reached over the edge of the casket and touched the folded hands with his index finger; they felt cold.

SLAM! The tall man hit Wendell in the face again. The shorter man screamed just inches from Wendell's nose.

"WHERE IS TIMOTHY?!"

"Timothy...oh you mean Tiny Tim...he died. So did Timothy Bell...died in the seventh grade from leukemia."

The tall man hit him again, and then rubbed his hand with his other hand, and Wendell could feel a tooth loose in his mouth.

...And then Wendell was staring at his high school sweetheart. Janet Sue was lying in a casket, her youthful beauty ravaged by unexplained liver cancer. He was bent over the casket, almost in the casket with her, touching her face, sobbing uncontrollably.

Suddenly she was behind him in the cabin, wrapping her protective arms around his duct taped torso, singing a sweet song he had never heard before, just as she had done for Doug so many years ago in the Green Dragon's turret, although it was only a split instant ago in her dimension.

"Oh...you mean Timothy Leary...the LSD guy...you guys would have liked him I bet...sorry, he's dead too." Wendell spit a tooth at the shorter man.

The tall man uttered an epitaph in Spanish. He said something to the shorter man in Spanish about "taking a shit," and he walked out the cabin door, headed for the outhouse.

Doug froze in place behind a large maple tree.

Ric followed the tall man's head just above the layered fog in the crosshairs of his night scope.

When the tall man was twenty yards from the cabin, Timothy quietly slipped through the open door with the Thirty-Eight Special raised.

Ric fired the M40. Through the smoky-fog he saw the tall man's head jerk to the side and his forehead blew away into the dark night.

The sound of the rifle shot brought the man lying on the bottom bunk to his feet with a shotgun in his hands, and face to face with Timothy's revolver. Timothy shot him between his black snake-like eyes.

Doug was on a dead run towards the cabin, twenty yards ahead of the State Police and Big Bay Police, when the second shot rang out, and then a third. When he reached the cabin and charged through the door with his shotgun raised, he saw Timothy on his knees, arms wrapped around Wendell.

Bright blood spurted with each heartbeat through a hole just above the right elbow of Timothy's camouflage jacket. Timothy could feel the bone grind in his arm.

"I think we're even now," Wendell whispered. "Who are they? What the hell, Timothy; why're they looking for you?"

"Tell you later, buddy."

Two men wearing dark Armani suits were sprawled on the cabin floor among the beer bottles, each with a single wound between their eyes.

"Well, Doug!" Wendell exclaimed through his swollen lips. "Thanks for coming to my party. That was a little reckless, charging through the door like that, even for you."

"No worries Wendell, she had my back tonight."

"She's spent a little time with me too," Wendell replied through swollen lips caked with blood.

Doug cut the duct tape away with his Buck knife.

Both men knew without saying another word.

Chapter Seven

Triage

"**G**et up here now…two victims!" crackled the State Police Lieutenant's voice through the ambulance radio.

"10-4," replied the ambulance driver. The ambulance with Stanley and a paramedic by the name of Mike headed up the last little hill, bouncing down the two-track road towards the cabin.

Timothy was nearly unconscious, slumped on his left side, when Stanley reached him. Doug had cut the jacket sleeve open with his Buck knife, and Chief Strait was attempting to stop the pulsating spurts of bright blood by applying pressure over the hole. Timothy was conscious enough to recognize Stanley.

"Help me, Stan, this one feels bad…" the old soldier whispered, looking up at his friend. Stanley noticed that Timothy's pupils were beginning to dilate.

Stanley pushed on the flesh above the wound, trying to compress the brachial artery against the humerus bone, and felt the shattered bone crunch.

"I'm not going to let anything happen, buddy; you're going to be just fine, Timothy," Stanley said, staring directly into his friend's eyes. "I can stop this."

They positioned Timothy on his back, and elevated his feet on the wooden chair, which had held Wendell captive.

The paramedic started an IV in Timothy's left arm, and was infusing normal saline rapidly.

"Doug, tighten this tourniquet until the bleeding stops, and then loosen it when I say go," Stanley instructed. Quickly and gently, he probed the large exit wound made by a hollow point bullet, using a hemostat from the ambulance's instrument bag, feeling for the ruptured artery. After numerous attempts, the brachial artery was located and clamped shut, stopping the hemorrhage.

"Damn, you're good," exclaimed Wendell, who had pushed off all attempts at attention, and was on his knees next to Timothy's head, watching through his left eye as Stanley worked. And then bending down, placing his face next to Timothy's left ear, he muttered through his swollen lips, "Stanley stopped it, buddy; gonna be ok now. Us guys are really some kind of team." And looking up at the assembled crowd in the little cabin, he proclaimed, "Semper Fi!"

"Semper Fi!" shouted the assembled in response.

"Let's get Timothy to the hospital, guys, now," Stanley said, looking up from his kneeling position. He stood up, motioning to the paramedics to bring their stretcher closer.

Timothy peered up at his friend. Stanley's pants were saturated with blood from his knees to his ankles. Blood specs covered Stanley's face and his glasses. Both hands were covered with blood, and several fingers stuck together. Stanley looked down at Timothy and said, "Told you I wouldn't let you die."

Timothy admired his friend from the stretcher, "Love you, man... you look a sight!"

Seeing his best friend covered with fresh blood recently lost from his own body left Timothy with a feeling of complete, absolute gratitude beyond any feeling he had experienced. Ten minutes earlier Timothy was certain he had fought his last battle.

Stanley's hands began to shake, just a little.

Chapter Eight
Honduran Prostitute's Orphan

Raul Veracruz stared at his lieutenant in disbelief, as he sat behind his desk on the top floor of the Gran Hotel Ciudad located at the intersection of 16 de Septiembre and Plaza de La Constitucion. His once handsome face twisted with anger. A nearly full cup of con leche bounced to the floor when he slammed his fist repeatedly on his desk. The lieutenant's name: Cesar Veracruz, Raul's grandson.

Raul was born to a Honduran prostitute 58 years ago. He grew up in a Tegus orphanage. When he was 15, he ran away, eventually finding his way to Guatemala. One evening in Guatemala City, he was arrested for stealing a chicken from the meat market. The police tied his wrists with ropes and suspended him from the jail ceiling. They took turns beating him with bamboo whips until he was unconscious, and they left him hanging by his arms and turned the lights off.

About 3 a.m. the following morning, 40 men attacked the jail using automatic weapons and grenades. They were rebels attempting to free fellow freedom fighters. It took 5 minutes to kill the sleeping jail guards. The rebels cut Raul down, and carried him to their camp in the mountains.

For the next 12 years Raul fought alongside the Guatemalan rebels. He learned organization and discipline, and to be fearless. When the civil war ended, he moved to Mexico City, and soon became acquainted with the various drug lords and the human trafficking business.

He brought to Mexico City his top lieutenants from the rebel ranks, Mexicans and Cubans. Together they mapped out a business plan in human trafficking. He also brought his pregnant wife, Mariel.

Three months after moving to Mexico City with her husband, Mariel went into labor, six weeks prior to the anticipated delivery date. Raul drove wildly through the dark streets, side-swiping a taxi on the way to the hospital. He carried his bleeding wife into the Emergency Room waiting area filled with battered and cut people, many drunk. Standing in the crowd, terrified, as Mariel cried out with another contraction, Raul screamed in desperation. Ramming people in the way, an orderly pushed a filthy stretcher towards them. Raul gently placed his wife down as she curled in pain.

In a large room divided into partitions by curtains, a doctor attended Mariel. Raul watched, refusing to leave.

The doctor turned towards Raul after taking Mariel's blood pressure for a third time.

"Eclampsia, very bad," the doctor muttered.

Raul shuddered with confusion.

Mariel's body twisted with seizures. Suddenly a baby's black haired head appeared, and then his entire little body plopped into the doctor's hands, followed by gushing blood coming in waves.

The doctor placed the crying baby boy on his mother's chest. He pushed hard on Mariel's distended belly with his left hand as he reached into her uterus, trying to expel the placenta.

Blood continued to gush with each contraction. In desperation, the doctor began to pack the birth cannel with gauze, trying to stop the hemorrhage.

Mariel Veracruz died twenty-three minutes after giving birth to a little boy that she and her husband had decided to name Diego, if they had a son.

* * *

"My son has his mother's spirit in his soul," Raul commented to several guests as they watched the three-year-old Diego play with a new puppy.

"He is very gentle, like his mother," he added, watching the child stroke the pup's back as the puppy licked his face.

"I have provided for his safety," he said, nodding towards two young men sitting on either side of the front door. "He has a caring nanny, and these two young men are his drivers." The tallest young man, whose name was Matias, had high cheekbones. He spoke with a sneer. His companion, Roland Chanchez, claimed to be seventeen.

"My soul will die should anything happen to my son." Raul sighed.

* * *

"I will have nothing to do with the evil drugs," he said with determination one evening to his parish priest as they dined. "Drugs... they killed my mother!"

Raul believed that helping destitute people pursue dreams, and escape from the nightmares of the stinking ghettos was God's chosen plan for him. "Why should I care about the line in the sand we should not cross; I did not draw the line, and that land was once ours."

When the subject of prostitution would come up, Raul would simply shrug, and comment, "Who is unhappy? Not the ladies; I ask them. Not the men; I see their smiles. Not the police when they're paid. Not the judges when they're paid...just the hypocrites I think, and I do care about hypocrites."

The business of transporting people through the border checkpoints and then north became a sophisticated and well-oiled machine. Over the years, Raul had gained the loyalties of border guards with bribes or intimidation--usually both. A series of safe houses were set up along highway 35, in Oklahoma City, Wichita, Kansas City, and Des Moines while en route to St Paul, Minnesota. The workers and ladies would travel in passenger cars. Each carried legal appearing passports, letters of reference, and work visas. In St Paul, they would be assimilated into the population to work at restaurants, construction jobs, hotels, and farms and as ladies of the evening throughout the Midwest. A small percentage of their earnings would be collected each month, and funneled back down highway 35 to Mexico City.

The employers were happy; they had eager, hard workers. The Mexicans were happy; they were employed and making more money than they had ever fathomed.

The Italians were not happy.

Vincent Bonifacio had emigrated from Naples, Italy in 1967. He owned the wholesale franchise for the olive oil and European cheese imports for the Midwest United States, with headquarters in St Paul, Minnesota. He incidentally had interests in Nevada, which involved various drugs and prostitution. The "Mexican Invasion" irritated his good humor. Over the following two decades, as the number of workers from Mexico grew and impacted his concerns, Vincent instructed his lieutenants to subvert the Mexican cause by involving the illegal Mexicans with the drug business, and offers of great wealth.

In response, Raul sent his most trusted lieutenant, his son Diego, to St Paul, with instructions to govern over the Midwest business and prevent any involvement with the drug business.

Vincent Bonifacio ordered his operatives to plant heroin and cocaine in the trunk of Diego's car, under the spare tire. Then he called Detective Timothy Fife, with whom he had had a working relationship since the time Timothy saved his son from a burning Corvette. He advised Timothy of suspicious drug activity, and that Diego's Mercedes Benz likely had narcotics in the trunk, and that the car could be found in a parking lot just west of the 10th street and Roberts intersection.

About 1:30 a.m., Timothy and two patrolmen in a separate car approached the black Mercedes, dimly illuminated by street lamps. Both patrolmen had their pistols drawn.

Ten minutes later, Diego walked down the dark steps from an adjacent office building.

"You stop right there; let me see your hands!" Timothy demanded, placing his right hand on his holstered revolver.

"LET ME SEE YOUR HANDS!"

"DROP THE GUN!" screamed the patrolman now standing next to the driver's door of the black Mercedes.

Diego froze, and then his right arm moved slightly. The patrolman next to the Mercedes fired his pistol.

Diego's eyes opened wide with surprise; his entire body shivered slightly, and his mouth formed the word "why." Both empty hands grasped at the wound in the middle of his throat just above his Adam's apple. Then bright blood gushed from his nose and mouth. His knees crumpled, and Diego collapsed to the concrete.

The very last thing that either of the two patrolmen saw on this earth were the muzzle flashes from a Thomson machine gun.

Roland Chanchez launched through the office building door and walked rapidly down the steps with the Thompson blazing, dropped the empty clip next to his friend's crumpled body, and with a new clip, continued to walk towards the downed patrolmen with absolute anger in his brown eyes, firing bullets into their lifeless bodies.

Then he turned and pointed the machine gun directly at Timothy's head. Timothy stood facing Roland. They were ten feet from each other. Timothy had his arms raised at the elbows, away from his body, with the palms of both hands facing forward.

"You didn't pull your gun," Roland said in broken English.

"There has been enough death here tonight, sir," Timothy replied. He knew that if he had reached for his sidearm he would have joined the patrolmen on the ground.

Roland studied Timothy's face intently.

"You are a strange one, amigo."

Timothy was now surrounded by six Mexicans who had followed Roland from the office building and down the dark steps.

The Mexicans stood in a tight circle around Timothy, each holding a pistol except for the tallest man. He had high cheekbones and a darker complexion than the others. A switchblade flashed open with a flick of the tall man's wrist, and he quickly swiped the tip of the blade across Timothy's right cheek, leaving a shallow slice one inch long.

Timothy continued to stare at Roland without flinching.

"I think we cut your throat. That is how we slaughter pigs in our country. We cut their throats and let them run." The tall man with high cheekbones sneered and his mind flashed back to the day when he slashed the Emergency Room doctor's throat, and watched as the doctor staggered into the swamp, infested with alligators. He moved closer and closer to Timothy.

Timothy continued to stare at Roland. They were three feet apart now.

"Who is in charge here?" Timothy asked Roland, "the weasel with the switch-blade or the man with the Thompson?"

"You go now, and tell your police that an innocent man was murdered here tonight. You tell them that," Roland said, staring at Timothy. Blood dripped from Timothy's chin. Roland waved the machine gun in the general direction of the tall man with the switchblade. "That's all now; we take my amigo and we leave." He pointed towards Diego's body.

He took several small steps closer to Timothy, and speaking directly into Timothy's face, continued, "You take great care, amigo. I have done you no great favor this night." He paused, and then continued, "Raul, or perhaps young Cesar, will have questions for you in the future."

* * *

Now Cesar Veracruz stood in front of his infuriated grandfather. Cesar had informed Raul that the plan, which had been intricately developed over the years--to find and kidnap Timothy Fife, and to fly him back to Mexico City for justice--had failed. And, it had been Timothy Fife who had killed the three men sent to bring him back, including his longtime associate Matias. Timothy and a sniper named Ric had killed them all.

"And," young Cesar continued with sarcasm in his voice, "a nurse they call Stanley saved Timothy Fife from bleeding to death."

Raul Veracruz stared at his grandson through eyes clouding with absolute agony.

From deep down inside, Raul groaned.

Chapter Nine

Endocarditis

Timothy's feverish head thrashed back and forth on the pillow in ICU bed 3. A baby raccoon was feeling Timothy's nose with its little hands. And then he was in the woods, playing cowboys and Indians with his buddies. The boys had gone home and brought back BB guns to eliminate disagreements over "got-ya" claims. Suddenly a BB hit him on the forehead, just above the right eye, and he looked up. Stanley was looking down at him and smiling.

"Welcome back, Timothy."

"My arm is killing me, Stan," Timothy complained. He lifted his right arm from the pillow used to keep it elevated, and stared at the stump.

The arm, wrapped with an ace bandage, ended at the elbow.

Timothy lifted his head off the wet pillow and stared at his right arm for several seconds then plopped his head back into the pillow and closed his eyes.

...And then he was back in Saigon after the fall of the U.S. Embassy, walking through a smoldering restaurant calling Thi Kim's name over and over with his heart aching, indifferent to the sniper's bullets ricocheting in the burnt rubble around him.

Timothy lifted his head again when he heard the commotion outside his room. The crowd, consisting of The Usual Suspects, police, and friends who had gathered outside his room, refusing to leave despite hospital admonitions, parted, allowing a path for Carla and Danielle to enter room 3.

Warm teardrops splashed on his face. Carla had arrived from Nashville. Nearly hysterical, kissing his face and crying, leaning over the side rails of the hospital bed, she crawled in the bed with her husband.

"Why is he so sick?" Danielle whispered to Stanley. "He seems out of it more than I would have anticipated."

"Dr. McCaferty just read his echocardiogram. He's got vegetation on his aortic valve, Danielle,"

"Endocarditis!"

"He's septic and may be showering emboli to his brain. Dr. McCaferty is talking to a classmate at Cleveland Clinic right now. We're going to fly Timothy out yet today."

"Damn."

"That's the only chance he has. He was born with a bicuspid valve and it's infected with this gunshot wound."

"This is awful, Stan,"

"It is, for a fact, honey. Let's take Carla and the guys to the conference room, and we'll tell them the plans."

* * *

Carla and Danielle sat in a lounge chair together, their bodies seeming fused, sobbing. Pete and Wayne, along with Doug, Morris, Ralph and Chief of Police Strait sat around the conference room table. Wendell stood in the corner, his swollen forehead sutured and bandaged, next to Dora. Ric stood in the corner alone, his arms folded. He stared at the floor.

"This is very serious," Dr. Jack McCaferty said. "The blood cultures are growing coagulase negative staph, so we have Timothy on several intravenous antibiotics. We need to transfer him to a hospital where they can replace his infected valve, and we need to move him today."

Carla sobbed and gently slumped her head on Danielle's pregnant belly.

"I've made arrangements for Timothy to be flown to the Cleveland Clinic this evening," Stanley said. "I'm going to tell him right now. You want to come with me, Carla?"

She shook her head "no," and sobbed on Danielle's belly.

Timothy raised his head when Stanley entered the room. Then he motioned towards the door with his left hand, in a waving fashion, as if to dismiss someone.

"Who you waving at?" Stanley asked.

"Two angels; told them I wasn't ready to go with them yet, and to come back another day."

"Good. They gone now?'

"Yup."

"How about a trip to Cleveland instead? Need to get you to a heart center, buddy. You have an infected heart valve because of that gunshot wound."

"You driving?'

"Thought we should probably fly. Dr. McCaferty has a classmate at the clinic that is world famous for fixing these things. I think we should fly you there today."

"Well, Cleveland ain't heaven, but I'll go if you go with me."

"I'd go any place with you buddy."

Stanley stood up, leaned over the side rails and kissed Timothy on the forehead.

"I'll go get Carla."

"Stan…"

"Yes?"

"Thanks."

…And then Timothy was riding in a horse drawn carriage on Mackinac Island, with his right arm around Carla. They were headed to dinner at the Woods Restaurant. Carla was laughing.

Chapter Ten

That's What Friends Do

The blue and white Sikorsky Helicopter lifted from the airport tarmac, rotated towards the southwest, and with the nose slightly down, headed into the sunset at 170 miles per hour. It carried two pilots, a flight nurse, flight physician, Stanley, and Timothy on a stretcher.

Timothy's skin color looked like gray clay, and perspiration seemed to be oozing from every pore. Red spots were now evident on his palms and on the bottom of his feet, and under several fingernails on his left hand.

The sound of the helicopter confused his feverish mind, and Timothy was once again a Special Forces Lieutenant Colonel. He began issuing orders, instructing the helmeted medical staff to sit on their helmets. Twisting his head towards the pilots, he ordered them to fly at tree top level and to put down just south of the Embassy on Thong Nhat Boulevard.

"Not a damn one of them is listening to me," he shouted to Stanley. "Hey, what are you doing here?"

"Heard you needed me, so I volunteered to help, Colonel."

"Well, we're in for one hell of a fight. General Nichols told me the Embassy is being over-run by regulars…."

The sentence ended in slumber.

"Morphine works great," Stanley shouted over the roar of the engines, and he reached over the stretcher to take his friend's pulse.

Carla and Danielle had seen them off at the airport. The Sikorsky helicopter's weight limit was at capacity with the medical team, patient, and fuel necessary to fly back to Cleveland. Carla pleaded in desperation to fly with her husband. Even the seasoned flight team felt her gut wrenching agony as they prepared to lift off.

The flight nurse was pulling the helicopter door closed when Carla broke free from Danielle's hug, and attempted to climb in with her husband.

The flight nurse signaled the pilots and jumped to the tarmac. Hugging Carla with both arms around her shoulders, she shouted over the noise, "Mrs. Fife, even if we had room, it's against hospital policy for family members to fly on our Medi-Vac flights. I'm so sorry."

"I'll drive you in the morning," Danielle said, clutching Carla as they watched the helicopter lift and fly away.

Then things happened rapidly. After three negative blood cultures were obtained, Timothy was taken to surgery for removal of the infected aortic valve that was showering his body with debris, and placement of a mechanical valve.

The open-heart aortic valve replacement surgery was successful.

"That was close," the cardiothoracic surgeon said to Stanley. "The infection had eroded into the aortic root, but we were able to cut it all away, and I think things will be fine."

It was 6 a.m. when Stanley called home to Carla to give her the good news.

Danielle's personal physician, Dr. Rink, answered the phone.

"Karen?"

"Yes, Stanley. How is Timothy?"

"He just came out of surgery, has a prosthetic aortic valve. Surgeon said it went well. What are you doing there?"

"Your wife is in labor. She spent the night with Carla, and called me an hour ago when the contractions became more frequent."

"It's a month too soon."

"Well, the baby doesn't seem to care. We're about to head for the hospital. Here's Danielle."

"I'm sorry, honey; my water broke in the car driving back from the airport, and now my contractions are about 8 minutes apart. Karen thinks we should go to the hospital now. Ramona is here too."

"Ah, nuts; I need to be with you. Shit! Sorry, ok, we'll figure something out here."

"Stanley...!"

"Yes?"

"You stay right there with your friend. He needs to see your face right now. Can you imagine how awful we'd feel if you left him all alone, and things went south? You stay right there. I can have our baby just fine, and we'll be here to greet you when you get home."

"You're right."

"I usually am."

"How's Carla?"

"A complete mess, but I think this baby will give her a distraction."

"Can you put her on?"

"Hi, Stanley."

"Carla, Timothy's out of surgery and he's going to be just fine."

"He's out already? Did you call me last night or did I dream it?"

"You and I and the surgeon talked; you gave him a verbal consent, remember?"

"I'm sorry, Stanley...nope. This is a nightmare."

"He has a new valve, Carla."

"Stanley..."

"Yes?"

"I love you. You're a good friend."

"I love you too, Carla. Now go take care of my wife, and we'll swap places as soon as we can, ok?"

"Ok."

Chapter Eleven

Returning Hero

"**H**ello, Rose, this is Stan McMillen in Big Bay."

"Well, hi there, Stan; it's been a long time. How's things?"

"That's why I'm calling… to invite you and Jonathon to a welcome home party for Timothy."

"How's he doing now? Been a week or so since my last call from Wendell."

"Really! You've been keeping track of us, huh?"

"He has a soft spot in my heart; all you guys do. Tell me about your baby; Wendell said Danielle had a little girl."

"Yup, we named her Chloe Norma. She just turned eight months old and is crawling all over the place."

"After Norma Bouvier!"

"We both loved that lady. She was my mentor, Rose."

"Chloe look like you Stan?"

"No, thank God. She is a clone of Danielle…has my dark curly hair, but has Danielle's blue eyes that look right into you, and that big smile."

"You're gonna have your hands full in fifteen years."

"No kidding."

"So what's the update on Timothy?"

"He's coming home from the rehab unit in Cleveland tomorrow. I spent last Tuesday and Wednesday with him."

"How's he doing?"

"It's a miracle, Rose. He's almost completely recovered from the stroke he had after surgery. He's still a little weak on the right side, but walks and talks and thinks like the old Timothy. He even joked, as I was leaving; said, "You know I can use this stump like a lethal weapon and don't even have to register it.""

"He's back."

"We're planning a celebration for early next month and hope you and Jonathon can join us."

"Wouldn't miss this, Stan. I'll bring the cello player that accompanies Jonathon; you'll like the way they sound together."

"I'm going to call David Chown and Miriam Pico and ask them to join us, too."

"Gonna be a special night, Stan."

* * *

A temporary stage had been constructed against the southwest wall in Poor Joe's. The old upright piano was pushed up on the wall next to the stage. David Chown sat at the piano. Jonathan sat on stage behind an electronic keyboard.

"How's things in Vegas?" David asked, leaning towards Jonathan.

"I'm having more fun than I imagined possible. Not much sleep playing six nights a week, but lots of fun. How's things in Traverse City; you still there?"

"Sure am, most of the time, plenty of gigs. Miriam and I just cut our third CD, and it's selling real well."

"I sure want one, and want you guys to sign it, too."

"You got it, friend," Miriam chimed in with a smile.

Rose was the self-appointed director of ceremonies.

"Ladies and gentlemen, please give a warm welcome to Miriam Pico

37

on vocals, Ralph on trumpet, Nick on cello, Jonathon on the key-board, and David Chown at the piano," Rose shouted over the racket of the crowded bar.

The old bar, packed to well past the occupancy rating, trembled with applause. Even the outdoor patio was crowded on this hot summer night.

Everything was free. The food and the beverages were on Rose.

When Stanley offered to help with expenses, Rose simply said, "I'm the owner; Timothy is a dear friend. This is on me, Stan."

Stanley and Danielle were acting as the hosts. Baby Chloe Norma had become the mascot for The Usual Suspects. She was passed around from man to man throughout the night as the festivities continued, with Wendell acting as her guardian.

And then a yellow taxi pulled up and stopped in front of Poor Joe's. Timothy looked through the taxi window at the crowd bulging out of his beloved old bar. With a cane in his left hand, he climbed out of the taxi, and with the help of Carla, up the steps and into Poor Joe's.

The band started playing, and Miriam sang, "For He's a Jolly Good Fellow." Timothy limped through the crowd towards the stage with Carla at his side. People reached out to pat him on the back, and just to touch him. Then he climbed onto the stage, and stood next to Miriam.

Timothy raised his cane over his head, and the crowd roared.

Stanley climbed onto the bar, facing the stage, with a glass of Basil's held high.

"A toast to our returning hero, and our best friend. To the man who saved Wendell's life, and the man who has defined the meaning of loyalty, and changed our lives forever. To Timothy Fife!"

"Salute!" the crowd shouted.

Timothy climbed down from the stage and walked to the bar. Looking up at Stanley, he raised his cane, and touched Stanley's chest.

"And a toast to the man who saved my life. I love you, man."

"Semper Fi!" shouted Wendell.

"Semper Fi!" returned the crowd.

Looking down at his friend, Stanley saw tears appear in his eyes, just for an instant.

The welcome back celebration continued until sunrise. The 2 a.m. closing time ordnance was suspended by Chief of Police Strait at 2 a.m.

Miriam and the band performed for at least six hours, and then took the occasional requests while coffee and breakfast sweets were being served.

Eight-month-old Chloe Norma had been passed around throughout the night from one member of The Usual Suspects to the next. She could be frequently found sleeping in Wendell's arms, or Doug's, coming back to Danielle only in times of "need."

Around 2:30, a grimy little man with black stringy hair, who had been sitting unnoticed on a wooden folding chair in the hallway leading to the men's room next to the pay phone, stood up.

The little man slowly squeezed his way through the crowd towards Wendell, who was holding Chloe on his chest, patting her on the back. When he approached Chloe, she turned her head slightly to the side, watching him, pursing her little lips slightly. The man snaked his arm between two people, stretching his hand towards the baby, trying to touch her.

Chloe grasped his grimy index finger with her little right hand, and with her pure blue eyes, smiled at the stranger.

Chapter Twelve

Machete

Machete Juarez killed for a living. He had never been influenced by a moral compass. After surviving a parentless childhood in the ghettos of Mexico City, his services were occasionally utilized when unpleasant justice needed to be dealt.

He was a little man, with no functioning teeth, only an occasional shard protruding from rotting roots. Black matted hair clung to his neck and forehead. He peered between the divisions in his bangs with dark brown eyes that seemed to have no expression whatsoever.

When he was twelve, one afternoon while shooting rats in the smoky city dump, he spotted a fourteen-year-old boy who had beaten him up two months previously. Without hesitation, he put the boy's head in the rifle's sight, squeezed the trigger, and watched the blood spray from the back of his skull. After that, killing a human was as easy as shooting kittens, which he used for target practice almost every day.

Even though his profession was profitable, Machete preferred to exist in the ghettos where he grew up. He did this for several reasons; the authorities were afraid to search for him there, and so were the people who hired him. And his women lived there. His wife had given him two daughters and a son. He had also sired a son with his oldest daughter and a daughter with his daughter-in-law.

From time to time, when money was needed, Machete would call a memorized telephone number, inquiring for employment opportunities.

* * *

And there he stood, in Raul Veracruz's office on the top floor of the Gran Hotel Ciudad in Mexico City. Cesar Veracruz sat in the chair next to his grandfather's desk.

The room reeked of a wet dog that had rolled on something dead.

"There is a job we have for you," Cesar said. "It is in the States."

"You get me there, I do the work," Machete replied with a smirk.

"We seek justice for my son Diego," Raul said. "There are men in a city called Big Bay that must pay."

"You get me to that city and the names, and I will cut the pigs' throats."

"We will get you up highway 35 to the States, and money for the bus to Big Bay. Remember these names: Timothy Fife, Stanley McMillen, and three men who live at a bar named Poor Joe's, Wendell, Doug and a man called Ric.

"How much am I paid for this?"

"Five hundred thousand U.S. dollars. Take it or not," replied Cesar.

"I will burn that Poor Joe's down to the ground for fun!" the little man said with a toothless grin.

Chapter Thirteen

Stone Cold Sober

Doug remained stone cold sober during Timothy's welcome home party. Three weeks earlier during an office visit, Dr. McCaferty had admonished him about the seriousness of his weak heart muscle.

"Doug, the last echocardiogram showed you have lost another 10 percent of the pumping strength. You lose another 10 percent and you'll be seriously ill. Alcoholic Cardiomyopathy…"

"Alcohol's killing me, huh?"

"Sorry."

"I don't give a damn, Doc."

"That's selfish, Doug. You may not give a damn, but you're not the only one to consider."

"What?"

"I can name at least a dozen people who would do anything for you, anything at all, and they would be devastated to watch you commit slow suicide at the end of a bottle."

There was a pause of at least thirty seconds.

Doug stared into Dr. Jack McCaferty's eyes. Neither man blinked.

"You're right, Doc…I quit"

"Good."

As the festivities rumbled through the night, Doug sipped a glass of tonic water with lime, and watched. Sometimes he held Chloe Norma, loving her.

He was holding Chloe when his sober mind spotted Machete Juarez sitting unnoticed in the corner next to the hallway, staring at him and the baby. Doug's skin prickled. He held the little girl even tighter. He walked up the stairs to his room, and took a Thirty-eight Special from his dresser drawer. He put the pistol in his pocket, went down the stairs, and handed Chloe to Wendell. He moved through the crowd to a place next to the popcorn machine behind the bar to observe.

With his finger on the trigger, he watched the filthy little man work his way through the crowd, reaching between partiers to touch the baby. Doug was about to come over the bar when Machete turned and walked out the front door, and into the darkness.

Doug immediately went to the corner where the little man had been sitting, grabbed the folding chair and took it upstairs to his room, and to Malcolm.

"We got a job in couple hours," he said to Malcolm, as he stroked his dog. "We're going to track that scumbag," he continued.

Malcolm sniffed at the chair.

* * *

Timothy and Carla had left the party early; so had those who had to work in the morning. The remaining partiers were drinking coffee and eating Dora's sweet rolls, hot out of the oven, when Doug and Malcolm came down the stairs. Doug carried a folding chair.

"What's up, Doug?" Dora asked from the kitchen. "Want some coffee?"

"In a little bit; Malcolm needs a walk."

Outside, Doug unfolded the chair, and his German Shepherd sniffed it again. He then gave a command, "Find him!"

Malcolm ran in a serpentine fashion for twenty yards and stopped, looking back at Doug, eyes sparkling, ears up, and tail wagging.

"We've got him now buddy. Let's go!"

Malcolm tracked Machete Juarez for ten blocks, losing the scent only once at Brown Creek. He picked up the smell twenty yards downstream, and followed it for another five blocks, coming to a stop behind a vacant house on Pine Street that had a *for sale* sign in the front yard.

With Malcolm on a tight leash, Doug went silently from room to room. The house was empty.

Peering through the window of a tool shed behind the house, Doug watched the house for ninety minutes while Malcolm slept at his feet. Then they walked back to Poor Joe's.

* * *

The babysitter called the hospital with a hysterical voice just after noon.

"MRS. McMILLEN...I CAN'T FIND CHLOE!"

Danielle sat down.

"What do you mean, you can't find her?"

"She was taking a nap in her bed with the rails up, and she's gone. I CAN'T FIND HER...ANYWHERE!" the young lady screamed.

"We'll be right home," Danielle replied. Her hands trembled. She dialed Stanley's office number.

"Honey, Chloe is missing."

"WHAT!?"

"The babysitter just called...." And then Danielle could only sob.

"Meet me at the car; I'll call Chief Strait, ... be right there."

Stanley also called Wendell at Poor Joe's.

The drive up the hill from Big Bay General Hospital to their condo on the bluffs was nauseating.

"She can't be far; we'll find her, honey."

"Stan, she can't climb out of that bed with the sides up."

Chief Strait's car idled in front of their condo with lights flashing.

The chief, a deputy, Wendell, and Ralph stood beside the car.

"We'll find her; she can't be far," Chief reassured.

"Someone had to take her, Chief," Danielle almost screamed. "She can't get out of that bed by herself."

"We'll find her, Danielle," he replied. He opened the door to his squad car and picked up a portable radio.

* * *

Doug had listened to the phone conversation when Stanley had called Wendell at Poor Joe's. From his room at the top of the stairs, he listened as Wendell exclaimed to Ralph that baby Chloe was missing. He watched from the top of the stairs while they charged out the front door and drove away.

"Come on, Malcolm. God damn, let's go buddy."

Tears filled both eyes. He walked down the stairs followed by an excited Malcolm, jumping with youthful enthusiasm. In his mind he could smell Chloe's sweet baby smell, and see her pure blue baby eyes looking up at him.

"Lord, help me make it….help me save her…I will never touch another drop…. I promise…" Doug gasped, running behind Malcolm. When they reached Brown Creek his world was spinning around and around, and Doug held tight to an old maple tree, gasping with gurgling respirations.

His knees started to buckle.

…And then she was behind him, holding him tight, and singing the same sweet song she had sung to him during the Battle of the Hump in Vietnam on that fateful day when he drove the Green Dragon directly into the Vietcong positions, and incoming rattled against the armor like hail from hell. She whispered strong encouragements for him to stand up, and to run faster, and that Chloe could be saved, and that he was the one to save her.

Doug ran the last five blocks at full speed. He did not know how; he just did as he was told.

Looking through the sunroom windows, he saw the filthy little black haired man rocking back and forth in a rocking chair. Chloe sat on his lap.

Doug briefly considered shooting through the window. *Nope, can't. Shit, she'll get hit by glass.*

For six minutes Doug carefully worked his way into the house through a basement door and then up cement basement steps, through two more doors, and then he was standing directly behind the man, who was rocking the baby and speaking to her in Spanish.

Doug stepped on the rocker, stopping it, and pressed the Thirty-eight Special hard against the man's left ear.

"One move... I will kill you."

"She is my baby sister, reincarnated."

"I don't care if she's Mother Theresa; put her on the floor. Right now."

Machete carefully placed the baby on the hardwood floor.

"Get her," Doug softly commanded Malcolm, who pulled the baby behind the rocking chair.

* * *

"Chief, you need to get back to the station ASAP," crackled the dispatcher's voice in the portable radio.

"10-4, what's up?"

"Our switchboard is all lit up. Doug is walking down the middle of State Street with a pistol against the head of some stranger. Doug has a baby under his arm."

People were coming out from the businesses and office buildings to watch the procession, consisting of a dirty little man with matted long black hair followed by Doug who had a pistol pressed to the back of the little man's head. Malcolm was attached to the prisoner by a ten-foot leather strap.

Little Chloe was under Doug's left arm, her head turned to the side looking at the gathering crowd on the sidewalk.

At the intersection of State and Cass, Machete lurched to the left and ran down Cass Street for three yards before Malcolm sprang up his back and grabbed him by the neck, throwing the man to the pavement. Malcolm had the man's throat securely in his mouth, growly softly, looking up at Doug for instructions.

"Good boy, Malcolm. Good boy."

Doug squatted next to Machete lying on the street. He pointed the Thirty-eight Special directly between the emotionless brown eyes.

"She is my baby sister."

"The world will be a better place without you, but first we talk, scumbag." And the procession again proceeded down State Street towards the city of Big Bay Police Department.

Except for Malcolm, no one could see the angel with her arm around Doug, whispering to him while they walked.

Chapter Fourteen

A Brother's Love

He was eight years old when his baby sister was slaughtered.

Machete's mother had a three-year affair with an American working undercover for the CIA on a clandestine operation to seek out communists.

The agent had his throat cut one night in the alley behind their shack. Two months later, Machete's mother gave birth to a baby girl. She had black curly hair and blue eyes.

She named the baby Maria.

Machete was his little sister's babysitter. He fed her, changed her diapers, and rocked her to sleep every night in a rickety rocking chair he had found in the dump. When she was sick with dysentery, he took her to a doctor's office and was refused treatment, until he leaned close to the nurse and said, "If you do not give me medicine I will burn down this office tonight, and find your house and doctor's house the next night."

He cared for Maria the next seven days with little sleep, giving her fluids and the medicine the nurse gave him, until she recovered. The bond between brother and sister was immense.

On the 7th of September when Maria was eight months old, a drug warlord and his gang of thugs drove through the streets and alleys of Machete's ghetto at 1 a.m., shooting into the shacks and businesses at random.

Maria's crib was against the front wall of their shack. She was hit twice in the head.

Even now, after all the passing years, Machete recalls that awful night, the terror of the blood, and seeing his beloved little sister dead in her crib. He remembers it every day, that and his mother's crumpled body next to the crib.

* * *

Now there he sat in the Big Bay Police Department interrogation room. Machete had been scrubbed clean and dressed in an orange jump suit. His left ankle was shackled by a short chain to a bolt in the floor. His black hair was pulled back into a ponytail.

"I think she is my sister. Maria has come back to me," he repeated several times.

Machete Juarez answered every question asked by Chief of Police Strait with that sentence, until Chief Strait asked, "Why are you in Big Bay?"

Chapter Fifteen

The Unexpected Gathering

Nine days had passed since Chloe Norma's abduction and Doug's march down State Street, when the phone rang at the McMillen residence.

"Stan, I'd like you to come down to the office. Timothy's here. We need to discuss a few things."

Stanley exceeded the speed limit down the hill by twice the posted number.

"They're all in the conference room," the dispatcher said to Stanley as he walked through the Police Department front door.

Captain Quinn O'Malley was sitting at the head of the conference room table. He was not smiling.

Rose Jackson sat next to him. Also at the table sat Timothy, Vincent Bonifacio, and Chief of Police Larry Strait.

"Grab a chair, Stan," Captain O'Malley said. "We have a problem."

"Quinn? ...Rose?" Stanley said, standing, stunned.

"Stanley, this is my friend Vincent Bonifacio that I've mentioned in the past," Timothy said.

Stanley shook hands with the man, and sat down next to him.

"What the hell's going on, Quinn? What are you doing here?" Stanley asked.

"I called him after Timothy called me with this Juarez situation," replied Vincent Bonifacio.

"Oh man, I'm confused...and Rose?"

Chief Strait stood up. "Stan, during our questioning of this fellow who kidnapped your daughter, he spilled the beans about a plot to kill you, Timothy, Wendell, Doug, and Ric."

"Shit. Why?"

"This guy, who says his name is Machete Juarez, claims to have been sent here by the same cartel that sent the three men who kidnapped Wendell, the ones killed during the rescue." Chief Strait continued, "These men have been sent from Mexico City by a Mexican Godfather named Raul Veracruz, and his grandson, Cesar."

"Why, what'd we do?"

Timothy cleared his throat and then spoke slowly with regret in his voice, "I was present when this Godfather's son was shot to death in St. Paul. It's me they want. I think it'd be best if you let me and this Machete fellow get on a plane and fly to Mexico City...settle things up with this Godfather fellow."

"HELL NO!" came a unanimous response.

"I'll vote yes, if you can get Carla to agree," Stanley said with a wry smile on his face, and then continued, "I'm still as confused as all hell. What ARE you doing here, Quinn, and Rose, and you, Vincent."

Captain Quinn O'Malley smiled the big smile that exposed his missing front tooth. "We have a common denominator, Stanley; we're all associated with the same company."

Events began to fall into place, and Stanley took a deep breath. The helicopter flying over Big Bay, finding the cabin in the woods, the phone call to Chief Strait describing the cabin location, the promise from the captain in the Green Parrot, "I can help here."

"Vincent and I personally know Raul Veracruz," Quinn continued.

"I know his grandson Cesar. His business associates rent two casinos from me," Rose added.

"Oooh...."

"They sent this Machete to Big Bay with orders to kill you, Stan, and Timothy, Wendell, Doug, and Ric, and then to burn Poor Joe's," stated Chief Strait.

"Why'd he fess up?"

"He's in love with your daughter. He thinks Chloe is his baby sister."

Stanley's body shivered with a chill all over. He clenched his jaw.

"Oh man, somebody give me a gun," Stanley moaned.

"That's not going to solve the problem, Stan. In fact, in a sick kinda way, that little scumbag just saved your lives," Chief Strait muttered. "He could have killed you all and left town without a trace, back to Mexico."

"Ok, men, here's what we need to do," said Quinn O'Malley from the head of the table. He winked at Rose.

"We need to have a face to face with Raul Veracruz and his grandson. I can arrange for a meeting in Cuba; they will feel safe there. Mexico is out of the question; doubt we would survive that adventure. We'll have a face to face and work this out, everybody here. You want to participate, Chief?"

"Yes, sir."

"Cayo Coco?" Stanley asked.

"No, save that for your anniversaries, Stan. Now, take me to my granddaughter." And the captain winked.

"Are they all CIA?" Stanley asked Timothy, standing in the parking lot.

"Well maybe, or FBI, I don't think the CIA can work in the States, but what do I know. Don't know about O'Malley."

"Did you have any idea that Vincent Bonifacio was some sort of Fed when you were a detective in St Paul?"

"Nope."

Chapter Sixteen

Malcolm's Plea

Ric and Wendell were up early, sitting at the bar, waiting for the coffee machine to finish its job when Doug stumbled down the stairs clutching his chest. Six steps from the top, his legs crumpled and he tumbled headfirst, rolling over and over, and then lay sprawled on his side on the landing next to the phone booth, unconscious.

Ric reached Doug first, and carefully rolled him to his back. Wendell called the police department.

"We have an emergency at Poor Joe's. Send an ambulance. Now. Please."

"No pulse," Ric said, looking up at Wendell.

Instinctively the two war vets began CPR.

Anxiously, they worked on their friend, Ric doing chest compressions while Wendell gave mouth-to-mouth respirations.

Malcolm licked the gash on Doug's forehead.

The ambulance with two paramedics arrived in 7 minutes.

The cardiac monitor showed ventricular fibrillation.

"Stand clear!" ordered the paramedic. He placed the defibrillator paddles on Doug's bare chest, and shocked him.

Malcolm leaped over Doug, knocking the paramedic flat on the floor, growling down at the man.

"Get this damn dog off me. Get him outta here!"

"Come here, Malcolm," Wendell said, holding his hand towards the dog.

"Get him outta here. Right now!" screamed the other paramedic.

Ric stood up and pointed at both paramedics. Glaring intently, he calmly said, "Shut up and save our friend. Right now. I'm not kidding."

The second shock converted Doug's heart rhythm to some sort of junctional rhythm with a weak pulse. The paramedics intubated him, and begin to "bag" him.

Malcolm leaped into the back of the ambulance.

"Get out!" yelled the paramedic bagging Doug.

Wendell climbed into the ambulance and sat next to the man.

Staring with stony cold contempt, Wendell whispered, "If my friend dies, this dog is going to be the very least of your problems. Now shut up and do your job. I'll hold the dog."

Wendell held Malcolm in the ambulance, and in the Emergency Room.

"Doug is in critical condition," Dr. McCaferty said to Wendell and Ric, standing outside ER room number 1. "His weak heart fibrillated. I'm going to put an intra-aortic balloon pump in him, and hopefully get him through this crisis. Prayers would help a lot right now, guys. Does Doug have any family?"

"Just us," Wendell replied.

"And," Wendell continued, "can Malcolm stay with him Doc; they're inseparable."

"Malcolm can stay in Doug's room," Dr. McCaferty said, looking down at the dog peering up at him. "Once we get everything all set up, I'll see to it."

* * *

Malcolm was lying on the floor, at the foot of Doug's ICU bed, listening to the to-and-fro sounds of the ventilator, and the rhythmic pulsating sound of the intra-aortic balloon pump, when she floated in. She settled on the floor next to Malcolm and began humming a sweet, sweet sound before she spoke.

"It is ok, precious one," she said. She stroked the German Shepherd gently. "We all leave our flesh, and it is beautiful when we do."

Malcolm lifted his head, with his ears pricked up, and looking directly into her brilliant aqua eyes, said with his brown eyes, *Don't want him to go yet. You stop him from going... please, for me?*

And then from the ceiling, just above the bed, Malcolm watched Norma Bouvier, and Chief of Police Charlie Johnson enter the room. They were joined by Doug.

Norma, Chief Johnson and Doug hugged above the bed. There was joy.

Please, Malcolm repeated.

The angel smiled as she watched Stanley and Danielle walking rapidly down the hall, around The Usual Suspects standing in a circle holding hands with their heads bowed, and towards the room.

"Yes," she said, "I will." She swooped over the bed and kissed Doug on the forehead. Doug's body quivered.

Hand in hand, Chief Johnson and Norma flickered through the ceiling and were gone.

Stanley cried, seeing his former patient and good friend looking moribund. He bent over the side rails and kissed Doug on the forehead.

Doug's eyes opened.

The sound of Malcolm's tail thumping on the floor added to the cadence of the machines keeping Doug alive.

* * *

On day three, Doug's blood pressure was stable with the balloon pump weaned off. The following morning Doug was extubated.

Stanley did the extubation.

When the endotracheal tube was removed, and suctioning completed,

Richard Alan Hall

Doug weakly pulled Stanley close to his face.

He whispered, "You ain't gonna believe the crazy dreams I've had."

Chapter Seventeen

Call Me Jim

Miriam Pico did not fly back to Traverse City with David Chown after the welcome home party for Timothy.

During lunch with Danielle and Carla following the party, she had mentioned she felt totally exhausted.

"If you guys know of a place I can rent, I need a rest."

"Stanley's old place on Grant!" Danielle exclaimed, "You guys wouldn't mind another guest upstairs, would you, Carla?"

Carla laughed. "We'd love it. We're renting Stanley's house on Grant Street, for free it turns out; he refuses to take our money. There's a spare bedroom upstairs, if you don't mind sharing the upstairs bathroom with a single mom and her little son."

"Same rent as Carla pays, Miriam ...deal?"

"Thanks, guys, I really need a little vacation. Thanks!"

Lounging alone on the beach, reading novels and magazines revitalized her spirit. And, in the evening she would frequently walk the seven blocks to Poor Joe's and play the piano, or her guitar, while singing, to the delight of The Usual Suspects and other patrons.

When word came from the hospital that Doug could now have visitors, Miriam grabbed her guitar and took a taxi to Big Bay General.

She walked down the hospital hall looking at the walls for room numbers with her precious Martin guitar under her left arm. She turned a corner and ran into a physician who was reading a patient's chart.

They collided hard.

Miriam's guitar flew against the wall in the company of the patient chart and the doctor's glasses. The whole mess hit the floor with a discordant sound, the flutter of chart pages scattering like fall leaves.

"Oh! I'm so sorry," Miriam exclaimed.

"My fault. Wasn't watching. Sorry," replied the young physician.

Miriam started to pick up the scattered medical record.

The doctor reached down and picked up Miriam's guitar. The neck was completely broken from the body just above the sound hole, and dangled by the strings.

Miriam stared at the young man holding her broken guitar. His blue eyes were wide.

"I am *so* sorry."

"Doug likes it when I sing a cappella," Miriam said. "It's only a guitar."

"You here to sing to a patient?"

"My friend Doug is in ICU….had a cardiac arrest."

"I was in the ER when he came in. I'm James Roosevelt."

"I'm Miriam Pico."

"Let me show you to ICU. Hey, I know a guy who repairs musical instruments; has a little shop down on Bay Street."

"That would be great, doctor. I love this old guitar."

"Call me Jim," he replied, and for a second they paused in the hallway, and glanced at each other, then continued to Doug's room.

"I'll take your guitar to my friend this afternoon. How can I contact you?"

They stopped at the ICU nurses' station. Miriam asked for a piece of paper, and wrote her phone number.

* * *

"Hi, Doug!" Miriam exclaimed.

She bounced into ICU room 3 and was greeted by Malcolm.

"Miriam! I didn't know you were still in town."

"I traveled all the way back from Indonesia to see you."

"I bet you did, too!"

Miriam leaned over the side rails and kissed Doug on the cheek.

"That's a nasty bump on your forehead."

"Thank God it's not a vital organ." Doug smiled, pointing to his head.

She spent the next 30 minutes singing softly to her friend, with Malcolm's head resting in her lap.

"One more, and then I should let you rest. Do you have a favorite?"

"Please sing *Amazing Grace*."

"Amazing grace how sweet the sound,
That saved a wretch like me.
I once was lost, but now I'm found.
Was blind, but now I see."

Miriam sang. Malcolm's tail thumped against the floor.

Doug stared intently at the ceiling with crystal clear brown eyes.

* * *

Miriam lay on her belly, sound asleep baking in the afternoon sun, when her cell phone rang. She rolled over off the beach towel and into the sand, looking for the phone.

"Hello?"

"Hi, Miriam, This is Jim Roosevelt. I have your guitar all fixed!"

"That was fast. Thank you, Jim."

"The least I could do. Thought maybe we could have dinner together, and I'll bring the guitar."

"I'm on vacation; what night is good for you?"

Richard Alan Hall

* * *

The light wind blowing in from the bay felt warm enough to sit on the outdoor patio, overlooking the city of Big Bay down in the valley.

"Your glasses are sitting a little cockeyed." Miriam laughed. She reached across the table, took them, gently twisted the frame, and then placed them back on his face. "There!"

Dr. James Roosevelt reached over the table, gently running his fingers over Miriam's left hand, and his face blushed a little.

Tingling sensations. Miriam felt tingling sensations all over her body when he touched her.

"You say you're a resident?"

"Yup, last year of my Cardiology Residency; here working under Dr. McCaferty. I'll be done this fall."

"Then what?"

"I had an interview with a cardiology group in Carmel. Last week they invited me to join them; I think I will."

"I've never been to Carmel," Miriam replied.

"You would love it, Miriam."

* * *

After dinner, with the sun setting behind the hills, Jim and Miriam walked down the wooden steps leading from the patio to the parking lot.

"Don't let me forget your guitar."

"Oh, yeah."

"Can I see you again?" he asked.

"Yes, I'd like that, but I fly back to Traverse City next Monday."

"I've memorized your number," Dr. James Roosevelt said, with a smile.

Chapter Eighteen
A Mother Can't Do That

Little Chloe pushed a plastic bowl of pureed peas from her highchair tray and watched it bounce.

The doorbell rang.

It rang again, and a third time.

Stanley stood up from the dinner table and walked towards the condo's front door, stepping over the green cascade.

"I don't mean to interrupt your dinner. Need to have a conversation with you and Danielle," Chief of Police Strait said.

"Well, join us....I'll start some coffee."

Watching Chloe play with the mess she had created on her food tray, Chief Strait said, "The State Police sent a Spanish translator so we could communicate with this Machete fellow better."

"What's the little creep have to say?" ask Danielle.

"He truly believes your daughter is his sister."

"This guy is nuts, Chief," Stanley interjected.

"Could be, but he believes it. And he wants to see his sister again."

"YOU HAVE GOT TO BE KIDDING. You can't be serious, Chief; there is no way that skanky man is going to get close to my daughter again," Danielle said. "NO WAY."

"What're you suggesting here, Chief?" Stanley asked. He reached over and held his wife's hand.

"I have two daughters, guys. I know how ludicrous this sounds. The guy wants to promise something to his little sister; we think something to make amends for his life. I know how crazy this sounds, but it might give us the break we need to handle the Mexicans. I had to ask."

Danielle picked Chloe out of the highchair, cleaned her face and hands with a washcloth, and sat down next to Chief Strait, stepping in the mess on the floor.

"This isn't going away if we don't, is it, Chief?"

"I don't know, Danielle."

"But this would help," he continued.

"A mother cannot just let her baby go into a room with an evil man, Chief. This is not something a mother can do." She continued, "And if anything happened..." Tears ran down her cheeks. "I can't."

"How about if Danielle and I were in the room, Larry? Danielle holds Chloe the entire time, and scumbag can only talk to her. No touching."

"Would you be willing to try that, Danielle?" Chief asked. "We could try it. And trust me, Stanley could take the runt out with one jab if need be, and I will be right outside the door looking through the window."

Danielle looked into Stanley's eyes with her deep blue eyes. "What did we ever do to deserve this nightmare honey? I just want it to go away. Ok, damnit. If he tries anything in that room, you guys get him good."

* * *

Thursday morning Danielle and Stanley walked into the Big Bay Police Department. Danielle held little Chloe tight against her chest.

The sensation reminded Stanley of the first time he walked towards the boxing ring in college. It was a mixture of excitement and fear, nausea, and pride that he was about to do it… and the urge to pee.

Danielle was pretty sure this was a nightmare, and that she would wake up any second, and tell Stanley she must be pregnant again, or just run to the bathroom and vomit.

* * *

The yellow tiled room had three green plastic chairs, two side by side, and the third facing the pair. That's all.

Stanley and Danielle sat side by side. Danielle held Chloe on her lap, facing the door.

The door opened and Machete Juarez entered, wearing ankle shackles. He stopped and stared at Chloe.

Baby Chloe giggled with delight and held her arms out towards Machete.

Danielle stood up, and slowly walked towards the little man whose brown eyes were now sparkling.

He whispered in broken English, "Thank you for bringing my sister for a visit. I have promises to make to her, and to the God who sent her back to me."

Danielle slowly handed Chloe to Machete.

Chief of Police Strait struggled with the strong desire to barge through the door and end the visit.

Stanley's hands begin to shake, just a little. He rehearsed in his mind the left jab that served him well in his Golden Gloves years.

Chloe giggled again, and pulled Machete's left ear.

"See...she IS my sister!" he exclaimed. "She always pulls that ear."

* * *

For twenty-seven minutes Machete sat in the green plastic chair holding Chloe on his lap, speaking to her in Spanish. Chloe played with his fingers, and pulled at his orange jump suit, and occasionally giggled. And sometimes she just stared at his face.

Then he stood up holding Chloe. Stanley and Danielle stood up. Machete walked towards Danielle and handed the baby to her.

"Thank you. You are brave mother; my sister loves you very much."
Then he turned to Stanley. "Thank you, amigo. Now I help you."

And with that, Machete Juarez was led away and back to his cell.

* * *

"Thank you guys, that was kinda intense there at the beginning," Chief Strait commented, walking into his office.

"Yeah, I looked down and saw my hands shaking." Stanley chuckled.

"My big brave men! Geez." Danielle laughed nervously.

"I couldn't believe my eyes when I watched you hand Chloe to him."

"I couldn't believe what was happening either, Chief. I just had a feeling all of a sudden that everything was ok, and that I should…. it just happened."

"The State Police translator was giving me a live translation of what Machete was saying. It was pretty incredible, guys."

"What'd he say?" Stanley inquired.

"It was a rambling confession of all his evil deeds, and that he'd lost his way when she was killed in her crib, that he lost his soul and hated everyone after he saw her and their mother's blood on the floor. He asked for forgiveness for all the evil deeds he had committed all the years since her death. He said that he is ashamed and truly sorry for embarrassing her in heaven. He said that he would do no evil ever again, that he would help those who fight against evil. He pleaded for her to intercede on his behalf with the Almighty God."

"Whew," Danielle and Stanley uttered in unison.

"Well, I'd say we have a friend now," Chief Strait said with a smile. "This should make for an interesting meeting with the Mexicans."

Chapter Nineteen

Made Whole Again

"That place isn't the Poor Joe's everyone once knew and loved since you've been gone," Rose said to Timothy. "It was obvious when we came over for your coming home party. The bar misses you."

Timothy sat on the porch of Stanley's house on Grant Street, looking out at the fall color changes, talking to Rose Jackson on the phone.

"I miss it, too, but life goes on. Carla has a five-year contract with Imagine Studios in Nashville. She's contracted to perform every Saturday night. She's working on an album and has two more to cut. We have to go back this Friday."

"What happens if Carla breaks the contract?"

"All sorts of clauses and penalties, and probably black-listed in the recording business."

"Imagine Studios, that's run by Karl Remington. He's a pissant Timothy; let me deal with him."

"You know him!?"

"I'm in the entertainment business, Timothy. You talk to Carla, and see what would suit her, and what will work for you two lovers so you can take over at the bar again. Call me back."

"Thanks, Rose."

* * *

Carla sat next to the man she adored.

"If you want to own Poor Joe's again, you have my support, honey. Remember when we were first talking about Nashville, I told you that we are the most important thing, and I didn't want my career or whatever you choose to do to ever get between us. I meant it when I said it on Mackinac Island, and I mean it now. When you were wounded, when you were so sick in Cleveland, I thought I might never get you back. I promised God that I would do anything if you came home to me. I adore you, Timothy. I just want us to be together."

The lovers sat on the porch and hugged without saying a word for several minutes.

Finally Carla said, "Let's buy the bar back."

"What about Nashville? How do you want to handle Remington?"

"I'd love to sing at the Tin Roof one Saturday a month, and I can fly back for recording sessions."

"I'll call Rose in the morning and tell her we'll buy the bar."

"I'll call Mr. Remington in the morning; he's such a hard ass Timothy."

"Let's wait for a couple of days, before you make that call."

"Why?"

"Rose knows him."

* * *

Timothy was at Poor Joe's the following afternoon, sitting in a booth with Wendell and Ralph, when the phone rang.

"Timothy! Karl Remington just called me. He said he has been made aware of your situation, and that he's happy you're recovering, and that he wants to help in any way possible. We talked, and he agreed to cutting back to once a month at the Tin Roof and I can fly down for sessions. He said he's happy to help. Can you believe it?"

Timothy immediately called Rose to thank her.

"You're welcome. Take care of Poor Joe's; I've got a few more parties left in me."

Then Timothy called Stanley's office at Big Bay General.

"Hi, Stan. Will you sell Grant Street to Carla and me?"

" What's up?"

"Carla likes that house a lot, and we just bought Poor Joe's back."

"I'm sure we can work something out. Welcome home, buddy."

Wendell and Ralph raised their mugs of Schlitz beer high in the air. Standing beside the grill, Dora had a really big smile.

Chapter Twenty

House Call

The "Closed for Private Party" sign in the front window of Poor Joe's did not deter the person who was pounding on the locked front door.

Timothy had closed the bar at 7 p.m. The Usual Suspects were having a quiet welcome home party for Doug, who had been discharged from Big Bay General at 10 a.m. that morning.

Timothy unlocked the door and opened it.

"Doc! What are you doing here?"

"Stanley says you have an ample supply of Basil Hayden's," retorted Dr. Jack McCaferty. He strode through the door and headed towards the bar. "And I need to make a house call."

Doug, Ric, Ralph, Pete, Wayne, and Wendell stared in amazement at the curly haired Irishman behind the bar, pouring himself a full glass of bourbon.

"Welcome to our world," Doug said with a grin. "You can have my share."

"I've heard about this place for years, guys, and since it supplies a steady stream of patients, I thought I should stop by and say thank you," replied the doctor.

"You're welcome anytime, Doc," replied Timothy.

"Do you think you can expand the inventory to include some 18 year old Elijah Craig, and maybe some Jamison Limited Reserve for us Irish boys?"

"You an alcoholic, Doc?" inquired Ralph.

"Nope, not yet…still take call."

"He ain't never gonna be either," Doug said with authority. "Too many people depend on Doc, and love him. That would just be selfish, right Doc?"

Their eyes met briefly, and Dr. McCaferty smiled. "Exactly right, Doug; that's exactly right. How you feeling?"

"Tired, but my breathing is ok."

"How *you* feeling, Timothy? I can hear your valve clicking"

Timothy laughed. "I'll call you if it stops clicking."

"Seriously, Timothy, if the click gets soft or goes away, you call."

"Ok."

"Doug was telling us about the dreams he had while he was in your joint," Pete commented.

Dr. McCaferty pulled a chair to the table, sat down with The Usual Suspects, and took a long drink of the Basil Hayden's. In the past few months he had saved two of their lives. He had grown to love and respect this band of men.

"I think maybe now it wasn't a dream, guys. I think I died in that hospital bed for a little while."

"What makes you say a nutty thing like that?" inquired Wayne.

Doug patted Malcolm's head while carefully thinking of his next words.

"I was looking down from above my bed, watching Malcolm and an angel talk together at the foot of the bed. And then Norma Bouvier and Chief of Police Charley Johnson joined me and we hugged. There was a great feeling of joy and I wanted to go with them."

"Sounds like too much morphine to me," commented Pete.

"She's the same angel who wrapped her arms around me in Vietnam, at the battle of the Hump in the Green Dragon; she wrapped her arms around me. She's the same angel who helped me when I collapsed running to find baby Chloe. She held me up, and made me run faster. I know she's real. Malcolm saw her, too."

Stunned silence filled Poor Joe's.

"You see Jesus, too?" inquired Ralph with a hopeful tone in his voice.

"I felt Him; I could feel Him, His presence. Kinda like being with Stanley, you know he loves you, and will do anything for you, will help you through anything--not a guy you wanna cross--always ready to forgive. I know I saw Him standing there smiling. I just can't remember His face."

"I know her," Wendell said.

Stunned silence again filled the old bar.

"She was with me in that cabin when they were beating the shit out of me. She wrapped her arms around me and sang to me. The bastards couldn't hurt me after that. I watched her talking with Malcolm at the foot of Doug's bed in ICU when we were standing in that circle praying for you, Doug. And I saw her swoop up from beside Malcolm and kiss you on the forehead before she left. She smiled at me."

"I've seen angels, too," Timothy added. "Before I went to Cleveland, there were two angels outside my room. I told them to scram when Stanley showed up, but I think he knew they were there."

"Well, Doc, aren't you glad you showed up for the mighty mystery hour at Poor Joe's?" Ric said, shaking his head. "You might want another one of those Basil's."

"I believe every word," Dr. McCaferty said. "I sure do."

"Her name is Janet Sue," added Wendell.

Chapter Twenty-One
Absolutely Not!

Stanley had just left his office located next to the Cardiac Care Unit when the phone rang.

He walked back and answered it.

"What's that piano player's name you told me was so great at Timothy's wedding?"

"Quinn...is that you?"

"Who the hell do you *think* this is?"

"Where are you?"

"Key West."

Stanley laughed. "I've come to believe you know everything about everybody, Captain. Why're you calling me?"

"The secret is to know the people who know everything, Stan."

"Are you in the Green Parrot drinking Mount Gay?"

"That's classified. Now, are you going to give me his name and number?"

"Is he in trouble?"

"Nope, I just need a good piano player, preferably one who plays Chopin."

"David loves Chopin."

"How about the rest of his name?"

"David Chown. Hold on, I've got his number on my Rolodex." He read the number.

"Thanks, Stan. I'll be in touch."

And he hung up.

* * *

David Chown was between piano students when the phone rang.

"Hello, David. My name is Captain Quinn O'Malley from Key West. Your friend Stanley McMillen supplied your telephone number. Is now a good time to talk?"

"Yes, sir. You're the captain who married Stanley and Danielle!"

"Guilty. Think the marriage will make it?

"Are you kidding; we're all jealous. How can I help you?"

"You play Chopin?"

"He's my favorite of all time, why?"

"I'm putting together a little symposium. The host loves Chopin. I'm hoping you can help me out here."

"When and where, Captain?"

"September 15th in Cuba."

"We can't go to Cuba!"

"No problem, we can get you a visiting artist visa. No problem, David."

There was an awkward pause, and then David continued, "How am I getting to Cuba? What about expenses?"

Quinn O'Malley chuckled. "You and Stanley worry too much. I'll call with all the details. Just keep a week on either side of September 15th open.

* * *

Danielle answered the phone at 9 p.m., and laughed.

Stan, it's Timothy. I think he's been drinking; announced himself as

Lieutenant Colonel Fife!"

"What's up Colonel?" Stanley answered. "Danielle thinks you've been drinking."

"Not over the phone; come on down."

"Ok."

"Timothy has something important to discuss, I'll be right back honey."

"At this hour on a work night?"

"Guess it's important."

* * *

They were sitting at the long table in front of the booths, when Stanley walked in: Timothy, Doug, Ric, and Wendell. Chief of Police Strait sat at the head of the table.

"I had a conversation with Quinn O'Malley on a secure line this afternoon," said the chief. "He has arranged for a face to face with the Mexicans… in Cuba. The meeting is scheduled for September 14th or 15th, in one of three possible locations, to be determined upon our arrival in Cuba."

Everyone stared at the chief.

"He's sending a plane to Traverse City on the 12th to pick up David Chown then here to pick us up, and on to Key West. We're going to Cuba on his boat."

"That boat knows its way to Cuba," Stanley muttered.

"Why is David Chown coming?" asked Ric.

"O'Malley said our host loves Chopin," Chief Strait answered.

* * *

Danielle, wrapped in a white bathrobe, lay on a lounge chair on the condo deck overlooking the lights of Big Bay far below when Stanley arrived home.

"What was that all about?" she asked Stanley.

He walked towards his wife, holding a glass of white wine for her and a full glass of Basil Hayden's.

"Quinn O'Malley has arranged for a face to face with the Mexicans in Cuba. He's sending a plane to pick us up in the middle of September."

"No, Stanley. ABSOLUTLEY NOT!"

"We have to, honey; these idiots tried to kill us. O'Malley knows what he's doing. We gotta settle this thing somehow, or we'll be looking over our shoulders the rest of our lives."

"I have finally found what I've been looking for. I have the love I dreamed was possible, and our baby. STANLEY, WE HAVE A BABY! The thought of me kissing you goodbye and you getting on that plane and never coming back… I can't deal with goodbye, Stanley. I don't want you to go."

"Remember the time when I ran Medic One, and all those kids were killed in that car accident on the way to the beach?"

"Yes"

"And you told me that we have known since we went into nursing-- that there are no assurances when we get up in the morning what the day will bring?"

"I remember."

"We're just trying to hedge our bets, honey, stack the deck in our favor. We really don't want those people coming back. Besides, it's not like I'll be alone. Larry, Timothy, Wendell, Ric, and Quinn, that's a serious contingent."

"They could do it without you. You're a nurse, Stanley, not some former Special Forces commando. Sorry honey, I know you were a boxer. Nobody was shooting at you."

"Quinn said the Mexicans need to see the faces of the people they planned on killing, face to face, smiling back at them."

"I remember getting you drunk the night of that accident."

"Want to get drunk, and call in sick tomorrow?"

"Yes."

Chapter Twenty-Two
All Cleaned Up

Machete Juarez, chin held high, walked alongside Chief of Police Strait towards the idling jet. It had just arrived from Traverse City. The little man was wearing a brown business suit, free from any shackles or handcuffs.

Stanley, Timothy, Ric, and Wendell followed. Doug stayed home on Dr. McCaferty's advice, under protest.

"Whose plane?" Machete inquired.

"Mine," answered David Chown from one of the tail seats.

"It's mine," came from the man sitting next to David, Captain Quinn O'Malley. With a wink, he continued, "We're both kidding."

Stanley introduced Machete to David then guided the little man to a seat and sat down next to him.

The shiny Lear jet 85 taxied to the runway as the sun rose over the hills east of Big Bay. The logo on the fuselage showed a roaring lion. The thrust of the twin Pratt & Whitney turbines pushed the eight passengers back into their seats. The jet left the runway heading south at 515 miles per hour, for a three and a half hour trip.

"You cleaned up real good," Stanley said, leaning towards Machete.

"I like my haircut," Machete replied, "and the new clothes. The teeth doctor wanted to give me teeth, but I said no; the smile may be helpful. Maybe no one knows me now, until I smile."

"You have quite the smile. Scares the hell out of most people."

"My sister likes my smile."

There is no way you are going to ever see her again, you little scumbag, Stanley thought, and he shivered. He smiled back at Machete, "That she does."

I like pockets, Machete thought. He unbuttoned his very first jacket and stuck his fingers into the liner pocket.

An hour into the flight, Quinn O'Malley stood up, walked to the front of the plane and turned, facing the passengers.

"We will be landing in Key West, and taking my boat to Havana. We will not know the location or date of the meeting until we arrive in Cuba. Fidel Castro has agreed to host this meeting, and act as the mediator. He moves around frequently for security reasons. He'll decide the night before where we meet."

"Fidel Castro, you're kidding right?" Ric exclaimed.

"Oh, am I glad Danielle doesn't know," Stanley said.

"Actually, Stan, it should be a great comfort to her, with Fidel helping here."

"Why?"

"The rumors you and Danielle joked about, that Fidel and I were college buddies in the late 40's, and that we went to law school together, they are facts. I have known this man for over 60 years. I saved his life in 1958. He is a brilliant thinker. He has a photographic memory; aced every test. I could only come close to his grades, never beat him. He comes from humble beginnings, the son of a single mother, a maid. He compensates with a giant ego and arrogance… until you know him, until you get to know the real Fidel. The distain for U.S. Presidents is real; he told me once that he wished they were smarter than they looked, and that he wished Bobby Kennedy had become a President."

Silence overtook the Lear jet except for the sound of the engines.

"He'll run a tight meeting. It'll be the safest place in the world, guys." And he walked to the rear of the plane and sat down next to David Chown, whose eyes were now wide.

The deceleration was as impressive as the acceleration on takeoff. The jet swooped down and landed on the short runway in Key West with roaring reverse thrusters and brakes screeching. The plane stopped as the runway ended.

"That was exciting," proclaimed Wendell.

The door opened and the humid hot air gushed in. Stanley's glasses steamed up, and he stumbled walking down the steps.

Quinn O'Malley grabbed him by the arm.

"Thanks, Quinn. Forgot how humid it can be," he said, looking up at the "Welcome to the Conch Republic" sign on the roof of the little terminal through fogged glasses.

"I have a van waiting for us on the other side of the terminal," Captain O'Malley announced, and the men followed him through the terminal, carrying small suitcases.

"Greene Street; drop us off at the Conch Republic Seafood," he instructed the taxi driver.

"Beautiful weather for a boat ride, men; the Gulf is flat today."

"Good, I get seasick real easy," Timothy admitted.

"Well, no problems today. We're headed to Habana the beautiful."

The Key West Dreamer was just as Stanley remembered her. The 1948 white, wooden-hulled 36 foot Taylor Craft cruiser with African mahogany and teak decking was spotless. Both 200-horse power engines rumbled softly.

Stanley immediately recognized the Cuban guard that had greeted him and Danielle when they arrived at the Cayo Coco marina in Cuba.

"Hello, Raul," Stanley said. He climbed on board and shook the guard's hand.

"Old friend," he said with a grin, pointing towards Raul. "Doesn't speak much English...as far as I know."

"Where's your machine gun, Raul?" Stanley teased.

Raul smiled.

"Take a seat men; got a little over one hundred miles to cover," the captain announced. The Key West Dreamer circled Tank Island, and headed towards the southwest at 10 knots.

"It'll be dark when we reach Cuba. The Cuban Air Force takes a dim view of planes leaving the U.S. mainland and flying into their airspace, as evidenced when they shot the Piper down a few years back. I like my boat. They have plenty of warning that I'm coming!"

It was 10 p.m. when a Cuban destroyer pulled up on the starboard side of the Key West Dreamer. A brilliant white spotlight illuminated the little boat and blinded the men for a few seconds.

Captain O'Malley waved up at the sailors on the destroyer. They waved back. He went below and talked on a handheld radio.

"We're being put up in the Hotel Saratoga in Habana tonight. We'll find out where the meeting is tomorrow. We're to meet a government attaché in the hotel restaurant at 9 a.m."

The men may have slept, but not much. At breakfast they stared out the restaurant windows.

"Can you believe this place?" Wendell exclaimed. "Look at those cars, 50's and 60's Fords and Plymouths, and Studebakers; reminds me of my garage days!"

Machete grinned, and helped himself to a second helping of fried plantains. As he reached for the platter with his right hand, he slipped a steak knife up his left jacket sleeve, and then into his jacket pocket.

Stanley wished he could call Danielle.

Two military vans stopped at the entrance to the hotel at 9 a.m. The green passenger doors opened on each vehicle and a soldier stepped out and stood at attention, holding a submachine gun. A government official entered the hotel. He spoke to Captain O'Malley in Spanish.

"We are going to the airport; they are flying us to Nueva Gerona."

"Where?" was asked in unison.

"City on the Isle of Youth, an island on the other side of Cuba, directly south of Havana."

Machete mumbled to himself. He flashed a smile at the guard.

Chapter Twenty-Three

The Broken Blade

Quinn O'Malley walked close to Timothy and whispered something as they walked towards an old DC-9 for the 90-mile flight to Nueva Gerona.

Timothy took the aisle seat next to Machete.

After the plane lifted, Timothy turned and put his forehead on the side of Machete's head.

"Give me the knife."

"What?" Machete responded, with his grin and a shrug.

"O'Malley saw you sleeve a steak knife at breakfast. Hand it to me right now, handle first."

"But amigo…"

"Right now or I will snap your neck like a twig."

Machete slowly reached into his pants pocket with his left hand and withdrew a stainless steel steak knife with a pearl handle. He quickly concealed the knife up his sleeve while a soldier slowly walked down the aisle looking from man to man.

Quinn O'Malley called to the soldier from the back of the plane, questioning him in Spanish about the length of the trip, trying to distract him.

Machete pushed the knife onto Timothy's lap.

"What the heck were you thinking?" Timothy whispered. He stood up.

Timothy walked to the restroom in the tail of the plane, past Quinn

O'Malley and the soldier who were conversing in Spanish. Quinn did not look at Timothy.

Timothy locked the door.

He looked around the cramped space, his mind racing, searching for a hiding place. He felt the structure under the sink, ruled it out. He briefly considered the wastepaper container next to the commode, discounting it. He was searching for a space behind the mirror when he looked down at the commode. "There," he exclaimed out loud. *Pieces will fit through that flapper valve and down the hole into the shit tank*, he thought. And he placed the knife on the floor against the wall and stomped on it. The knife blade bent, but did not break. Timothy scooped the knife from the floor, and forced the bent blade into the space between the mirror and the wall. "Both hands would be helpful," he muttered.

With all the strength he could muster, Timothy pulled. The knife snapped, leaving the fractured handle in the palm of his hand. The broken blade fell into the sink. Blood splattered up on the mirror and into the basin.

"Oh shit!"

Quickly, he deposited the knife pieces into the commode. He flushed the commode twice, wiped the splattered blood from the mirror and sink, wrapped his hand with paper toweling, and flushed the bloody towels down the commode, one at a time.

He opened the door and stood face to face with the soldier.

The soldier looked down at the bloody paper towel in Timothy's left hand.

Quinn O'Malley stood up and looked over the man's shoulder. In Spanish he asked, "Did that cut start bleeding again?" He nodded his head *yes* behind the soldier.

"Yes," Timothy answered instinctively.

"Do you have a First Aid kit aboard, Lieutenant?" He continued, "My friend Timothy cut his hand on the boat trip from Key West, and I fear it will become infected."

The DC-9 circled the Isle of Youth in preparation for landing.

Quickly, the Cuban Lieutenant applied silver nitrate salve to the laceration in Timothy's left hand and wrapped it with gauze.

Captain O'Malley handed the soldier 5 twenty-dollar bills, and smiled. The soldier smiled back and placed the money in his shirt pocket.

Timothy sat down next to Machete.

"You little idiot," Timothy uttered.

Machete stared at Timothy's wrapped hand, and then looked out the window at the pine trees and grapefruit trees getting closer and closer.

* * *

A destroyer moved slowly back and forth on the Gulf of Batabano. Three MiG 21 fighter planes circled the island, leaving contrails.

"He's here," exclaimed Quinn O'Malley, looking up at the contrails, and at the destroyer off shore.

The twin turbines on the Russian Mi-8 helicopter whined softly. The rotors turned slowly.

Three soldiers approached the men: one had a submachine gun, one held an electric wand, and the third had rubber gloves on both hands.

"Well, men, we are about to be searched for weapons," Quinn said.

Timothy stared at Machete. "Ask him in Spanish if he has anything else hidden, Quinn. If he does, we turn him over right now. Maybe we should anyway."

Machete shrugged and shook his head no.

Everyone else had a puzzled look.

The helicopter lifted and circled the airport several times, waiting for a MiG fighter to join alongside, and then they headed south at 155 miles per hour.

"Guess we're important enough to get a fighter escort!" Ric announced.

"Or they don't trust us," chuckled Chief Strait.

The helicopter landed on a pad next to an expansive villa on top of a hill overlooking the ocean. They were met by a government attaché who spoke to Quinn in Spanish.

"We have dinner with Castro and the Mexicans at seven, and then the meeting will follow. This fellow over here will show us to our rooms. And, Timothy, a doctor wants to take a look at your hand."

"What?!"

"Fidel travels with his personal physician. Told you guys they wouldn't miss a thing."

* * *

The dining room sat on the top floor of the three-story villa. A large round room sixty feet in diameter with walls consisting of wood framed glass windows extending from the floor to ceiling overlooked the ocean. The domed ceiling was constructed of mahogany. A large grand piano sat next to an oak desk. A round oak dining table filled the middle of the room, large enough to seat thirty people.

The Mexicans were already seated.

The elevator door opened. "What did the doctor say about your hand?" Quinn asked Timothy.

"He thanked me for saving the meeting. Said my hand would heal nicely."

Quinn shook his head.

Cesar Veracruz sat next to his grandfather, Raul Veracruz. Roland Chanchez sat next to Cesar. Timothy remembered Roland immediately, and the night in St Paul when Roland had walked down the steps of the office building with a Thomson machine gun blazing.

The Mexicans studied their faces intently. Raul nodded in recognition at Quinn. Timothy stared back at the three men, rubbing his right arm stump. Wendell glared at Raul, the scar over his right eye highlighted by his frown. Ric wished he was on a Baghdad rooftop with a M40 sniper rifle, or back in Avon, Ohio. Stanley could feel the muscles all over his body tremble, and he had the urge to pee. Chief of Police Strait thought the three Mexicans sitting across the table looked like poster boys for the Mexican

Cartels. Machete wished he had the knife. David Chown smiled from the piano bench, wishing that he had never left Traverse City.

"I imagine you still feel your hand," Roland said to Timothy from across the table.

"Sometimes," Timothy replied.

"So, amigo, we meet again."

"You predicted we might."

When Machete smiled, the Mexicans recognized him.

Cesar Veracruz stood up, livid. Pointing at Machete, he shouted in Spanish, "You are a dead man!"

Raul grabbed his grandson's arm and pulled him back down into the chair.

Machete grinned again, and pointing at the Mexicans, he calmly and deliberately spoke, "I know where you live, each of you, and your families. You will never find me. I am the cat on a foggy night. I see you. You never see me."

The elevator door opened. Three security guards exited, looked around the room, and nodded towards the open elevator door.

Fidel Castro entered the room.

Quinn O'Malley stood up.

Everyone stood up.

His six foot three inch frame now bent with age, Fidel walked into the room with authority. He held a cane in his left hand. He wore a camel hair jacket and a black beret on his head.

He stopped at the piano and spoke to David, in English.

"We both love Frederic Chopin."

"Yes, sir."

"Slide over, please." Fidel Castro sat on the piano bench with David Chown.

David watched as Fidel played the *Minute Waltz.*

When he finished, Fidel smiled, leaned close to David and said, "We have at least started the evening on a civilized note." He handed David a list of requests to be played during the dinner, including the *Revolutionary Clavier, Revolutionary Etude,* and the *Funeral March.* "My favorite works by Chopin," he said. "I am told you are from Traverse City."

"Yes, sir."

"I love cherry pie."

Fidel walked to the dining table. He greeted Raul Veracruz first.

"I was saddened when I heard of Diego's death, my friend." And they shook hands.

Looking down into Cesar's brown eyes, Fidel shook his hand. "Life without a father is unfair. I never really knew my father."

He shook Roland Chanchez's hand. "I could have used you at my side in 1959, amigo."

Then he rounded the table and greeted Chief Strait. "I hear you know how to polish a jeep!" And he laughed.

"Yes, sir, anytime!"

And then he was eye to eye with Timothy.

"You, young man, have quite a story: Vietnam, St Paul and the woods of Big Bay. I would have treasured you at my side when we were fighting for justice. I hear your wife is a wonderful singer. Perhaps someday I will visit your Poor Joe's. I hope your hand heals quickly."

Fidel looked down at Machete.

Machete grinned up at the President of Cuba.

Fidel spoke in Spanish, "You, little man, need to be watched. We count the steak knives at the Saratoga, and I personally chose the dinnerware here. Behave."

The President of Cuba looked down at Wendell's deformed right hand.

"It is my honor to shake the hand that caught a grenade, and meet the man who saved Timothy's life at the Embassy battle."

"I admired Benito Mussolini in my youth," Fidel said, shaking Vincent Bonifacio's hand. "He was a great journalist, you know, before he lost his way. You Italians have a flare that I admire. You do things with passion."

"Thank you, Mr. President."

He studied Ric for a moment before he spoke.

"They say you can hit a basketball at 1000 yards. Our revolution would have been shortened by months if you had been with us, young man." And they shook hands.

"I hear you enjoyed our hospitalities at Cayo Coco not too long ago, young man," Fidel said, shaking Stanley's hand. "Dr. Blue informed me that you are the greatest critical care nurse he has ever known. We have a wonderful medical system here in Cuba. If you would ever like to join us, you are welcome; you and your wife, Danielle, and daughter would all be welcome here. I would see to it."

"Thank you, Mr. President."

"I am serious, Stanley."

Quinn O'Malley and Fidel Castro stared at each other for several seconds before they embraced. Fidel dropped his cane.

They whispered in Spanish.

"We've been over bigger hurtles, Quinn; we can resolve this dispute together."

"These are my friends, Fidel. If anything happens to my friends, I will turn the Lions loose."

"Those Lions saved my life in 1958, amigo. I thank God for your help every day in my prayers."

"We were quite a team," Quinn said. He patted the President's back.

"We had the great General Eisenhower quaking in his boots."

The men hugged again.

Fidel Castro sat down at the table between Quinn O'Malley and Raul Veracruz.

President Castro nodded in the direction of the piano, and David Chown began to play the concertos of Frederic Chopin.

"We will have a civilized meal together, and then we shall work out our differences in a civilized manner tonight," Castro announced.

Gazing at the Cuban feast, Stanley wished that Danielle was with him.

The meal started with deviled crab rolls, followed by white bean stew, and then sea bass or mojo chicken with rice. The meal ended with flan Cabana.

After dinner, a Cuban drink consisting of rum, lime juice and ginger ale was served. A box of Cohiba Esplendido cigars passed from man to man.

"These are my favorite cigars," Castro announced. He sniffed a cigar. "I no longer smoke on my doctor's advice; you enjoy. I smoked them from age 15," he said with a smile.

Following dinner, the dishes were cleared, and the wait staff dismissed. The meeting began abruptly.

Fidel Castro pointed at Stanley and commanded, "Stand up."

Chapter Twenty-Four

Trembling Legs

Stanley stood on trembling legs, and swallowed hard.

Why did this man have a death sentence?" he asked, looking at Raul. "What did he do to deserve that sentence? The runt stated you had Stanley on the list." He pointed at Machete.

The Mexicans stiffened and glared at Machete.

"He helped the man we were hunting, the man responsible for my son's death. He saved Timothy's life."

"So you are saying this man who did what he has done for many people over the years--saving lives--and would do for each of you I am certain, if you were injured--making every effort to save your life--deserved to be killed? Is that what you are telling me?"

The Mexicans remained silent.

Stanley felt dizzy. He braced his legs against the table.

President Castro waved at Stanley, indicating he should sit down.

He then pointed at Wendell, indicating he should stand.

"Tell me, Raul, what did this man, who confuses grenades with baseballs, what did he do to deserve his mistreatment?"

"We apologize, Fidel. Our operatives went rogue. They arrived in that city and could not find Timothy Fife. They became desperate in their search. We are sorry, Mr. President."

Wendell sat down.

Ric stood up as instructed.

"And did this man have any involvement in your son's death?"

"He is the one who shot my longtime friend Matias outside the cabin. Shot him like a coward, using a sniper rifle."

"One of the men beating Wendell, correct? One of the men sent to kill or kidnap Timothy?"

"Yes."

"Would you have done differently, if it was your friend?"

Silence ensued. Raul stared at Fidel.

And then Fidel Castro indicated for Timothy to stand.

"Did Timothy Fife kill your son?"

"He was the detective in charge. His subordinates murdered my son."

Fidel motioned for Roland Chanchez to also stand.

Timothy and Roland stood facing each other across the round table.

"Did Timothy order his subordinates to shoot Diego?"

"He did not."

"Did Timothy point his weapon at Diego?"

"No. His pistol remained in his holster."

"Tell us what you witnessed."

"Timothy was talking to Diego. The police on the street shot him."

"What happened to the men who shot Diego?"

"I killed them both. I shot them with my machine gun. I filled their bodies with holes."

"What was Timothy doing at this moment?"

"Standing on the steps next to Diego, his hands out, with a sad face. He told me there had been enough killing this night."

Fidel looked directly at Raul.

"I am sorry Diego was killed, and that you lost your son in this way. The men who killed your son paid with their lives. If Timothy had intended to cause your son harm, he could have, but did not. My information is Mr. Bonifacio (he pointed towards Vincent Bonifacio) plotted this arrest and set Diego up."

"That is the truth," Vincent replied. "I did that to maintain my cover for the company I am employed with."

Richard Alan Hall

"You can say C.I.A. in this room," Fidel said with a smile. "We have no secrets today."

"Yes, sir."

"And you still work for the C.I.A.?"

"Does one ever truly retire?"

"You could take your revenge on Bonifacio; your son's death is on his hands. You could do that; just know that the C.I.A. will hunt you down like Mongoose hunting snakes."

Young Cesar exploded with rage.

"This is bullshit! These guys killed my father, and you allow your friendship with this old man (pointing at Quinn O'Malley) to poison the well, and cloud your judgment. This is bullshit!"

A shiver trembled over everyone in the room.

Three bodyguards sitting next to the elevator stood up. Each had a handgun drawn.

Fidel started to stand. Quinn stood first, put his hand on the President's shoulder, and whispered something in his ear.

Captain O'Malley walked towards Cesar Veracruz. Looking down at Raul's grandson, he spoke in Spanish. "Do not add to your grandfather's grief by adding your funeral to his burdens. When you have time to reflect, you will understand the honesty of this meeting today, and that justice has been served; the innocence of these men has been exposed. In a younger time, you would now be gasping your last breath. Your life would now be flowing out on this floor. Take this as a lesson; revenge extracts a heavy worthless price."

Raul reached over and grasped his grandson's hand.

Quinn began to walk back to his chair then turned and faced Cesar again. "If you do not accept Mr. President's words as facts, if you do not call off your henchmen, you have no idea what will be unleashed on you and your family, starting with a cat in the fog." And he nodded towards Machete.

Fidel grabbed Quinn's arm when he rounded the table. Quinn and Fidel put their heads close.

"You are still the Great Lion of the Pride." Fidel chuckled.

"And you are still the master in the courtroom, Mr. President!"

The President patted Quinn on the back.

Machete grinned at young Cesar.

Chapter Twenty-Five

I've Got News For You, Too

The men walked towards the helicopter the following morning, emotionally exhausted. Quinn noticed the MiG fighters were no longer circling the Isle of Youth. The Naval destroyer had left as well.

The Russian helicopter did not stop at the airport in Nueva Gerona, but rather continued out over the Gulf of Bataband, then over Cuba, landing on the marina lawn next to the parking lot.

"We need to top off the fuel before we head back," Quinn commented. He started the blowers.

Quinn had started the starboard engine and was about to start the port engine when a green military van came through the parking lot, driving across the lawn, stopping 20 yards from the boat. Three men climbed out of the vehicle. He immediately recognized the driver as one of the three bodyguards with President Castro during the meeting.

Quinn shut the engine off. A Navel destroyer slowly moved past the break wall. He walked to the men, and had a short conversation with the driver.

Quinn turned, pointed at Machete, and waved at him to join them. Machete trotted to the van, nodded his head yes, and turned, waving back at the boat. He climbed in the van's back seat, closed the door, and grinned out the window.

"Machete will not be going back with us," Captain O'Malley said.

After filling both fuel tanks, the Key West Dreamer idled out of the marina, headed for the Straits of Florida. The Cuban destroyer shadowed them for 12 nautical miles. When they reached international waters, the destroyer pulled alongside with sailors lining the port railing, saluting. The ship's foghorn blew three blasts.

"Who are you, O'Malley?" ask Ric.

"Same as you, Ric, just a guy with a little history."

Stanley stared down at the mahogany deck and smiled. When he looked up, Quinn was staring at him.

"Let's get you home to your family," the captain said.

Passing the dark Mallory Square ten minutes after midnight, the festivities at Schooner Wharf Bar could be heard echoing through the marina.

"Let's go hang with the Big Dogs over at Schooner Wharf!" the captain shouted over the engine noise. "I'm buying."

The men secured the Key West Dreamer in her berth. They walked past the shuttered Seafood Company, around the marina and up the sidewalk steps, passing Jimmy Buffett's gray concrete windowless recording studio, and under the lights strung from pole to pole, into the glorious old outdoor bar. A country and western band played *How Do You Like Me Now*. They were greeted by several mongrel dogs, tails wagging.

The bartender looked up, watching the group walking under the large umbrellas.

"Welcome back, Captain, first round is on the house," he said with a smile.

Two hours later, tired and inebriated, the men stumbled into the La Concha Hotel.

Timothy called home using the lobby phone, under the slow moving paddle fan.

"Hi honey, we're back in the U…S…of A…!"

"It's 2:30, Timothy."

"Oops…I forgot."

"You boys been celebrating, haven't you?"

"Sorry."

"Well, when you get home we've got a little celebrating of our own to do!"

"What?"

"I've got a surprise for you," Carla teased.

"Tell me…!"

"I want to surprise you. When you get home."

"Stop it. You can show me when I get home tomorrow. Just tell me."

There was a pause.

"You still there, Carla?"

"Yup…Timothy, you're going to be a daddy!"

Timothy's mind flashed to the first time Carla walked into Poor Joe's, how amazingly beautiful she looked to him, and the look in her eyes the night she said, "You are adopted, that makes us not cousins." He thought of the night in the Grand Hotel when she grasped him by the shoulder, spun him around, pinning him on the bed, her soft long blond hair coming over her shoulders and tickling his face.

"Timothy?"

Timothy slumped on the couch. Stanley and Wendell started to walk in his direction.

"Thank you, Carla. I'm so in love with you. You're going to be a wonderful mother."

"I'm very happy for us, Timothy."

"Carla is going to have a baby!" Timothy said, looking up at the men standing in a semicircle around the couch.

"Congratulations, old man," Wendell said.

"Yeah, who do you suspect?" Ric asked in jest.

With speed which defied his age, and before anyone could react, Timothy sprang off the couch, and with his nose on Ric's forehead, said, "You can razz us guys…never say anything like that again about my wife."

"I'm very sorry, Timothy."

"Ok then."

Chapter Twenty-Six

The Bus From Avon

Wendell ran up the stairs. He never ran up the stairs. He knocked on Ric's door, and entered without waiting for a response.

"What the hell?" responded Ric. He tossed Steinbeck's *In Dubious Battle* on the bed, and stared at Wendell.

"She's here."

"Who?"

"You know."

She was standing next to the piano with her back to the staircase, wearing a light blue summer dress with a thin long sleeved white sweater, talking to Timothy, when Ric came down.

"Michelle?"

She turned around and they were face to face.

The Baptist girl was as beautiful as he remembered from that night eight years ago.

The bar became very quiet. Ric and Michelle stared at each other, and then embraced tightly. She could feel his heart pounding.

"How'd you find me?" he asked.

"Always known where you are Ric, even when you were in the service, I knew where you were stationed."

"How?"

"Your brother Ted. I'd see him at the IGA, and sometimes at the Shell station. Once in a while, I'd just call him at his shop. He'd give me any news; said you'd call him from time to time, but not very often."

"I've thought about you every single night since I left Avon. Every night, Michelle," he whispered in her ear.

Timothy shooed some patrons from the booth under the staircase, and then came back and gently led Ric and Michelle to it.

"Ted said you've never been married," she said after they were seated.

"No. Dated the secretary at the body shop for a few months, and a nurse; that's it. How about you?"

"Yes, to Art Crothers."

"The churchy football guy from high school?

"Yup, I was a cheerleader and he was the football star. We both ended up at Ohio State together. He went to seminary afterward, and then we got married. He's the assistant pastor at the Baptist church in Avon now."

"How'd you get here?"

"The bus. I just left. Got on the Greyhound when he went to Thursday evening bible study."

The conversation paused. They stared at each other.

"I can't go back Ric." She paused.

"He says I'm disrespectful when I question him, that wives are to be submissive to their husbands."

"Holy shit!"

"We got married when I was twenty-two. I was young. I was naïve. I never even achieved a career of my own; I teach Sunday school and give piano lessons."

"Well, I hardly have a career myself; I help out here at the bar, and work part-time at Barrett's Auto body shop."

Ric reached both arms across the table. They held hands, staring at each other for several minutes. Through the white sweater, Ric could see multiple bruises on both of her arms. Michelle glanced down at her arms. "I can't believe you're here."

"Me either. I hope I don't wake up on my side of the bed facing the wall and find this is a dream."

"It's a dream, all right," Ric said.

"Have any children, Michelle?"

"I can't; that's one of the things he blames me for. And he says I misled him, that I was not pure at the altar."

Ric's body tensed and his fists clenched, "I'm going to take a little trip to Avon."

"No, don't. I don't want you in trouble. I'm afraid he'll come here after he calls the Greyhound office."

Ric looked over at the bar where Timothy and Wendell stood, watching him. He waved, beckoning them.

"Guys, this is Michelle. She's in trouble and needs our help. Her husband beats her."

Michelle looked startled and frightened for a second.

"Would you like a place to stay?" Timothy asked.

"Yes, please."

"She can stay with me," Ric interjected.

"Not now, Ric, not yet," Timothy replied. "We have an empty bedroom at our place. You can stay with Carla and me until we get this all sorted out. I'll give my attorney a call in the morning, and get you an appointment, Michelle."

"Thank you, Timothy."

"You're welcome. Want a job?"

"Sure, need a piano player?" she answered, pointing at the upright.

"You're a piano player? Good, hasn't been played much lately. That'll liven up the place."

"I know lots of hymns!" Michelle said, laughing.

"That'll go over great! Ok, let me take you down to Grant Street and introduce you to my wife. She's pregnant."

"Help me find some sheet music tomorrow," Michelle whispered to

Ric. "I love you very much, Ric; I always have. I don't know what I was thinking."

"We were too young to think for ourselves. Not anymore," Ric replied, and there was anger in his eyes.

* * *

It took the assistant pastor two days to track his wife to Big Bay.

The man filled the front door at Poor Joe's.

He blocked the entrance looking in. He stood 6 foot 4 inches tall. Doug sized him at 230 pounds.

The big man walked to the piano player and grabbed her arm.

Michelle stopped playing.

"Go on and get your bags; you're coming home with me right now."

Michelle trembled with terror.

Timothy reached under the bar and grasped a baseball bat with his left hand.

Doug reached into his jacket pocket and fingered a Thirty-eight Special. With his left hand, he took the leash off Malcolm.

Dora dialed the police department.

Wendell and Ric stood up from the southwest table. Pete, Ralph and Wayne hopped off their bar stools.

The big man looked at the assembly staring at him.

"I'm here to take my wife home. You're not going to stop me," he said as he lifted her by the left arm. Her feet came completely off the floor.

"Art, put Michelle down," Ric said calmly. "She's not going with you. Michelle's filed for divorce. She's staying here."

With the flick of his wrist, the big man tossed Michelle against the piano, and she crashed down on the keys. He walked rapidly towards Ric.

"YOU! You are the defiler!"

He was nine feet from Ric when Malcolm lunged at the big man's testicles and twisted them with a growl. Timothy hit the preacher in the back with the baseball bat. The big man tossed Malcolm to the side and headed for Ric again, when four old war vets tackled him. As the preacher struggled to his feet, Doug hit him over the head with a wooden chair, shattering it, without dissuading the angry man.

Chief of Police Strait, along with an officer, ran through the front door, their guns drawn. Doug breathed a sigh of relief and shoved his pistol back into his pocket.

"I'll be back!" he yelled. "I'm never going to sign divorce papers." And Chief Strait led the big man out the door.

As he placed the big preacher in the back seat of the patrol car, Chief Strait leaned close to the man's head, and whispered, "You are *never* coming back to Big Bay. And I'm certain you'll sign those divorce papers."

"REALLY!"

"Promise, big fella."

* * *

Chief Strait opened the door to the empty holding cell and ushered Art Crothers in without removing the handcuffs. "Have a seat," he said, pointing towards the cement bench on the back wall.

Art Crothers stood, glaring through the black steel bars at the Chief of Police.

"I want a lawyer."

"Well, of course you do big fellow, but let me tell you what's going to happen if you call a lawyer: the front page of the Big Bay News Review is going to carry a story, pictures and all, about how you busted up Poor Joe's Bar, and in addition to those charges, a charge of domestic abuse has been filed by your wife. Yes sir that will make quite a splash on the front page. Been kinda starved for exciting news in town for quite a spell. And, I'll make sure that copies are sent to the appropriate folks in Avon; I am sure they would like to be apprised of your situation."

Chief of Police Larry Strait pulled a green plastic chair close to the bars and sat down.

"Sit down," he ordered.

The big man sat down on the cold cement bench.

"As I see it, you have several options, young man. Let me list them for you. Pay attention, Art. First option: you take a vacation, say down to the Florida Keys, do a little shark fishing, think about life. I have a friend who has a charter service, he'd be happy to take you shark fishing. Kinda dangerous though; most guys make it back. Second option: I call an old war buddy, served in Vietnam together. He was the chaplain and I was the sinner. He grew up to be the president of a Baptist Theological Seminary, is a Doctor of Philosophy in Bible stuff. I call him with your situation; bet he would have an idea on how to help you. Third option: you go back to Avon with your tail between your legs and tell everyone that your wife has succumbed to the ways of the world, and has left you. Why, you'd save face. And people will feel sorry for you. That'd be good for a couple of sermons. Fourth option: you go back to Avon and tell the truth, ask for forgiveness. The hell with what the people think. You ask our Lord and Savior for forgiveness, get on your knees and plead for His grace, then get on with your life. There you go, Art, there're your choices as I see 'em. Pick one. But Art, I want you to know one thing for certain, if you ever come back to Big Bay, or if you bother Michelle in any way, you *are* going to take that fishing trip. I know just the men who will oblige you."

Chapter Twenty-Seven
We're Still Alive

"**I**t could have been worse," Timothy commented.

The Usual Suspects and Stanley surveyed the rubble on Monday morning.

"Doug could have shot the place up with his shotgun again," he continued with a grin, looking down at the buckshot holes in the hardwood floor, a souvenir remaining from the night New York City bikers calling themselves HELLS SPAWN had invaded the bar.

"Boy, that big guy was strong," Wendell said. He rubbed his neck with both hands. "He threw me off like I was a rag doll."

"You missed quite a fight, Stan," Ric said. "I'm very grateful that I stopped here for some clam chowder and never left," he continued. "Maybe I'd have never discovered friends like you guys."

"Ain't it something, us guys!" Wendell said, and then shouted, "Semper Fi!"

"Semper Fi!" everyone in the room responded, including Stanley, even though he never served as a Marine.

"Ok, let's clean this mess up; I have a bar that wants to be open tonight," Timothy commanded.

The men were busy cleaning and moving tables when Chief of Police Strait's car pulled into the parking lot. The chief got out, and opened a rear door. Art Crothers climbed out. The two men talked for several minutes.

The chief handed the big man his wallet and car keys, and shook his hand. Art Crothers started his red Buick Riviera, and drove away.

"Did you see that!" Ric exclaimed.

Chief Strait walked into Poor Joe's and surveyed the mess.

"Well, you're almost back together, Timothy. Gonna be open tonight?"

"Yes, sir. Thanks for your help Saturday night."

"Your tax dollars at work. You're welcome. Ric, need to have a word with you."

Larry Strait and Ric walked out the front door.

"You know, I sure as hell was wrong about that guy," Pete said. "I thought nobody could measure up to Charlie Johnson, but geez, Larry is... just different."

"Hard to know a guy until you do," Wendell added.

* * *

The Chief and Ric walked down the sidewalk on Basswood Street.

Chief Strait handed Ric an envelope.

"What's this?"

"I had the Prosecutor draw up some boilerplate divorce papers, and Art Crothers signed them."

"What!?"

"He seemed most eager to sign them, put the past in his review mirror, and leave town as soon as possible. Now you have Michelle sign above her name and date it, and turn it in at the courthouse. I spoke to Judge Linsenmayer. She'll take care of the rest when the time is right."

"Thank you, Chief."

"You're welcome, young man. You have my best wishes for much happiness in your lives together."

Ric walked through the front door of Poor Joe's with a giant smile on his face, waving the envelope.

"Art Crothers signed the divorce papers. I have to take them to Michelle." He left, walking the seven blocks to 737 Grant Street.

"What the hell?" commented Ralph.

"See what I mean," Pete said. "Chief Strait is in a league of his own too."

"I think this calls for a celebration!" exclaimed Wayne.

"Yes it does," Timothy said. "We've seen more than most would believe if we told them. Let's have a party Saturday night, a party for Ric and Michelle, and for us. We're still here."

"I'll call Lisa's Meat Market. They have a pig roaster now," Stanley volunteered.

"A pig roast Saturday night!" Pete shouted.

"Oh boy!" Doug exclaimed.

"You know, if somebody made a movie of our lives, the critics would say, 'Nope, that couldn't happen,'" Stanley said. "Nope, they would say our lives are not plausible." And he laughed.

* * *

The Saturday evening festivities were well underway when the old man with shoulder length white hair walked up the steps and into Poor Joe's. He walked with a cane.

"I have grown to like pork over the years," he said to Stanley, who was bent over carving meat from the pig's shoulder. "The Cubans marinade it with orange and lime juice...delicious."

Stanley turned.

"A.W. Blue!"

"Hi, Stan. Hi, Danielle."

Danielle hugged the doctor; her mind flashed back to Cayo Coco, Cuba, and the night they talked on the beach while the tide came in and a wave almost tipped her over.

"Wow, what a surprise, Doctor. What are you doing here?"

"I heard there was going to be a pig roast at Poor Joe's, so O'Malley gave me a free ride to Key West, and I booked a flight."

"That's a likely one, A.W.," Stan said.

"I need to be home right now, Stan .Will you give me a tour of the hospital next week?"

"Love to. Lots of changes over the past 20 years, Doc. Come with me, I want to introduce you to the guys."

Chapter Twenty-Eight
A Very Evil Day In Big Bay

Michelle signed at the designated spots with tears dripping on the divorce papers. "They weren't all bad years; he just changed after his knee injury at the chief's rookie camp, and then there were the times he was passed over and stayed the assistant pastor," she said, turning the pages. "And I have always wondered what it would be like if I was with you."

"You're about to find out."

"I'm excited. Let's date; I want to start out slow, for us to get to know each other."

"Ok, Michelle."

* * *

No one noticed the red Buick Riviera parked in the dark alley off Grant Street for three consecutive nights.

Art Crothers watched each night as Ric walked Michelle home at 10 p.m. He watched while they kissed on the front porch, and Ric walked back towards Poor Joe's. He looked up at the dark upstairs window, waiting for the light to flash on. He stared through the curtains while Michelle undressed and put on pajamas, and turned off the light.

Richard Alan Hall

On the fourth night, Art was hiding in the shadows behind a large beechnut tree when Ric and Michelle passed on the sidewalk, down the block from 737 Grant. Michelle was laughing when Art struck Ric in the back of the head with a tire iron then put his large hand over her face, smothering her until she lost consciousness.

He placed duct tape over her mouth and nose, and tossed her in the trunk. He drove all night and for six hours after sunrise. He drove into Kentucky, up into the mountains and mining country, finally stopping at an abandoned mine he and his cousins had explored as teenagers.

The big man opened the trunk and lifted the limp body. He removed the duct tape from her face. He walked to the edge of the vertical mine shaft and sat on a tree stump. For twenty minutes he stroked her long hair. Then he stood up, tossed her body down the shaft, and listened. Twenty seconds later he heard a splash.

He walked back to the Buick and took a screwdriver and the registration papers from the glove box. He removed the license plate, and walked back to the mineshaft, throwing the papers and plate down the shaft.

Finally, he climbed over the logs blocking the entrance to the mine, and jumped.

* * *

That afternoon, two teenage boys hunting squirrels walked down the two-track road leading to the mine.

"Hey, somebody's here," the taller boy whispered, and they slunk from tree to tree, looking all around.

After ten minutes, they were standing next to the automobile.

"No plate," the shorter boy said, pointing.

"Bet it's stolen. Keys are in the ignition, too," the taller boy said.

"Let's drive it to my daddy's garage. This'll make an awesome Stocker. Daddy'll help us."

"Yeah, we can race over at the fairgrounds Saturday nights," the shorter boy exclaimed.

The tall boy started the red Buick.

* * *

The flashing red lights reflecting through the window on their bedroom wall, along with the sound of a lone siren, woke Timothy. He looked at the clock radio on the dresser; the clock hands pointed to 3:22. Carla rolled towards him.

"What's wrong, honey?"

"There's something going on down the block. I'm going to check." He jumped out of bed, grabbed his blue jeans and a tee shirt, and headed out the front door.

A night shift police officer had spotted a man lying under the big beechnut tree on Grant Street. "Damn drunk," he muttered. The young officer stopped the patrol car, turned on the overhead lights, and walked towards the tree.

The man was lying face down in the grass, both arms crumpled beneath him. In the light of his flashlight, the young patrolman saw a pool of coagulated blood in the grass, and a large gash on the back of the man's head.

The patrolman squatted down and felt for a carotid pulse. The pulse was weak and very fast.

"Man down 748 Grant Street. Requesting an ambulance and backup," he radioed to the police dispatcher.

Timothy ran barefoot down the sidewalk, and arrived at the scene just as the ambulance pulled up. Carefully, the two paramedics, Timothy, and the patrolman rolled the man over to his back, while supporting his neck.

Timothy sucked in a deep breath and sat down in the wet grass when he saw the man's face.

The patrolman looked up in the sky. "This is Ric from Poor Joe's."

* * *

Timothy ran back to his house. Carla was standing on the porch.

"It's Ric. Go upstairs and check on Michelle."

Carla came back, pale. "She's not here; her bed is still made."

"Oh my God, Carla." And the old war vet who had weathered agony over and over, sat down on the porch steps.

"Something very evil has happened."

Timothy and Carla were still sitting on the steps of the porch when Chief Strait arrived. He walked to the porch and sat down next to them without saying a word.

* * *

The phone rang at the McMillen residence.

"Stanley, this is Dr. Smith."

"Hi, Lavern, what's up?"

"Sorry to call you at this hour. Our friend Ric is in the ER."

"What happened?"

"It looks like he was attacked sometime last night. He has a head injury, a serious one, Stan."

Stanley walked down the darkened ICU hallway without saying a word. The young night nurses stood aside and watched. One of the young ladies reached out and touched his arm. He stopped for just a brief instant, long enough to see tears in her young eyes.

She had dated Ric.

Dr. Smith met Stanley before he entered ICU room one.

"This isn't looking good, Stan. His pupils are fixed."

Ric had been intubated and was on the ventilator, making its whooshing sounds. His swollen eyelids were taped shut. Stanley put the side rail down with a clunk and pulled up a chair. He reached under the covers and held Ric's hand; it reminded Stanley of scraping frost off the windshield without gloves.

The respiratory therapist suctioned pink froth from the endotracheal tube.

Stanley looked up at the cardiac monitor, showing sinus tachycardia at 138 beats a minute. Ric's blood pressure registered 80/42.

"Does he have family we should contact?" asked the night charge nurse.

"He's from Avon, Ohio; left when he was eighteen years old and has never been back. I asked him once, and he said, 'that was another life' and refused to talk about it."

"What should I do?"

"I'll take care of it. Guess the guys are his family now."

Stanley was sitting with his forehead resting on the bed mattress still holding Ric's hand when he heard a voice behind him.

"I'm sorry your friend's been hurt, Stanley."

Stanley looked up. Dr. A.W. Blue was looking down at him, leaning on his cane, with his long white hair in his face.

"A.W.! What are you doing here?"

The old man shrugged, and smiled a little.

"Just wanted you to know I'm here. You know your friend is not here, don't you?"

"Yup," and Stanley started to cry. "I know. I just don't know how I'm going to tell Michelle."

"Stanley."

"Yes?"

"Ric and Michelle are together."

Stanley looked up at the old man.

And he knew.

Chapter Twenty-Nine
Tunnel Of Swords

They all gathered at Poor Joe's the morning Ric died.

His friends sat in that big room silently, looking at the booth where Ric and Michelle had been not too long ago.

Even the men of steel sniffled and wiped at their eyes from time to time.

Finally Timothy spoke, "I remember him telling me he was raised a Catholic; should we contact Father Stanton, and see if we can have his funeral at St Joseph's?"

"Ric didn't go to no church, except in his heart," Doug commented.

"This is for us guys, not for Ric. Let's have his service over at the Methodist Church, same as we did for Chief Johnson, and for Norma when she died," Wendell said.

"I think Wendell is right guys, and I agree; let's use the Methodist church. I'll call Pastor Long, and make arrangements," Stanley said.

"We don't need him for the service, Stanley, just the church. Us guys are gonna do the talking. We're his friends," Doug said.

* * *

The funeral was the following Saturday morning at 10. Even the balconies on either side of the worship hall were crowded.

Stanley walked slowly past the closed casket, reading the notes attached to the banks of flowers surrounding Ric, including flowers from Vincent Bonifacio and Rose Jackson.

The largest arrangement, a glorious selection of red, white and blue flowers, standing 4 feet in height, had a simple card signed by Fidel. It said, "I am sorry, Ric."

In the front row sat Dr. A.W. Blue, next to the Catholic priest from St. Mary of the Immaculate Conception church in Avon, Ohio. Captain Quinn O'Malley sat next to Father Raftery.

The pews on the left side of the church were filled with uniformed men, United States Marines and British Special Forces, both active and retired.

Timothy walked up the steps to the lectern first.

"I did not know Ric as long as some of you. I was out of town when he moved here. In the short time I knew him, and traveled with him, I discovered a genuine human being without pretense. He did what needed to be done, loved deeply, and cared for others. I sure am going to miss him."

Wendell spoke next.

"We would sit at our favorite table and talk almost every night. Ric shared his heart. He was the most unselfish, kind person I have known. His great regrets were that he had hurt other people; he hated that about his life, that he had ever hurt another person. I am *sure* he has been forgiven."

Stanley spoke.

"Ric was the most genuine person I've known. What we saw is who he was, Ric cared for people and it grieved him that sometimes he had hurt others. The Gulf War haunted him. He told me that he prayed for forgiveness every day."

Stanley took a deep breath. "He loved Michelle with his whole being, and I am sure they will spend forever together, hand in hand."

Richard Alan Hall

A.W. Blue and Father Raftery from St. Mary's looked at each other. Carla, and Ralph carrying his trumpet, walked into the choir loft.

"I just keep hoping this day is a dream, that I will wake up and tell Timothy all about it in the morning," Carla said. "But it's not, this is life, and sometimes life is a nightmare. I don't know if Ric had a favorite hymn. This one is for all of us that are still here."

Carla sang the first line a cappella. Then Ralph joined in with the trumpet.

"What a friend we have in Jesus
All our sins and griefs to bear
What a privilege to carry
Everything to God in prayer
O what peace we often forfeit
O what needless pain we bear
All because we do not carry everything to God in prayer."

Ric's casket was carried out of the Big Bay Methodist Church by his friends, through a tunnel of swords raised high. He was buried on the bluffs, next to Norma Bouvier and Chief of Police Charlie Johnson, overlooking the valley of Big Bay.

* * *

Chief Strait's wife, Dawn, called the McMillen residence Sunday evening. Danielle was rocking Chloe when she answered the phone.

"Hi, Danielle, this is Dawn,"

"Hi, Dawn."

"Stan home?"

"Yup, I'll get him. Just a second."

"Just tell him to come down. Larry's not himself. I'm scared"

Stanley's beloved Avanti slid in the gravel and he almost lost control on the S curves at the bottom of the hill, going 80 in a 35 mph zone.

"Lord, help Larry. Whatever's wrong please help us tonight. Please help us. We've been through too much pain, Lord. Please," Stanley prayed out loud. His right foot pressed the accelerator to the floorboard and the black Avanti's 425 horsepower engine roared.

Dawn was standing on the covered porch with the outside light on. Stanley kissed her on the forehead, and hugged her tight. Her eyes were frantic. Silently she turned, pointing through the open front door, towards the closed bedroom door.

He walked into their bedroom alone. Dawn watched from the hallway. Stanley entered, and without saying a word, laid down on the bed next to her sobbing husband. He put his arm around the quivering man, and pulled the chief's quaking back close to his chest, and hugged him tight.

The chief's service revolver lay on his wife's pillow. Stanley hit it with his head, and then rested his head on it, even though it hurt his ear.

Neither man said a word for a very long time.

"I really screwed this one up, Stanley."

"How'd you know it was me?"

"Old Spice, you and Timothy are the only ones who use Old Spice, and he doesn't have a right arm."

"That's why you're the Chief of Police."

"I really messed-up this time. It's all on me. Ric would still be alive if I followed the book, but no…had to be a cowboy. And who the hell knows where Michelle is and what Art Crothers has done. We haven't found a trace, not even a credit card trail."

"So how is using this pistol going to make any of this better, Larry? How is Dawn finding your bloody brains all over the bedroom ceiling going to help a damn thing? All our hearts ache, and we're all wishing that we'd done this or that differently. Poor Timothy is livid that he didn't have Michelle stay upstairs at the bar where Malcolm and the guys could have kept her safe. Wendell just sits alone in agony at the corner table and stares at the booth under the stairs. When I close my eyes, I see Ric's big grin, and feel the love he had for Michelle. Like Carla said at the church, sometimes life is a nightmare, but Larry, we've been through nightmares before, and

113

we'll have them again, until we're all buried in a row up on that bluff. The way we get through this shit is by loving each other, no matter the fault; we just hug each other and get on with life while we wait for the pain to become a bad memory."

Dawn cried.

"Damn it!" Larry Strait said. He stood.

"Let's drive over to Poor Joe's and wake the guys up," Stanley said, now facing the red-eyed chief.

"I could use a big glass of that Basil's you brag about."

"Me too--several. You are about to get your first ride in the Avanti."

"My life will now be complete." And the chief laughed, a little.

The men walked down the hallway. Dawn Strait hugged her husband. She squeezed Stanley's hand without saying a word.

Chapter Thirty

Red Haired Irish Preacher

The young lady walked through the front door of Poor Joe's at 8:30 p.m., interrupting the sacred men's night poker game. For as long as anyone could remember, Wednesday night was poker night at the bar. While never explicitly stated, the participants were men. The Usual Suspects were always present, as well as various patrons who would come and go. Sometimes Stanley would participate, although not as frequently since the birth of his daughter. More frequently now, Dr. McCaferty would join in, and sometimes Chief Strait.

Actual cash never exchanged hands. The poker chips had various denominations and could be exchanged for Dora's clam chowder, and there were beer chips redeemable for draft Schlitz, as well as prime chips that could be exchanged for top shelf bourbon, or a steak dinner.

Wendell was shuffling the cards when she walked in. He glanced up and half the deck scattered across the floor.

"Good evening, young lady," Timothy greeted from behind the bar.

"Good evening right back atcha. You must be Timothy."

"Correct…you have me at a loss."

She laughed. "Well if you guys made it to church for more than funerals, you would know that Pastor Long has been transferred to Fargo and I'm the new pastor."

The men around the table stared at her.

Timothy estimated her age about 30.

She stood 5 foot 6 inches tall with an athletic muscular build, and curly red hair, barely tamed, in a short bob cut.

"My name is Katherine Kennedy McGinnis. You boys may call me Kate," she said.

Her green eyes smiled when she spoke with a gentle Boston Irish accent.

"I like cold Guinness," she continued. She pulled a chair towards the poker table. "And I like poker."

The men could smell her fragrance of honeysuckle.

"You married?" Doug blurted from the end of the table.

"Not yet. How 'bout you?" she shot back.

Timothy stood at the bar and smiled. These tough men, who had been hardened by the horror of wars and recent heartache, were completely befuddled and acting like high school sophomores discovering lust.

"Timothy, give Kate a starting stash," suggested Ralph.

"Where's your home?' asked Wendell

"124 Roosevelt, right next to the church."

"I mean where were you raised, Kate?"

Her green eyes twinkled. "Oh." She rubbed her pixie nose.

"Yeah, what city?" Ralph chimed in.

"You guys are a curious bunch," she said, looking down at her cards, and peering through her red curls at the men. "What'd you do to your hand?" Kate asked, pointing towards Wendell.

"He was playing catch with live grenades," Timothy responded from behind the bar.

"I was born and raised in south Boston...in Dorchester actually. My mother emigrated from Ireland when she was 7. My father's parents emigrated from Ireland in 1937."

Wendell won the hand and collected his chips.

The game stopped and the men waited.

"More?" Kate asked.

Everyone at the table nodded affirmative while Ralph dealt the next hand.

"I'm an only child...spoiled rotten," she continued with a grin, "really spoiled.

"…and no …what's your name?" she asked Doug.

"Doug."

"I'm not married. Never have been. And no, I'm not gay. No cards for me."

"How come you ended up a Methodist preacher? Thought you Irish girls were all Catholic?" Pete asked.

"My mom is Catholic. She's a Pediatrician at Boston Children's Hospital. My dad is a captain with the Boston Fire Department. He's 'a practicing fireman, District 7, Engine 27 and Ladder 7, 36 Washington Street, Dorchester.' That is a direct quote I overheard at a baptism when Father Haller ask him why he didn't come to church more often."

"How'd you end up a Methodist?" Pete repeated.

"In the eighth grade Sister Marissa showed us a documentary on the life of Mahatma Gandhi. During one interview he said, 'I like your Christ. I do not like your Christians. Your Christians are so unlike your Christ.' That quote never left my mind. I watched denominations criticize each other, and religious zealots kill each other and innocent people all over the world; it made me sick. I couldn't wait to throw that school uniform away. Oh look, I win." And she plopped a full house on the table.

"I had a scholarship to Duke. I studied law."

"You're a lawyer?" Timothy said from the bar.

"That I am, Timothy. My parents were so proud. I felt empty inside. Duke has a Methodist Divinity School, too. That quote of Gandhi's flitted across my mind one night, and I thought, *if I can preach love and acceptance, I'd be a happy girl*, so I looked into it, and now I have a doctorate in theology, too."

"How old are you?' Ralph blurted.

"35…And look who won this pot, too; why it's me!"

"Do you practice law on the side?" Wendell asked with a smile.

"Just the practice of love. The logic of love is so clear to me, guys. I can win that argument every time. Anybody want to try me?"

Everyone at the table shook their heads *no*.

Timothy grinned from behind the bar. *This gal's something else,* he thought.

"So can I expect to see you guys in church for more than the occasional funeral?"

"We go to church in our hearts," Doug said with determination.

"Fair enough, Doug. Tell you what. I win this hand, and we get together once a week and talk about stuff."

"Here?" was the unanimous response. "This is a bar," Ralph said.

"Right here at this table, every Wednesday, just like now. This is the perfect place. I think Jesus would hang out with you guys."

"You believe in angels Kate?...cuz we do. Some of us have even seen them, and some miracles too," Doug said.

"Yes I do, Doug, but that will need to wait for another poker night. We have a deal?"

Everyone nodded in the affirmative.

"Well, boys, speaking of miracles, look at this hand." Kate tossed a royal flush on the table.

Yup, Timothy thought to himself, *this town is never going to be the same*.

"Ok," Kate said. She looked over her shoulder while she walked out the front door. "See you next week, boys."

Ralph groaned.

Chapter Thirty-One

Consequences Of Not Cooperating

Machete Juarez stalked Cesar Veracruz all around Mexico City for five weeks. He followed him every morning using a different cab, from his condo to his Grandfather Raul's office on the top floor of the Gran Hotel Ciudad. He watched and memorized the daily routines of lunch with his grandfather and business associates at their favorite restaurants. Machete memorized the established evening routine, too.

Every Wednesday night following the evening meal, Cesar stopped at a massage parlor located next to a 5 star Thai restaurant high in the hills overlooking the business district. The routine was established. At 9:30 Cesar's silver Mercedes 500 circled the block twice, and then stopped in the parking lot. The driver would get out and survey the area while walking around the car and opening the passenger rear door. Cesar would exit and enter the massage parlor through a side door, and return in 40 minutes.

The driver stood outside the Mercedes with an AK-47.

On a cloudy, foggy Wednesday night, Machete watched the silver Mercedes drive up the hill and park in the usual spot.

Twelve minutes after Cesar entered through the side door, two young ladies emerged, one topless. The ladies teased Cesar's bodyguard, kissing him and rubbing against his body. The topless girl sucked the end of the AK-47 barrel and winked.

He wilted. The young ladies led the man through the side door, with his rifle slung over his shoulder.

Like a cat slinking in the fog, Machete left the alley and crawled under the automobile. With a bolt cutter, he severed both front brake lines, and then after several attempts, cut the emergency brake cable. Just as quickly, he returned to the alley and watched.

The guard returned within 5 minutes, buttoning his shirt and zipping his pants. He was standing at attention when Cesar emerged and climbed into the back seat.

The silver Mercedes slowly left the parking lot, its headlights shining into the fog as it crested the hill and started down the steep incline.

Machete grinned. He whispered into the fog, "You will have exciting finish, amigo, compliments of Fidel." Then he entered the side door where the young ladies awaited. He handed each an envelope and left after kissing both breasts of the topless one.

* * *

Stanley was playing peek-a-boo with Chloe on the deck after work Friday evening when the phone rang.

"Stan...O'Malley here."

"Hi, Captain. How are you?"

"Just received news from a friend in Cuba. It seems young Cesar Veracruz was killed in an automobile accident last Wednesday night."

"That's news all right, Captain. I thought that young hothead would be killed in a gun fight."

"Dead is dead, Stan. The appropriate thing now is for you guys to send a big bouquet to his funeral. His grandfather is grieving. Send it F.T.D. overnight to Sacred Heart Church on Plaza de La Constitucion."

"See to it first thing in the morning, Quinn."

"Good." And Quinn O'Malley was gone.

* * *

The spring stock car racing season had begun for the 47th year at the Muhlenberg Fair Grounds. Every Saturday evening, weather permitting, stock car racing would begin under the lights at 8 p.m. Sitting on the very top row of the bleachers, side by side, Vincent Bonifacio and Machete Juarez watched the cars race around the 2 mile oval track. Leading the pack of Fords, Chevys and Dodges, was a battered red Buick Riviera with the number 6 hand-painted in white on the driver's door.

The red Riviera won two races, and placed second and then third in the final race of the evening. At the end of the final race, Bonifacio leaned over to Machete. "Let's go pay the driver a visit."

In the crude pit area, a 40ish year old man with a short beard climbed out of racecar number 6 through the driver's window. Two teenage boys greeted the driver with high-fives, a tall boy and a short one.

Vincent and Machete approached the race team.

"We're with the Target Pizza Company, and are always looking for stars to sponsor on the racing circuits," Vincent said.

He shook the driver's hand. "I think you're a winner."

The bearded driver smiled. "I just put a rebuilt engine in her this winter," he said. "Puts out about 500 horses now."

"Don't believe I ever saw a Riviera on the race circuit before," Vincent commented, looking through the driver's side window.

"Bought her off a guy had it on a flatbed, taking it to the scrap metal yard. I said, 'That's a fine automobile to scrap, let me make a stocker out of it,' and he sold her to me for the scrap metal price."

"You've got a good eye for automobiles, young man. Let's all go down to that little restaurant on Front Street and talk about getting you sponsored."

The driver and the teenage boys sat across from Vincent and Machete in the diner's booth. A family style platter of onion rings and French fries had been placed on the table.

Then the young blond waitress with acne brought a platter of gator bits, while they waited for burgers.

"One thing our company insists, our CEO is a real stickler on this, is that we are assured of a clean title prior to giving our Target endorsement and sponsorship. We had an ugly thing happen a few years back where a guy we sponsored was driving a stolen car. The boss was mad as hell when the cops called his office."

The driver looked down at the onion rings. The taller of the teenage boys started to slide out of the bench, muttering, "I gotta pee."

His dad grabbed him by his shirtsleeve.

"You stay."

The teenage boys looked at each other, then started eating French fries rapidly.

Finally, the driver looked up from the onion rings.

"We ain't got no clear title, sir. Just bought it off the guy and didn't ask no questions. She's just a junk racer."

Machete watched the teenage boys intently. Their eyes shifted between the French fries and each other, and the floor. Then he smiled a big smile with a full set of teeth. "You boys want to tell the truth now? "

"It will not be difficult to check on the scrap metal story," Vincent added.

"We just found it, mister," the shorter boy said. He chewed rapidly, looking at the floor.

"Yeah," the taller boy added, "and it must have been stolen cuz when we found it there's no papers in the glove box and no plate or anything…promise."

The driver looked at the boys, "Didn't figure there was any harm in racing a stolen car they found out by the old mine. Figured we'd just use her at the track."

"Ok, here's the deal," Vincent said. "We keep our mouth shut about how you found your racecar…You guys just show us where you found it."

"You guys ain't really pizza guys are you?"

"And sorry," Vincent continued, "no sponsorship. The boss would be really pissed if we sponsored a stolen car."

* * *

"Timothy, we've found Art Crothers' Riviera in the hill country of Kentucky, being used for a stock car at a race track."

Timothy had answered the phone at Poor Joe's during breakfast.

"How'd you find it, Vincent?"

"We've been monitoring used parts traffic between junk yards since the car disappeared. Saw a request for a rebuilt Riviera engine and a purchase made from a yard outside of Lexington last winter. We just followed it to the buyer, and bingo!

"We?"

"Yeah, Machete kept me company. He's cleaned up real good; has teeth, a short haircut, and horned rimmed glasses compliments of our friends in Cuba."

"Really!"

"The car was found near an abandoned mine shaft up in the mountains. Sent a team down that shaft. They found Michelle floating at the bottom. No evidence of Crothers."

"Oh shit!"

"We've recovered her. Put her in a closed casket."

"Send her to us, Vincent. We'll bury her next to Ric."

"I knew that; she's on the plane right now. Meet her at the airport at 3."

Timothy hung up the phone and looked at The Usual Suspects eating breakfast.

"You guys. They've found Michelle's body at the bottom of a mine shaft in Kentucky."

"How'd she get there?" asked Ralph.

"Probably Art Crothers threw her down the shaft. They're still looking for him."

"Who's looking?" asked Doug.

"Bonifacio and Juarez."

"What's that little scumbag doing back?"

"I don't know, Doug."

Timothy called Stanley at the hospital with the news.

"We'll have a funeral for her," Stanley said. "Before we bury her up on the hill by Ric, I need for Michelle to have a funeral. All of us do."

"What about her family in Avon?"

"When Chief Strait notified her family when she went missing, her father said something about the 'wages of sin,' and hung up," Stanley answered

"Unbelievable," Timothy uttered.

"I'll call the new pastor Kate at the Methodist Church," Timothy continued. "She was just here last Wednesday night, playing poker with the guys."

"What!"

"Just wait until you meet her, Stan."

* * *

Saturday morning and the Methodist Church had no empty seats for the Baptist girl from Avon, Ohio; even the balconies were crowded with people standing against the back wall.

Pastor Kate stood up to deliver her first eulogy.

"I did not know Michelle. Most of you in this church today did not know her either. The fact that we are here today is a testament to the love she shared from her soul. She touched each of us in some very special way during her short time with us. I KNOW THAT RIC AND MICHELLE ARE TOGETHER RIGHT NOW... and I bet smiling at us."

Pastor Katherine McGinnis paused and looked out at the large sanctuary without an empty seat. "I know this because I have visited their world, the dimension where they exist." She paused again, and took a very deep breath before she continued. "When I was in the 10th grade, my boyfriend gave me some pills at a party and I accidently overdosed. I suffered a respiratory arrest and was on a ventilator, unconscious for 3 days.

I clearly remember my grandmother Kennedy sitting on the side of my bed, both of us side by side, looking at my body in that bed hooked to all the machines. She said, 'Don't be frightened, Katie,' and I wasn't, not in the slightest. My grandmother hugged me and then we were joined by a great feeling of love and joy...that I think was Jesus. I don't remember His face, just the love." Kate took a deep breath. "I wanted to go with them, but instead I'm right here with you today. So what I'm saying is this: it's ok for us to be sad and to grieve with the loss of this special soul that stopped and spent a short time in our lives, but just know that Ric and Michelle are in the presence of glorious love, and will be waiting to greet us when we make that wonderful trip."

Kate wiped tears from her cheeks and smiled.

"As C.S. Lewis wrote," she continued, "'There are far better things awaiting us than what we leave behind.'"

And she sat down.

The Usual Suspects sitting in the front row looked at each other, astonished.

High up in the left balcony, Machete Juarez and Vincent Bonifacio sat side by side. Machete leaned close to Vincent and pointed down towards Stanley and Danielle exiting the church. "My sister can walk now. See her walking!" he said, pointing towards little Chloe.

Chapter Thirty-Two

No Greater Love

I t is not during the wonderful times, when laughter and smiles abound, but rather it is during the sad days and the frightening times when friends are revealed. It is during the times of danger we discover those who are willing to stand by our sides regardless of personal consequences, and hold our hand. On this sad funeral Saturday, this truth became evident.

* * *

The long screeching sound of locked rubber tires sliding on concrete ended with a violent crunching of metal bending metal, and the tinkling of glass, followed by several seconds of silence.

People walking on the sidewalk in front of the Big Bay Methodist Church pointed towards the intersection at the end of the block, and some began running in that direction.

"Stay here," Stanley said to Danielle, and he ran.

At the intersection, a large, yellow Public Works City of Big Bay dump truck rested on a blue Pontiac, which was rolled over, with the front tires still spinning. The mangled vehicles leaned on a metal utility pole, tilting forward from the impact. The truck was leaking fuel, creating a little stream trickling past the wreck and down the street towards the Methodist Church.

The pregnancy test was positive, and worries raced through her teenage mind as she drove down Carver Street on the way to her boyfriend's house. She had grand plans, graduating the top of her class and attending Yale next year. She'd already been accepted at Yale and was assured of a scholarship. She had been so careful. *Maybe this is God's punishment for sinning. How am I going to tell Jeff? Geez, my dad is going to blow a fuse, maybe kick me out. Mom is going to cry for days. The girls at school are going to have a blast with the Mennonite girl getting pregnant. Maybe Jeff can help me get an abortion and nobody will know. No…no…I can't do an abortion.*

A violent smashing force hit the passenger side. She had not even looked at the traffic signal. The car slid 10 yards before the tires caught on the curb and the big yellow truck rolled the car over, stopping on top of the blue Pontiac.

"I'm sorry, Jesus," the young lady cried, dangling upside down, her braided blond hair hanging in her face.

Without hesitation, Stanley crawled through the diesel fuel and glass shards, barely squeezing into the Pontiac through the shattered windshield. Hanging upside down suspended by her seatbelt, she sobbed. Blood dripped from her nose and splashed on his forehead.

"You hurt?" Stanley asked, looking up from his back.

"No… scared," the young lady with blue eyes answered.

"What's your name?" Stanley asked.

"Sarah Phillips."

"Sara with an A?" Stanley asked, checking her level of consciousness.

"No, Sarah with an H, like in the bible; my folks are Mennonite."

"Brace yourself; I'm going to release the seatbelt," Stanley instructed, "and get you out of here."

A fire truck pulled up at the intersection and shut off its siren.

Suddenly a soft woofing sound and a gasp from the crowd. The little river of fuel running past the wreck ignited. Dark smoke drifted into the wreck. The southern breeze pushed heat with the smoke.

Dave Rickett had dreamed of being a fireman since grade school. He had a collection of small cast iron fire trucks. In high school, when the various career choices were presented by his counselors, he steadfastly stuck to his dream of being a fireman. Three months ago he had graduated from the Fire Academy at the top of his class. His heart pounded a little when the call came into the station: "PIA with entrapment intersection of Carver and Washington. Reports of a fuel spill."

Dave jumped off the pumper in full gear and pulled a high-pressure line towards the burning wreck. His mind raced back to the simulations at the academy when he had encountered similar situations. He activated the nozzle and began to spray water in a clockwise fashion, advancing towards the wreck.

Chief of Police Strait pounced on the rookie, knocking the fire hose to the pavement where it twisted on the ground like a snake.

"Damnit, son, there's people inside. You're blowing burning diesel on them."

Larry Strait stepped on the hose, reached down and pulled the nozzle to *off*. When the Fire Chief, wearing a white helmet, rounded the front of the fire engine, Chief Strait shouted at him.

"That was a close one, Chief; the kid was blowing burning fuel right into the wreck. I'll be right back."

He ran into the flames and disappeared in the smoke, pulling the fire hose with him.

"Hurry," Stanley said as he started pushing Sarah through the broken windshield. Through the smoke crawled Chief Strait, pulling a high-pressure fire hose by the nozzle. He pushed the young lady and Stanley back, rolled over, aiming the nozzle towards the street, and sent a stream of water outward.

"The rookie was hosing the fuel right into the wreck!" he shouted.

"Your pant leg is on fire, Larry!"

"Thanks," he said, hosing both of his legs.

The metal above them groaned and crunched again. The roof of the Pontiac made a grating noise against the pavement. The utility pole tipped towards the ground. The wreck shifted forward, crushing the top of the

Pontiac even more, and narrowing the windshield opening.

"Shit," Chief Strait uttered.

The mustard yellow dump truck tilted towards the left, and fuel poured from a hole in the tank. A little river of fuel ran into the flames. It ignited with a concussive force.

Inside, Larry Strait tucked Sarah's head into his armpit, covering her face with his jacket, spraying water at the encroaching inferno. He searched for a spot to shield his face from the heat. His mind flashed back to Vietnam, and the time when his F-4 had been shot down.

Sarah's quivering body now rested across Stanley. His legs burned, and he reached up, gripping something in the smoke, trying to pull himself further into the wreck. The metal burned his hands. He shrugged and rested his head on the chief's hot, wet leg. Resolutely, Stanley turned his eyes towards the flames. "If you want me to come home, I'm ready, Lord. Take care of Chloe and Danielle," he whispered into the smoke, and he wondered if Danielle would remember the combination to the safe.

Dark smoke obscured the entire wreck when the fire engine from the Big Bay Airport arrived at the scene minutes later. With great precision, the airport crew sprayed foam into the flames.

From inside the crushed Pontiac, the three-trapped humans watched the flames growing closer and more intense. Then white foam bubbled towards them in waves, replacing the flames. Through the foam crawled a little man covered with the white stuff, followed by a Big Bay fireman. The little man pushed a hydraulic jack he had taken from the rescue rig without permission.

The front of the truck shifted forward again with a grinding, crunching sound. The truck's smoking front tires almost touched the road now and the cavity in the twisted metal mess shrunk. The fireman tried, but could not squeeze through the narrow opening to the Pontiac. Little Machete Juarez wiggled through.

"Hi, amigos." He grinned with a foam-covered face. With the help of Chief Strait, he placed the jack against the bent frame and began to pump the handle. The opening slowly expanded. And then through the twisted metal, Stanley watched as multiple sets of legs clustered together on the left side of the wreck, standing ankle deep in the foam and fuel. Wendell, Pete, Wayne, Ralph, Doug, Timothy, Vincent Bonifacio, and Dr. McCaferty, as well as many more parishioners, pushed against the leaning dump truck, ignoring the danger and direct orders from the Fire Chief to "stand back," stabilizing it while the hydraulic jack slowly lifted.

When the opening was large enough, Dr. Jack McCaferty crawled through the foam and diesel fuel. Stanley and Larry pushed Sarah through the windshield and into the doctor's arms.

Crawling out of the wreck, the cool foam on the pavement felt soothing on Stanley's burned hands. At the edge of the wreck, a kneeling Pastor Katherine Kennedy McGinnis prayed, her robe soaking up water and diesel fuel. Danielle was kneeling beside her, one hand holding Kate's and the other holding her daughter's.

Stanley crawled towards them.

"Thanks, ladies," is all he could manage before he hugged them.

The three adults hugged and little Chloe watched.

After kissing Danielle, he said, "Great to meet you, Kate."

Before they stood, young pastor Kate put her arms around Stanley and Danielle. With her head still bowed, she said, "Sometimes it's during the saddest moments when our faith is tested the most, and it's then we are made strong again."

* * *

Vincent Bonifacio and Machete Juarez walked down the wet street and climbed into the back seat of a black car with darkened windows.

"Good job, little fella," Vincent said.

"My sister needs her father. I never had a father."

Chapter Thirty-Three
It's A Boy!

S tanley was sitting at his desk reading the new budget constraints when the Director of Nursing walked in.

"How're your hands?" Ramona asked.

"Healing great. I love Bag Balm."

"You and that Bag Balm. Danielle off today?"

"Yup, taking Chloe for more vaccinations."

"Carla is in labor, just came in… dilated 5 cm."

"Timothy with her?"

"You'd think he was 17, just grinning and getting in everyone's way."

In addition to family members visiting other new parents, The Usual Suspects paced about the O.B. waiting room, feeling very uncomfortable. Doug called pastor McGinnis, and she joined the men.

"How long does having a baby take?" asked Pete.

"As long as it does," Pastor Kate answered. "I've never had one."

Stanley and Ramona smiled, listening to the conversations between the bewildered, excited men awaiting news.

Danielle met Stanley and Ramona outside the delivery room. She was dressed in scrubs.

"Carla called me on her way here. Chloe's with the girls down in the E.R. Carla's doing a great job; she's dilated 8 cm. We'll meet baby Fife pretty soon!"

"How's Timothy doing?"

"Holding Carla's hand and grinning."

At Poor Joe's, Dora walked in to start cooking lunch, looked around at the vacant building, turned the *open* sign around to *closed*, and locked the front door. She drove to Big Bay General, smiling and praying.

At 9:26 p.m., Charles Dwight Fife joined the population of Big Bay, weighing in at 7 pounds, 3 ounces and 21 inches long.

The nurses at the OB nurses' station tried to stop Timothy. He carried his son, bundled in a soft white receiving blanket, towards the waiting room.

"You can't take him out of the room yet, Timothy."

"Sure I can; I'll be right back. The guys gotta meet Charles. Be just a second."

With a smile and sparkling eyes, Timothy walked into the waiting room with his son.

The men gathered around and stared in awe, speechless.

Kate took a small vial from her purse and unscrewed the top. She dabbed her finger with olive oil. She approached Timothy who was sitting in a recliner now. Timothy looked up.

"I'm going to bless your son," she whispered.

"Thank you," Timothy replied.

Pastor Kate made the sign of the cross on tiny Charles Dwight's forehead.

"Will you bless me, too?"

Kate dabbed the end of her finger with olive oil again, and made the sign of the cross on Timothy's forehead.

"Us too, Kate," Doug said from behind her. "We all need to be blessed too, cuz we'll be helping with his raising."

Standing in a single file line, Doug, Wendell, Pete, Wayne, Dora, and Ralph waited to be blessed.

Stanley and Danielle, Ramona, and the OB nursing staff watched from the nursing station while each received a blessing.

"I really don't know what to say," Stanley said, "except we have witnessed several miracles today."

Ralph was last in the line waiting to be blessed. When he approached

Kate, she smiled.

Putting her lips close to his ear, she whispered so only he could hear, "No more cheating on Wednesday nights."

"You either," he shot back.

Chapter Thirty-Four

Not A Fan Of Religion

"**A**nybody know where Doug is?" Wendell asked the congregation of Usual Suspects as they consumed scrambled eggs, thick sliced bacon, and hash browns while sitting at the bar. "I just checked his room again, and he's not there."

"He told me he was going to church. He took Malcolm and left," Dora said from the grill.

The men looked at each other's reflections in the Goebel Beer mirror and shrugged.

"He ain't been the same since you and Ric did CPR on him," Ralph said, turning towards Wendell.

"Not since he saw Malcolm talking with that angel and watching Norma and Charles above his bed when he died. Not since then, Ralph."

"That'd do it for sure," chimed in Pete. "He told me once, after lots of Wild Turkey, that he had been an altar boy at some Catholic Church in New York City. His face got real sad and he changed the subject to the Yankees."

"Well, he and Malcolm are in church today," Dora said. She smiled, and scraped the grill with her spatula.

* * *

Pastor Katherine McGinnis stood and walked to the podium after the gray haired man wearing wire rim glasses finished reading the announcements. She wore a short-sleeved green summer dress that made her red hair appear even redder.

"Last Sunday a parishioner asked why I was not dressed in my robe. The simple answer is that the dry cleaners could not salvage it after the accident last month, and the replacement has not arrived yet, and we had only one in my size. The truth is that I do not consider a robe important. It is no more important than when you men put on a coat and tie, or you ladies pick out your favorite Sunday dress before coming to church. These are traditions, I suppose, and a sign of respect, too, and traditions have their place. We follow traditions because that is what we do; it gives structure to our lives, and it is nice to look nice for other people to see, but I doubt God is impressed."

Kate looked down, and for the first time saw Doug in the front row. Malcolm was sitting in front of him, watching her intently with his brown eyes.

"That is the great danger which we all face when religion becomes a tradition: that we do what we do because we always have, just like our parents and their parents, too...like putting on a robe or putting on our special pretty clothes and going to church."

She paused and looked down at Malcolm again.

"I am not a fan of religion. There is very little connection between faith and religion. I have watched with disdain over the years as horrible things have been done around the world in the name of religions. When I was in college I would ask how such things could be done in God's name, people hurting other people when we are all God's children, and thought how angry He must be.

"The Bible tells us that God is love. That hit me one night when I was trying to decide what to do with my life after I had graduated from law school."

There was a soft whispering in the congregation.

"God is love. It is through faith that each of us grows close to God.

Richard Alan Hall

Religions are traditions, manmade traditions, built to meet our own societal needs, which may pit us against each other because our human needs differ. No, I am not a fan of religion, but I sure am in love with God. The fruit of faith in God is love. If there is no love, then my recommendation is run as fast as you can.

"*What about the infidels who don't attend church?* you may ask. And I ask, how do you know a person's heart? My mother is a gentle person. She is a Pediatrician at Children's Hospital in Boston. Growing up, I watched her work with sick children without concern for reimbursement. Sometimes I would make rounds with her on weekends, and envied the adoration she received from the little children and their parents, until I grew to realize that the adoration was, in a way, payment for the love she was sharing with each child, regardless of their appearance, skin color or status in society. I think sometimes the children recovered because she loved them. She once told me, 'Love heals, Kate. Never forget that. Love heals. And a broken heart can make one sick. Never forget that either Kate.'

"My mom is a devoted Catholic.

"My father's appearances in church can be counted on one hand, for baptisms and funerals. I remember watching him working in our lush green back yard, and walking around the big fishpond that he had built when I was 5. Sometimes he would be talking all by himself. When I was 9, I finally asked Mom, 'Why does Dad talk to himself all the time?' Mom smiled and hugged me when she answered, 'He's not alone Katie; your dad is talking to God. He goes to church in his heart, and they are talking in the garden.'

"Now I truly understand what my mother was telling me. Faith is a very personal relationship we may each have with God. It's what He wants. It has nothing to do with robes and suits, and dresses, or traditions. It has to do with love. And yes, we can go to church in our hearts. We should every day; I think God likes it when we start our day talking with him."

She paused. "Not that I don't enjoy seeing each of you every Sunday." The congregation chuckled.

Kate looked down at Doug. He winked at her, standing behind the podium in her green summer dress.

136

Doug waited until the line of parishioners had dwindled to just a few people before he and Malcolm got in line to exit the Sunday morning worship service. Several children had pointed towards them, and the parents shook their heads with disgust. Doug noticed that some of the people had left through the side doors rather than shake hands with the pastor on the way out.

"How did Malcolm like the sermon today?" Kate asked with a smile.

"I think he liked it a lot, Kate. I know I sure did."

"Good. That was *not* the sermon I had in mind for this morning, Doug. When I spotted you and Malcolm in the front row, the words just poured into my mind and I spoke. I was just a messenger. I could hear myself speaking and thought, *oh man, this sure will get some of them upset*, but the words kept coming, and I kept speaking."

"You spoke your heart, Kate. I loved what you said."

"Thanks."

"Can we go out on a date sometime, Kate? I know I must be as old as your daddy. Just want to know you better."

Kate studied Doug's face for several seconds before she replied, "Is that why you asked if I was married that first night I crashed the poker night?"

"I saw you walk in before the other guys did, but mostly I felt you walk in, even before I saw you; I felt you being there, Kate. I can't explain."

"I wanted to take that empty chair next to you that night, Doug, and sit right next to you and hold your hand under the table. That's what I wanted to do, but thought that would be a little forward, even for a redheaded Irish Methodist preacher from Boston, so I sat across the table."

"Really?!"

"And our souls are the same age, Doug. I would be happy to go on a date with you."

"I don't own a car."

"That's ok, I do, but let's just walk downtown to that little diner on Gulf Street."

"Tuesday night at 7?"

"That'd be perfect. It'll give the guys something to talk about on Wednesday night." Kate grinned.

Chapter Thirty-Five
A Puddle Of Urine

Timothy was actually present for the Wednesday night poker game. He had not attended on a regular basis for 10 months, preferring to stay home with Carla and their son. Carla had flown to Nashville to record her second album, and Charles Dwight went with his mom.

Carla returned to her studio condo from the recording studio at 6 p.m., after a long recording session. She had flown to Nashville Sunday evening for an anticipated weeklong recording schedule at Imagination Studios. The studio had hired a nanny to watch Charles, who was a busy boy. The nanny gave Carla a good report and left saying, "See ya in the morning!"

She had not been gone long when the doorbell rang.

"Latraia?" Carla questioned.

She unlocked the door and opened it.

Roland Chanchez pushed the door open and quickly closed it, with his finger to his lips.

One week earlier, Roland had been standing in Raul Veracruz's Mexico City living room. "I want them brought to me," Raul said, poking his finger in the air at Roland while seated in an overstuffed red leather chair, his lieutenants standing around him. "That Timothy Fife has destroyed my family. My son is dead. My grandson is dead. Timothy Fife is to blame. I want him to suffer a most terrible pain worse than death. Bring me his wife and son."

Roland nodded, "I will take care of this personally. I will bring them to you in this very room."

"And I will make Timothy Fife a dead man in his soul. First we send him a finger from them both, and a week later we send him the wife's right ear, and his son's. Then a month later we will send pictures of their naked dead bodies."

"Yes, sir."

"Is he loco?" asked one of the young lieutenants after the men exited the living room.

"I think he has the dementia," the other young man added with fear in his voice.

Roland stopped walking and grabbed the two younger men by their shirts. "He is the boss. While he is the boss, we do what he commands. That is how things are."

"He is going to get us all killed," retorted the taller of the young men.

"That may be true. Do you want to tell him this, or go back in that room and kill him, and then run until you are caught and fed to the fishes?"

"Sorry."

"Damn right you are sorry. This conversation never happened."

"Yes, sir."

Now, Roland pushed Carla against the wall, and with cold dark eyes staring directly into her's, said, "Get your son and we walk out of this place together like old friends. Any warning sound and I will put a bullet in your baby's head as you watch."

Urine trickled down Carla's right leg and formed a small puddle on the floor.

"NOW!" he shouted.

Carla cuddled her son tight to her chest as she trembled. The trio left the studio condo in a brown Ford Ranger. They stopped at the Nashville airport.

And then they were airborne, traveling directly to Mexico City.

* * *

"Timothy, we need to talk...in private," Vincent Bonifacio said.

Vincent walked briskly through the bar's front door towards the poker players.

"Well, hi to you too, Vincent. Go ahead, no secrets at this table."

Vincent hesitated, then pulled a chair over to the table and sat next to Timothy.

"We've been advised that there's a threat against your family by the Mexican Cartel.

"This information is supplied by our friends in Cuba."

"Carla and Charles are in Nashville," Timothy replied.

"I know. We have a team headed to the studio right now. They will transport her home."

The poker players' pupils dilated and they felt cold. Several jaws begin to clench with anger. Kate reached under the table and grasped Doug's fist. His entire body was shivering.

"Sir, we have news from team Nashville," a young man wearing sunglasses announced from the open doorway.

"Be right back, Timothy."

"I'm going with you." The two men walked to a black Suburban with all the doors open in the parking lot.

Why's he wearing sunglasses at night? Ralph wondered.

"We're too late, sir," the voice said on the radio. I'm sending you a video from the studio surveillance cameras. The video screen in the back of the vehicle flashed on. Timothy and Vincent watched Roland Chanchez leaving with Carla. Roland had his arm around Carla, who was holding Charles tight against her chest.

"Roland Chanchez!" Timothy shouted.

"We've got a team headed for the airport," the voice said on the radio. "The studio security guard is missing, too."

Vincent Bonifacio walked to the front passenger door and picked up a different phone. "Quinn, we have a situation here. Timothy Fife's wife and son have been abducted in Nashville by Roland Chanchez. A flight plan was filed for a Lear to travel from Nashville to Mexico City 30 minutes ago."

"I understand," Quinn replied.

Timothy turned and walked back into Poor Joe's. He was just inside the front door when he bent over and vomited. He looked at the poker players. "They got Carla and Charles. The Mexicans got my family."

An involuntary shiver spread over the room.

Stanley went to the bar phone and called Danielle. "I'm going to be late, honey."

"What's happened?"

"I'll call you back."

* * *

"We gotta do something," Wendell said. "We gotta get down there and save them."

Everyone surrounded Timothy. They all touched him, giving love and trying to provide hope.

"I want us to stop right now and pray," Kate said, standing next to Timothy. She held his hand tightly. "Lord we have evil attacking us right now. We're asking You to keep Carla and little Charles safe. Wrap them in Your arms and protect them. Their lives are in Your hands."

* * *

Carla now stood in Raul Veracruz's living room, holding her crying baby. Roland stood beside her. It was 3:30 a.m.

"You are quite beautiful," Raul said loudly.

She stared back at the old Mexican Godfather. On his right, hanging from the wall, she saw portraits of a beautiful young lady, and next to her, a larger portrait of a handsome young man. A smaller portrait of a young man hung next to the handsome man's portrait. Twelve candles burned on a shelf below the portraits.

"You are a very evil man," she replied.

"I am a very sad man," he retorted. "I am sad because your husband killed my son and then my grandson. He has destroyed my life, and now I am going to destroy his life."

"Please be with Timothy," Carla prayed silently. "Hold him close to You…and help Charles not to suffer."

She smiled at Raul. "You can't destroy us; evil cannot destroy love."

Raul snapped open and closed, repeatedly, a small bolt cutter.

He motioned for Roland to bring Carla closer.

* * *

Vincent rejoined everyone at the poker table.

"I just spoke with O'Malley. The Lions have been loosed."

"What?" came in unison from the table.

Timothy, Stanley, and Wendell looked at each other and nodded.

* * *

In the darkness they arrived. Almost silently, twelve men dressed in black, scaling the wall around the compound, walked stealthily from building to building with guns that had silencers, shooting anything that moved.

Slowly, Roland led Carla by the arm towards Raul. *The young men are correct*, he thought.

They approached the Godfather. *Raul has gone loco. Shoot him right now; put a stop to this madness.*

Richard Alan Hall

A hollow point bullet struck the back of his head. Roland Chanchez's skull exploded, splattering bloody matter over Carla and Charles.

Carla collapsed to the floor, covering her screaming baby with her body.

Three seconds later Raul Veracruz was hit by hollow points twice in the forehead. Two young lieutenants in the room pulled their pistols and threw them to the floor, raising their arms. Five men dressed in black, except for a small golden lion on each left shirt cuff, entered the room. The young lieutenants were shot dead immediately.

From outside, came a dull chop-chopping sound, shaking the house and causing things inside to rattle and squeak. Two strange looking black stealth helicopters circled the compound. The lead helicopter landed on the courtyard. A second hovered above the compound. Twelve men emerged from the house, along with Carla, holding her baby, and ran towards the helicopter, its blades turning. Two Mexican police cars pulled up at the front gate with overhead lights flashing. A policeman opened his door and began shooting at the hovering helicopter. The strange looking helicopter rotated slightly in the direction of the police cars, and with a roar of fire from a Gatling gun located on its underbelly, reduced both cars to complete rubble in seconds.

The twelve men and Carla ran across the compound and into the waiting helicopter, which lifted immediately. Side by side, the two stealth flying machines flew at treetop level, in the direction of El Paso.

From the floor, Carla stared at her rescuers. One man reached over and wiped the blood from baby Charles' face, then hers. She looked up. Above the men's heads on the bulkhead, stenciled in bold red letters she read, TRUE BELIEVERS.

"I love you, guys," she sobbed, rocking her son back and forth.

"Welcome," the man who had wiped the blood away answered.

* * *

"Timothy!" Vincent put his hand on the back of Timothy's head, which was resting on the table. In his mind he was thinking of the first time Carla walked through the front door of Poor Joe's.

Timothy's head jerked up.

Everyone in the room stared.

"Just received word from O'Malley. The Lions were successful. Carla and your son are on their way out of Mexico."

Timothy stood up and hugged his friend hard, trembling.

Kate whispered, "Thank You."

Stanley and Timothy hugged and said nothing.

Then Stanley walked to the pay phone next to the men's room, and closed the door. He dialed a number from memory.

"Hi, Quinn. Thank you my friend."

"Welcome, Stan. Fidel told those idiots not to mess with us at the meeting, but no, they had to go and pull this shit."

"I think it was you who told them, Captain."

"Could have been, don't recall. Anyway, they got the message now. By the way, are you and Danielle coming down next December for your anniversary?"

"We're hoping to."

"Good, we'll maybe take a little boat ride to Cayo Coco again. Fidel asked if you're interested in his offer."

"You're kidding."

"Nope. Give your wife a hug for me; it's been a long night." And the phone clicked dead.

Chapter Thirty-Six
Marry Me, Kate

"It's no accident, you know, that this Irish Catholic girl from Boston is sitting next to you on this porch in Big Bay."

"I thought you're a Methodist."

"Now," Kate smiled, "but I'll always be that red-headed Catholic girl, Doug."

"How does that work?"

"I think we see life through the filters of our childhood. All we can do is add more filters as we learn."

"If you say so; sounds like college talk to me, Kate."

"Actually I thought that up one night in a Boston bar. Drinking 18 year old Jameson, I was."

Kate snuggled closer to Doug on her porch swing, watching the sunset.

"I can't believe some guy didn't sweet talk you into marriage a long time ago," Doug said. He put his arm around Kate.

"Oh, several have tried, trust me. Even got serious a few times, but then I would wake up in the morning and look at him and ask myself, *Do you really want to spend the rest of your life with this man?* and the answer has always been, *absolutely not.* How about you, Doug; ever been sweet on some lady?"

"Nope. I've had friends. Dora is a good friend. Never felt like all the guys who get all excited about their girlfriends. Never met anyone who made me feel excited and eager like I can't wait until we're together again, and just want to be alone. Never have felt that way…until now."

Doug turned his head and kissed Kate on the cheek.

"That's what I've been waiting for too. That's the very feeling I knew I would wait for; knew if I didn't wait I would regret it. The thought of a mediocre life scares me, Doug. I've been waiting for the strong urge to make my man very happy, and to meet the man who has the same urge to make me happy. I refused to settle for less."

I hope I'm not blowing this, Doug said to himself. They snuggled.

They sat silently, watching the sun disappear behind the west hills of Big Bay.

"Could you see yourself waking up next to me for the rest of your life?"

"Yes, I can."

Kate squeezed his hand. They sat side by side, staring at the afterglow.

"Will you marry me, Kate?"

"That's why I'm here! I wasn't kidding when I told you it's no accident that I'm here in Big Bay. What're the chances of this happening between a college girl with two doctoral degrees and a Vietnam war vet who lives with his dog in a bar? Zero. I was sent to be with you."

"I worry about that: that I never went to college."

"Doug, we have several things in common: we're both very smart, and we're in love, we live life intensely, and we can't wait to spend the rest of our lives together. I know couples who, on the face of it, are perfect matches. They are attractive, have similar backgrounds and intelligence, and great jobs. When the lust was exhausted, they became bored, and most of them parted ways. What we have is an intense desire to please each other. We are in love. We're going to be just fine."

"I'm twenty years older than you, Kate."

"What's that got to do with forever? You'll get to greet me on the other side, if that's the way things work out. Life here is short, no matter how old we get."

"You're right."

"And don't you forget that answer. It's a good one." Kate laughed.

"Your father is going to blow a gasket."

"Don't worry about Dad. I'm his only child and he's spoiled me rotten. Really, all he wants is for me to be happy girl. He actually laughed when I told him I was going to become a Methodist preacher. 'Whatever floats your boat, Katie,' he said to me."

"Your mom going to be ok with us?"

"She already knows, Doug. When they visited me last spring, I pointed to you and told her someday you'd be my husband."

Doug simply stared at his fiancée.

"I don't have much money for a fancy diamond ring."

"Next week let's go shopping together and pick out some simple rings that we'll give each other when we get married."

"Ok. Hey, who's going to marry us?"

"Doug, as long as I've been looking for you, that is the last of my concerns. It'll work out."

* * *

Danielle walked out on their condo deck and looked down at the illuminated city of Big Bay, and called Miriam Pico in Traverse City.

Miriam answered, "Hi, Miriam here."

"Hi, Miriam, this is Danielle McMillen."

"Hi, Danielle, it's nice to hear from you."

"Carla needs our help Miriam. What I'm about to say has never been shared with the public. There are powerful people who kept this from the public and the press. Just between us ...ok?"

"Yes."

"Three months ago while working in Nashville, Carla and her baby were kidnapped by men from a Mexican Cartel, and flown to Mexico City. I don't know many particulars except they were trying to even some sort of score over past events with her husband when he was a police detective in St Paul."

"Oh my God."

"She was rescued by a private Special Forces team. Carla told me that men dressed in black charged into the room where she was being held, and shot all the Mexicans, and that she and her baby were covered with blood."

"I feel like crying," Miriam said.

"I just spent most of this afternoon with Carla. She's suffering from anxiety, afraid to leave the house or be left alone. Timothy only goes to the bar now when one of us can stay with her. Dr. Rink tried to start her on some meds for anxiety, but Carla refuses.

"We were talking today," Danielle continued, "and she told me that the Mexican Godfather was about to cut a finger off little Charles with a bolt cutter when the Special Forces guys shot him in the head. Carla then told me that while she was standing in that room, waiting to die, Norma Bouvier came through the wall and stood next to her, held her hand and whispered that everything was going to be ok, and not to be fearful. Carla started talking about Norma's funeral, and how glorious it was when you and she sang together up in the choir loft all alone. She said, 'it felt like there were angels all around us while we sang. I sure would like to see Miriam again.'"

Miriam interrupted, "I'm going to cancel my gigs. I'll fly out tomorrow on the early flight; it's never full. If we can, let's take Carla out for lunch, get her out of the house," Miriam added. "Lunch together at Benjamin's Seafood. I love that place. Special things happen there."

"By the way, how're things between you and Doctor Roosevelt, if you don't mind me asking?"

"I'll fill you in tomorrow!"

* * *

Danielle sat on the deck, hoping that Stanley would be home soon from the administrative meeting he hated.

The phone rang.

"Hi, Danielle, it's Kate!"

"Hi, Kate."

"Doug just asked me to marry him and I said yes, of course."

"Wow. I'm happy for you guys. Exciting! Wait till the boys at Poor Joe's get ahold of this."

"I'm very happy, Danielle. It'll be fun telling the boys at the bar on poker night."

"Hey, I want you to meet a friend who's flying in tomorrow. Her name is Miriam Pico. Carla wants to see her. They actually sang together for a funeral at your church a few years back. Anyway, we thought we'd try to get Carla out to lunch tomorrow; it'd be great if you can join us."

"I'll be there."

"Let's meet at my place at 11. You can fill us in on the details on Doug tomorrow over lunch."

"Poor guy never knew what hit him; he fell in love before he could catch himself." Kate laughed.

Chapter Thirty-Seven
Napkin Notes

Carla opened the front door at 737 Grant Street and stepped back. Miriam Pico opened her arms wide. Carla took two steps outside into her embrace.

"Miriam! I'm so tickled to see you," Carla exclaimed.

"It's great to see you too!" Miriam said. "Let's all go up to Benjamin's and have lunch. I have some exciting news."

Carla looked bewildered for a moment and stepped back past the threshold.

"I can't; it's not safe," she said with clouded fear in her eyes. "I don't want you guys to get hurt."

Miriam walked through the open door and hugged Carla again.

Kate and Danielle joined them inside.

With her right arm around the two hugging friends, Kate placed her forehead against them. She said softly in their ears, "The evil ones were not allowed to hurt you in Mexico City, Carla. What could possibly happen at Benjamin's?"

Carla tilted her head back and stared at Kate.

"We said a prayer for you at Poor Joe's that night; we all asked God to protect you from the evil ones. I think He's still on duty."

"You guys prayed for me at Poor Joe's!?"

"Very hard. I thought Doug was going to break my hand he was squeezing so hard to keep from crying. And look what happened, here you are."

"Ok. I'll try. Thanks. God even answered your prayer from the bar."

She walked inside and grabbed her purse. "Stay close to me."

"I have something to tell you guys about Doug and me," Kate blurted. "And I have something to tell you about Jim Roosevelt and me!" Miriam chimed in, as they walked towards Kate's BMW.

Timothy listened from the living room while he rocked his son. He smiled, listening to their chatter, and as the car drove down the street.

"I saw Norma when I was being held captive," Carla said from the back seat. "She held my hand and told me everything was going to be ok."

"I bet she's sitting in the back seat with you guys right now," Danielle chuckled from the front passenger seat, "asking for a Camel."

"I don't think they smoke in heaven, Danielle," Carla retorted.

"Probably not, Carla. It sure is good to have you with us."

"Just stay close."

The warm gusty wind rustled the trees, shading the outdoor patio and causing the red and green umbrellas to twist about. The four ladies walked up the long wooden stairs.

"Let's eat outside; I haven't been outside in forever," Carla said.

Kate, Danielle and Miriam smiled, and Danielle squeezed Miriam's hand.

"I don't know about you guys, but this Irish girl is going to have a drink."

"How about we just get a bottle of Pinot Grigio for the table? I want a nice big glass of Pinot with my lunch," Carla said.

"OK, who wants to go first with their man story?" Danielle asked, looking between Miriam and Kate.

"Let's hear Miriam first; she traveled the furthest," Kate said, smiling broadly.

"Well, ok! Jim has taken a position with a cardiology group in Carmel, California. We've been in touch almost every day. He flew to Traverse City last winter and we went snowshoeing, and dated, and fell in love. Six weeks ago he flew me out to Carmel and put me up at the Carmel Country Inn. The last night before I flew home, we were having dinner at Flaherty's, and just before dessert was served, he reached into his pocket and brought out this..."

She held out her left hand.

"When are you getting married?" the ladies asked in unison.

"We haven't decided. I'm so happy. I finally hugged my dream."

"And, Carla, I know it's kinda sudden, but will you be my Matron of Honor?"

"I will, Miriam!"

The ladies sat silently and drank white wine for several minutes.

Kate pushed a napkin with the inscription, *Will you be my matron?* towards Danielle.

"Kate, tell us your news," Danielle said after she finished her first glass of wine and poured a second. "These are kinda small glasses," she added with a smile.

"I'd almost given up finding him. Here I am, a 35 year old with two degrees working as a small town Methodist preacher for reasons not totally clear to me, and then there he was, sitting at a poker table in Poor Joe's bar, long white hair almost to his shoulders, and a dog named Malcolm lying at his feet. The very first words out of his mouth that night were, 'Are you married?' and somehow at that moment I knew why I was in Big Bay."

Kate smiled.

"He asked me to marry him last night. We were watching the sunset, and he looked at me, and said, 'Will you marry me?' Silly boy didn't know I'd picked him the first time he spoke. We're going to look at rings next week."

"You pick a date yet?"

"Nope."

The ladies sat at the table and smiled at each other. Kate ordered another bottle of wine, same vintage.

Danielle pushed the napkin back with the word 'Yes' scribbled on it.

"What a glorious afternoon, ladies. Here we are, four girlfriends, celebrating life. Carla's smiling--someone pour her one more glass, please--both Kate and Miriam are about to bust with happiness. I'm so happy for us."

"What about you, Danielle?"

"Stanley and I are celebrating number two this December, and I have him almost house trained."

Danielle paused, her eyes sparkling with excitement.

"I have a great idea, maybe my best ever. Stanley and I are planning on celebrating our anniversary in Key West...remember Captain O'Malley married us down there after our trip to Cuba? How about if we all go to Key West this December and you guys get married there and we all have a glorious vacation? Better yet, Stanley knows the Events Director at Truman's White House...name is Paul...you guys could have a double wedding at Truman's White House. Oh man, I'm full of good ideas. What do you think ladies, Kate and Doug, Miriam and Jim married at Truman's White House? And then I bet we can get Captain O'Malley to take us all to Cayo Coco. There is a beautiful huge pink hotel right on the beach. We wouldn't even run into each other unless we wanted to. And the beach there is beautiful."

Kate looked bewildered briefly and asked, "She always get this way after a little wine?"

"Yup," answered Carla.

"I like it," Miriam said with a smile. "It sounds like a dream. I'll call Jim tonight. He's always up for an adventure; I'll bet he gets excited."

Kate hesitated and then said, "That sounds expensive, Danielle."

"How's it sound if expense wasn't a consideration?"

"Are you kidding? As Miriam said, like a dream."

"My father died a very rich man," Danielle said, looking at the wine glass in front of her, twirling it around and around. "He's the reason we live in that condo on the bluffs; he bought that for me when I moved here, before I had ever met Stan. When he died--he was divorced--he left all his money to me. I've never mentioned it because it's not important, except when we can help somebody. Kate, you don't need to worry about expenses."

Danielle paused, and blushed a little. "Please keep this just between us. I don't want people to know."

The astonished ladies nodded their heads.

"Doug will have questions, and so will Dad."

Danielle laughed, "Ain't that the way dads are, always worried about their little girls? Tell your daddy that God has provided. That might work for Doug, too. No, better yet, tell Doug; he wouldn't tell a soul."

"Wow, what an afternoon," Miriam proclaimed. "I'm so happy that you could join us, Carla."

"I'm happy, too," Carla answered. "I'm not sure I can travel all the way to Key West to be your Maid of Honor though."

"Sure you can; we'll all travel together. It'll be safe, Carla," Danielle said.

"Ok. We'll see. Let me talk to Timothy."

"Who's going to marry us in Key West?" Kate asked.

"Here's another little secret that only a few people know," Danielle said. "Over the past 5 years Stanley has been going to school, mostly on-line. He had lots of credits already from the University of Minnesota before he went into nursing. Those vacations we took to St Paul last year were for dissertations and interviews. He now has a PhD in Theological Philosophy. With that degree he is granted marriage privileges."

She paused.

"So, Stanley can marry you guys if you want."

"How long were you going to keep that a secret?" Kate asked.

"Probably forever. Stanley's like that; he'll just study because he wants to know, and never tell anyone. I'm not sure he's going to be tickled that I let this cat out of the bag, until I give him the news about who he's marrying. Then he'll be thrilled, especially for you guys."

"I want to sing at your wedding too, Miriam. You sang for Timothy and me when we got married, sang Tupelo Honey and every time I hear that song my mind flashes back to that happy, happy day. I want to sing at your wedding. The singing Maid of Honor. I think I want to sing *Fly Me to the Moon*, if it's ok with you."

Miriam reached across the table and held Carla's hand.

"I would like that very much."

"Well, ladies, let's go home and let our men know what their plans are. Check your calendars. I think December 15th is a good day to get married."

* * *

"How was lunch?" Timothy asked.

"It was wonderful. Miriam Pico flew to town and joined us. She's getting married to Dr. Roosevelt. She asked me to be her Maid of Honor!"

"That's great! When are they getting married?"

"Date hasn't been set yet, but it looks like they might be getting married in Key West. I'm afraid, Timothy. I told Miriam yes, but I'm afraid."

Timothy hugged his wife.

Chapter Thirty-Eight
Thanks For Not Shooting

Looking past Danielle from the grocery cart seat, two-year-old Chloe began clapping wildly. Danielle placed a bunch of celery in the cart, and staring into the produce section mirror, saw Machete standing 10 feet behind her, grinning. She reached into her purse to grasp a pepper spray, and turned, facing him.

"Machete, what are you doing here?"

"I am on vacation."

"You can't sneak up on us like this. I mean it!"

"Sorry, just wanted to say hi to my sister."

"You can hold her for a second, and then leave."

Machete lifted Chloe from the grocery cart. He spoke to her in Spanish while she played with his black-framed glasses, and laughed when she put them on her head upside-down. He walked down the produce aisle, turned the corner and returned, placing her back in the cart. Smiling, he said, "Thank you, Danielle. We must give her Spanish lessons." He carefully chose a carrot from the produce bin and walked out, eating it.

* * *

"You are not going to guess who surprised us in the grocery store today," Danielle said to Stanley across the dining room table.

"Machete," Stanley answered with a grin.

"How'd you know?"

"Timothy called me today. Machete was at Poor Joe's last night, asking for some sort of Mexican beer that they don't have. One thing led to another and Machete got himself invited to stay upstairs for a while in the room next to Doug's. Timothy asked me what I thought about him hiring Machete as some sort of guard for Carla while he's out of the house. We're going to talk it over with Larry Strait this Saturday."

"You're kidding, right?"

"Nope."

"I don't know Stan, having him around gives me the creeps. I know he helped save your life, but geez. He gives me the willies. And besides, he wants to teach Chloe Spanish!"

* * *

"There is no way I can get a man who is probably an illegal alien a concealed gun permit," Chief of Police Strait said from behind his desk. "You sure you want to do this, Timothy?"

"My wife is terrified to be alone. She has nightmares about that night in Mexico City, Chief. I feel horrible. She refuses any medicine; told me the other night she knew I'd seen bad things in Vietnam, but I wasn't holding Charles when it happened, didn't see our baby covered with bloody brains. She washes Charles three or four times a day. I've got to do something to help her, Chief."

"Think she will be comforted by the presence of a Mexican?"

"Some of the Special Forces guys were Cuban. She mentions the rescue team dressed in black almost every day. I think she'll feel safer with him here."

"You know I can make a phone call, and get whatever papers you need, Chief," Stanley said.

"I believe you can, Stanley. You get that little man some citizenship papers and I will hire him as a special detective and assign him to you. How's that sound? That'll give them something to chew on down at City Council next month. To hell with them."

"Thanks, Chief."

"You're welcome, Timothy. This is what friends do."

* * *

Two weeks later Machete walked into Poor Joe's Bar dressed in black slacks and a black long sleeved shirt with button down collar. Even the buttons were black. There was no golden lion on the cuff. Timothy and Machete talked at the table under the stairs.

"You have a driver's license now?"

"Yes. The chief passed me yesterday."

"And you can actually drive?"

"Since 12 years of age I have driven…in Mexico City. A person can drive anywhere after Mexico City."

"How'd you have a car at 12?"

"Stolen," Machete grinned. "Making a little money. I like Mercedes."

"Well you're in luck; Carla has one. Your job is to drive her around town, escort her to appointments, and guard our house when I'm not at home. In exchange, you have a room upstairs next to Doug, free of charge, free meals and drinks at the bar, and twenty-five dollars an hour. Deal?"

"Yes. And can I see my sister also?"

"You have to take that up with Stan and Danielle. But I'll put in a good word."

"Deal." And they shook hands.

Richard Alan Hall

The Usual Suspects watched from their bar stools.

* * *

Carla hugged Machete. "Were you there the night I was rescued?" she asked.

"No, my friends were there and I have heard how brave you were that night."

"Oh I wasn't brave, trust me. I peed my pants. I was just trying to protect my precious baby."

"I am here now to protect you. Do not be worried."

The sight of the little Mexican man dressed entirely in black, driving Carla and her baby around Big Bay brought smiles to the faces of her friends as the silver Mercedes passed on the street. Seeing Carla out of the house shopping and talking with people in the stores gave a sense of relief to her husband.

Carla's nightmares began to subside.

Timothy came home early from the bar on a Wednesday evening, and surprised Carla.

"I thought you would stay and play poker with the gang tonight," she said with a smile.

"Just want to be with you tonight, honey," he replied. "I'll fix some steaks on the grill." Then he walked back out on the porch to talk with Machete.

"You take the night off. Go join the poker table and let Kate take some of your money."

"We'll see who has the money tomorrow, amigo," Machete said with a smile.

* * *

The teenage boys, Juniors and Seniors at Big Bay Central, were drunk. They were also under the influence of something the tallest boy, who happened to be the football team's star receiver, had concocted in chemistry lab the day before.

The six boys wandered down Union Street. In the near darkness, they spotted a little man walking under a streetlight, just down the block from Poor Joe's.

"Dudes, look at the freakin' leprechaun!" shouted the star receiver. In their chemically contorted minds, the teenagers watched a little green leprechaun dressed in black walking towards the bar. They ran and quickly surrounded the little man, taunting him, yelling obscenities.

One boy left briefly and returned to the lighted sidewalk with a broken branch the size of a baseball bat. He hit Machete in the back, knocking the wind out of him, and the boys tackled him to the pavement. They took his wallet and emptied the contents, flinging money and papers into the darkness like confetti.

Machete leapt to his feet, and like a mongoose teasing a cobra, jumped first at one boy and then another while making hissing sounds, and screaming in Spanish.

The boys surrounded him, jabbing in his direction, not quite sure how to handle the crazy little man. The boy with the broken branch began swinging it, and eventually hit Machete again, knocking him to the ground. The boys gathered close and began kicking him. He rolled first one-way, and then another, protecting his head with his arms.

From their poker table at Poor Joe's, the card players listened to the commotion and yelling from down the street. Dora went to the front door and looked into the darkness.

"Some sort of fight down there," she said, looking back at the poker table.

The assembled jumped to their feet. Wendell, Pete, Wayne, Stanley, Ralph, Doug, Dr. McCaferty, and Kate headed down the dark street towards the intersection.

Malcolm got there first. With a high bound, he hit the tall boy in the chest, knocking him flat on his back. Snarling at the other boys, Malcolm turned and stood with his front paws on Machete's chest.

Kate outran all the men. When she arrived at the scuffle, the boy with the broken branch took a hard swing at her. Nimbly, she stepped back, and as the branch completed its arc past her head, she flattened the young man with a sidekick.

The men looked amazed. Malcolm and the redheaded Irish girl had defeated two star athletes, and the remaining four boys walked backwards in bewilderment.

"My daddy insisted I take Tae Kwon Do all through high school and college," she said with a smile. "It works!"

Chief Strait's car, followed by two patrol cars with their overhead lights flashing, pulled up. Dora had called.

Dr. McCaferty kneeled on the payment, examining Machete, who was grinning and grimacing. Feeling Machete's legs, he stopped and pulled up the right pant leg, exposing a small handgun in an ankle holster.

Everyone stared in the dim light at the ankle holster in silence. The teenagers' eyes widened.

"Thanks for not shooting the boys," Chief Strait said. He turned towards the teenagers. "This unfortunate occurrence is not going to enhance your football careers, boys. I'll have a talk with Coach in the morning. Now you boys go with these nice policemen and I'll call your parents."

"Can I still play poker?' Machete asked, sitting on the curb.

"I think we'll take you to ER for some x-rays," Dr. McCaferty replied.

"No, amigo, I am fine. Trust me on this. Fights like this happened every week in Mexico City. I am fine."

The police drove away and The Usual Suspects walked down Union Street towards the lights of Poor Joe's.

"Damn, Machete, if I was getting the shit kicked out of me like that and had a gun, I would have shot 'em," Pete proclaimed.

"They are only silly boys having fun," Machete grinned through bloody false teeth. "They are no danger. We have all been silly boys at one time."

"You were a bad one, huh?" Wendell asked.

"That was a long life ago, amigo."

Chapter Thirty-Nine

Spurned Lover

The collection plates passed from person to person as the choir finished singing, *Just a Closer Walk with Thee*. Waiting for pastor Katherine Kennedy McGinnis to start her sermon, the domed sanctuary became quiet, except for an occasional cough from the pews, and a baby crying from the right balcony.

Kate said, "Good morning," and the congregation echoed the same greeting.

A man dressed in a tailored suit and a red tie stood up in the left balcony, leaning over the brass guard railing, looking down at the podium. His black hair was slicked back. Speaking though cupped hands, he shouted down, "When we were in law school, I slept with your preacher girl. We were going to get married. The word back in Boston is that you ended up in Big Bay, a Methodist preacher engaged to a worn out drunk. We could have been something special, Katie. You could've been a renowned Wall Street lawyer. Look at you now; aren't you grand looking in your robes."

Complete silence in the building, except for the baby crying intermittently in the right balcony.

Doug started to stand from the front row. Kate motioned for him to sit down.

She looked up to her right into the balcony.

"I love my life, Garrison," Kate replied, looking at the man, "and I love my finance. I've found the life I've been searching for. I knew the moment I accepted Doug's proposal that I was making the right choice, and now too, do all the people here today."

"You're pathetic," the man shouted back.

"If you see me after the service, Garrison, I'll give you a recording of today's service to take home. Your mom will be so proud."

And Kate opened the Bible on the podium.

"In about 59 A.D. the apostle Paul wrote a letter to the Corinthians. It is one of my favorite letters. He wrote, 'When I was a child I talked like a child, I understood as a child. But when I became a man, I put away childish things. Now we see things through a glass darkly. Then we shall see face to face. Now I know in part. Then I shall know fully. And now abideth faith, hope, and love. These three, but the greatest of these is love'."

Kate closed the Bible. For the next forty minutes she spoke without notes about the power of love, how it had changed her life, and the changes she had witnessed in the lives of others. At the end of the sermon, she opened the Bible to Corinthians again, and read, 'Eye hath not seen, nor ear heard, neither has it entered into the heart of man the things which God has prepared for those that love him.'"

She closed the Bible and looked at the congregation. "I sure do love you guys."

Halfway back in the center pews, a young teenage girl wearing a light blue cotton dress with tiny white polk-a-dots stood up. She appeared to be about five months pregnant. The young lady began to clap slowly while looking up at Kate.

The entire congregation began to clap. Everyone stood and clapped.

Kate left the podium and walked down the center aisle towards the entrance. The Usual Suspects left the front row pews and walked on either side of their friend. Doug looked up at the man, giving him the finger.

As he turned to leave, the man bumped face to face into Chief of Police Strait, who flashed his badge.

"We'll be going out the back entrance, young man."

"And if I don't?"

"I will arrest you for disturbing the peace," he answered.

He nodded towards two uniformed officers standing at the top of the stairs.

"That'll never stick, Barney."

"Probably not, but you *will* get to spend some special time in the holding cell with a couple of drunks who hate the Boston Red Socks."

Chapter Forty

What's Time Got To Do With Forever?

"**H**i Danielle, it's Miriam. I'm in Carmel with Jim!"

"Hi, Miriam. What'd he say about Key West?"

"He's sitting right next to me. We're at Nepenthe. I'll let him tell you."

"Hello, Danielle. Miriam just shared the plan you and the girls concocted for the wedding. I love it. I've only been to Key West once as a kid, but it sure did seem like a romantic place. As far as having a double wedding with Kate and Doug, I love that too. I really like different, and this will fill the bill, for sure."

"Great. We were holding our collective breath waiting for Miriam to tell you."

"I'm not sure about going to Cuba for the honeymoon though; I'd hate to have things ruined with an arrest or something. Miriam told me you and Stan have been there. We were thinking about going to Copal."

"Stan and I went to Cayo Coco when we were on vacation in Key West."

"How'd you get there without getting into trouble?"

"We met a man in a bar; that sounds reassuring, doesn't it? Jim, I will promise you this, it will be the vacation of your life, and it is completely safe."

Jim laughed." We'll talk about it; here's Miriam."

"I hope you can talk him into Cayo Coco, Miriam. We'd have such a great time together."

"Yes we will, Danielle. I'll give you a call when I'm back in Traverse City."

"Good night."

Danielle looked at Stanley across the living room.

"Miriam and Jim are excited to have you marry them in Key West alongside Kate and Doug."

"What'd they think about Cayo Coco?"

"Jim was thinking about going to Mexico for their honeymoon... They'll be going with us," Danielle replied. She smiled a really big smile.

"I better make another call to Paul Hilson and confirm Truman's Little White House for December 15th. When we talked last week, he said he would hold it until I called back. He's going to close the entire compound and open the White House just for our party. I asked him if David Chown had permission to play Truman's personal piano after dinner, and he told me, 'Well, of course, and it's just been tuned.'"

"Wow! That piano had a big 'Do Not Touch' sign on it when we took the tour."

"This is going to be a very special time, honey."

"That doesn't even begin to describe how excited I am. I love this for us, and for our friends."

"I want us to fly the guys down for the wedding," Stanley continued. "Did I tell you that Doug asked Timothy to be his Best Man? I want for all the guys, and Dora, to be there. I'll talk to Timothy; his old war buddy runs the charter service at the airport. See what kind of deal we can get to fly all of us to Key West."

* * *

Kate McGinnis didn't see Dr. McCaferty standing in the doorway of her study. Waiting there, he watched the young red-haired pastor hunched

168

over her desk, writing on small cards.

Finally, he knocked on the door casing.

She startled and looked up.

"Hi, Doc, how long you been here?"

"Several hours, Kate." And he winked. "Is this Catholic boy allowed in?"

"Sure is; this Catholic girl beat you in. I'm writing out my wedding invitations and have one for you." She shuffled through the pile of cards and handed the one addressed to him. "I hope you and Kathy can come; I would be honored."

Dr. McCaferty sat down in the chair next to Kate's desk. "We wouldn't miss this; *we* are the honored ones, Kate."

He paused.

"This is a little awkward, but I want to talk about Doug's health."

"That sounds like a HIPPA violation, Doc."

"Yup. I'm not sure you're aware of the full extent of Doug's heart problems. His heart is very weak. You do know he suffered a cardiac arrest before you moved to Big Bay, don't you? It's a miracle he's still with us."

He paused again. Kate reached over the desk and touched his hand.

"Thank you, Jack," she said. "Doug told me all about his heart problems, and the reason he doesn't drink alcohol any more. He told me about the time in the hospital when he watched Malcolm and an angel talk at the foot of his hospital bed, and that he saw Norma and Charles waiting to take him home. I know."

Her green eyes stared directly into Jack McCaferty's brown eyes.

"I know he may not be here long. What's that got to do with forever, Doc? I don't believe for a second that life begins at the moment of conception any more than it ends at the moment of our death."

Dr. McCaferty took a deep breath and squeezed Kate's hand.

"I think we knew each other before we ever came here," Kate continued, "and we'll be with each other after we leave. It's ok, Jack. Thanks for caring."

"They teach you that in the seminary?" Dr. McCaferty asked.

"Nope, came up with that over a glass of Jamison's."

"I need to switch to Jamison's!"

Kate pulled open the bottom drawer of the desk, and retrieved a green box of Limited Reserve, and two communion glasses.

"Ask and you shall receive. I love you, Doc. Both Timothy and Doug predicted you would pay me a visit."

* * *

"Stanley stopped by Poor Joe's yesterday," Timothy said, sitting next to Carla in the swing on their covered front porch at 737 Grant Street. "He told me that they're going to fly all of us down to Key West; wanted me to talk with Sammy and reserve a plane for December 12th. He and Danielle are flying all the guys down. I'm closing the bar, and we're all going!"

"We can help, too."

"That's what I told him; he said we could help with the wedding party. He's reserved Margaritaville the evening before the wedding!"

"I'm scared, Timothy. Every time I think about going, I get scared and get stomach cramps. I don't think I can go."

"What scares you the most?"

Carla shrugged. "Afraid of being kidnapped again, I guess."

"Those Special Forces guys who rescued you, what if they joined us?"

"How could that even be possible?"

"Stanley and I know their leader. If those men join us in Key West, if they're there for us, and if we take Machete with us, would you feel better?"

"It'd be kinda embarrassing with those guys shadowing us."

"Trust me; they'll be out of sight. And anyway, they would fit right in with the rest of the space aliens you'll see wandering up and down Duval Street."

Carla rested her head on Timothy's shoulder and took a deep breath of his Old Spice.

"I am going to do it. Thank you for helping me."

"Of course I'll help you, sweetheart. You were the one sent to save me. Remember that night on Mackinac Island when you told me that? Now it's my turn to save you. We were sent here to help each other, Carla."

"I believe that," Carla replied. She took another deep, deep breath of her husband's aftershave, and her mind wandered back to the carriage ride to the Woods restaurant.

"I want to go back to Mackinac Island next summer."

"Me too!" Timothy said, smiling with his cheek snuggling against her hair.

* * *

Stanley picked up the phone in his office and dialed the number he had memorized.

"O'Malley Charters."

"Hi, Quinn. Stan here. We have a wedding scheduled for December 15th at Truman's Little White House."

"Did Dr. Roosevelt capitulate to Miriam?"

"He never had a chance."

"We'll all be flying down on the 12,th staying at the Duval Inn for a week, and then the newlyweds and anniversary couple would like to vacation at the Hotel Blau Colonial on Cayo Coco for two weeks, if you can arrange it."

"No problem, Stanley."

"And one more thing; Timothy is worried that Carla may freak out when she leaves Big Bay. Can we have some sort of security at the Inn and at the wedding to reassure her?"

"You guys bringing Machete?"

"Yup."

"Good. Ok, there will be security that will make the Secret Service jealous. In fact, I'm going to call Carla myself and reassure her."

"Thanks, Captain."

"You and Danielle given anymore thought to Fidel's offer?"

"Not really, why?"

"He asked me about it last week. Talk to you later. It'll be nice to see you again, Stan."

"It'll be nice to see you, too. I'm buying at the Green Parrot."

"Damn right you're buying... Oh, I almost forgot: Dr. A.W. Blue is missing; can't find him anywhere."

"How long?"

"Last week he took a small motorboat from the Cayo Coco marina at sunset; told the guard he was going to talk to Rita. Just disappeared. We can't even find the boat. Thought you should know before you come down."

"Thanks, Quinn. He's quite a man. Danielle will be sad to hear he's missing. She loves him."

"We all love A.W."

"He's been missing before, Quinn."

"True, but I always knew where he was."

* * *

Timothy handed little Charles to Carla and answered the phone.

"Hello, Timothy, Quinn O'Malley here. I want to talk to your wife."

"Yes, sir." And he took the baby back.

"Carla Fife, you've never met me. I'm the charter boat captain who took your husband to Havana a while back. I'm aware of the awful things you've experienced in your life recently, and the fear you have to travel. Carla, I'm acquainted with the men who rescued you in Mexico City. I can promise you that those very men will be protecting you and your friends the entire time you're in Key West."

Carla looked at Timothy with eyes widening.

"Thank you, Captain. You have no idea how much peace this gives me."

"Yes I do, Carla. And one more thing, I want you and Timothy to vacation on Cayo Coco with the rest of the wedding party, my compliments."

"Thank you, Captain. I think I love you."

Quinn O'Malley laughed. "See you at the wedding. Good night."

Carla turned and looked at her husband holding their son.

"He's going to have the True Believers guarding us, Timothy! And he invited us to come to Cayo Coco with him!"

Chapter Forty-One

I Ordered You A Guinness, Katie

Even the strong ones have fears, hidden beneath their armor.

Kate shared a lifelong fear with Doug during the Friday night all-you-can-eat smelt and steak special at Mark's Diner on Basswood Street.

"I need to fly home and tell Mom about our engagement," Kate said

A waitress slid a plate of hot dinner rolls between their plates.

"You haven't told your mother yet?"

"You don't know my mom. She is the Queen Mother. Kids and strangers love her; her patients love her. She has always scared the crap out of me. For as long as I can remember, I've been afraid of what she might think of this or that. I have to tell her in person, face to face, honey."

Doug smiled. *NO...No...no...no...no* raced through his frightened mind.

"Want me to go with you?"

"This is something I need to do alone."

She paused.

"My parents liked Garrison. They were quite disappointed when I left him."

Doug's skin prickled a cold feeling. He felt nauseated and lonely inside. His mind wandered to Vietnam, the Battle of the Hump, and the angel hugging him as he drove the Green Dragon behind enemy lines. He wished she would hug him right now.

"DOUG!" Kate shouted again; he had not heard her the first time.

"Doug, I love you. Dad and Mom are my problem." She paused. "Not for long. I'll fly to Boston and talk to Mom. This will be fine, either way. You are my knight in shining armor, honey. We are us... forever."

Doug sighed; his body shivered a little.

"I wish your parents were still with us. I would've loved to meet them," Kate said.

"My mother was a very special lady, always trying to fix things for everyone. I lived with her for a while when I came home from 'Nam-- before I started wandering and drinking. I barely remember my father. He left when I was five."

* * *

Reverend Katherine Kennedy McGinnis boarded the first flight on a Monday morning and flew to Boston. She had a luncheon date with her mother at Cheers.

She stared out the window, watching while the pilot tested the flaps up and down, and then brakes. She listened to the engines warming up to a dull roar.

The plane slowly moved towards the runway. *Mom was so impossible the last time I gave her news not to her satisfaction*, Kate thought.

It had been a hurtful fight with more agony than the teenage fights. Kate had driven her new red BMW, which her parents had given her as a graduation gift, home to share her changing plans, and to inform them that she had broken up with Garrison. Her mother had been livid.

Kate replayed the memory. "I thought you came home to tell us that since you passed the Boards, you had signed with Jacobson and Serney like we discussed. I pulled strings for you Katie, went out on a limb, spent some goodwill capital to get you a position. And now you say you're going to Seminary...and a Methodist one at that. Good God, Katie. I suppose you want your father and me to pay for this, too? Well, you are on your own with this one. And Garrison, he'd make a fine husband. Most young ladies dream of a man like Garrison."

The plane accelerated down the runway and lifted, leaving Big Bay. *It's not going to matter. I don't really give a damn what she says this time. I'm a grown woman. It's my life,* Kate thought as the city with its bay grew smaller, finally disappearing in the clouds. *I have to do this. Be with me. Help me, Lord.*

* * *

The old restaurant was busy and smelled of French fries and onion rings. Kate's mother knew the manager, and had saved a corner table. She was waiting when Katherine walked down the steps.

"Hi, Mom."

"Hello, Katie. I ordered you a Guinness draught. How are you?"

"I'm happy, Mom; have some exciting news to share."

Kate's mother looked at her daughter silently.

"You remember the man I pointed out as my future husband when you and Dad visited?"

Silence ensued.

"The silver haired man I told you would be my husband someday...the Vietnam Vet?"

Silence continued.

"Doug...remember?"

The ladies sat across the table from one another and stared at each other.

Kate picked up her glass of dark beer and drank several gulps. She prayed, *Please help me.*

"You ready for all the criticisms?" Kate's mother asked, looking over her reading glasses. "Sounds like you've reeled him in. You ready to hear that he's too old for you, that he has PTSD problems, that you will likely be a young widow, that you should have married Garrison? Your father and I liked Garrison; he's almost as smart as you."

"Doug asked me to marry him, Mom!"

"And....."

"I said yes, of course!"

"Well this is going to surprise you, I'm sure, but I'm happy for you, Katie. You have always marched to a beat no one else can hear, and I've watched with a pride I can hardly contain some days. If this is the man who loves you, and you love in return, if you are truly in love, I could not be happier."

"Wow. Gosh, Mom. THANKS!" *Kate responded. Oh, thank you Lord. Thank you, thank you.*

"To hell with the critics, if they don't like it," she said, after another gulp of Guinness.

"Spoken as a true member of the clergy."

"Really, Mom, half of them either have or wish they could get a divorce, and secretly wish they had a genuine man like Doug. I could care less."

"Good point."

"Guess who showed up at a Sunday service? Garrison."

"What!?"

"Yup, made quite a spectacle of himself from the balcony. Yelled out to the entire congregation that we had slept together during law school, and that I should have married him. Said something about wasting my life."

"Oh my. I'm so sorry, honey. That must have been terribly embarrassing."

"Not really, Mom. I just shouted back that I knew the moment Doug proposed that I'd made the right decision, and now so does everyone who was in the room."

"Good retort, Katie."

"I'm a good lawyer, too," Kate said with a smile then added, "I felt sorry for him. I think he'd been drinking. And, Mom, the entire congregation gave me a standing ovation after my sermon. And the guys from the bar--they come to church now--they walked like an honor guard beside me. I wish you could have been there. I melted inside."

"How did Doug handle this?"

"He gave Garrison a definitive hand gesture."

"In church? You got yourself quite a man there, honey. You guys set a date?"

"December 15th...in Key West, at Truman's Little White House. It's going to be a double wedding with Miriam Pico and her fiancé Dr. Jim Roosevelt. And remember Stanley?"

"The Critical Care manager?"

"Yes. He's going to marry all of us. He has a degree in theology."

"When you moved to Big Bay, and took that job at the Methodist Church, I worried that you would feel out of place, and would be lonely. I worried every night. Look at you: you've found your friends and the life you've longed for. Garrison give you any more trouble?"

"Never heard another thing. Doug told me that the Chief of Police escorted him out the back door, took him to the hotel to pick up his stuff, and then drove him to the airport. That was a relief. I was afraid the guys would put him in Intensive Care, or worse, sic Machete on him."

"Who's Machete...what a peculiar name."

"You'll meet him at the wedding. He's a man you want as a friend. I saw him attacked one night by six drunken teenagers. He reminded me of a Badger on National Geographic. Oh, tell Dad all those martial arts classes paid off."

"Katie...?"

"It was six against one little man. Had to even up the advantage, so Malcolm and I charged in and mixed it up. We won."

"Malcolm?"

"Doug's German Shepherd."

"Of course. Someday someone should make a movie of your life. Do you and Doug need help with expenses?"

"You're not going to believe this either, Mom. Stanley and his wife are flying us--all of us--on a charter plane to Key West. Timothy is going to be Doug's Best Man, and his wife Carla is my Maid of Honor. They're flying all of us--our friends from Poor Joe's too."

"Your dad is going to be tickled, Katie. He likes those men. I never told you, he sneaked over to the bar one night after I had gone to bed, and played poker with those guys until 1 a.m. Timothy drove him back to the hotel and guided him to the elevators. Seems your dad had been 'over-served,' in his words. He still mentions that poker game after a few Jameson's."

"That explains a lot. It's my daddy's fault."

"What?"

"Poker and Jameson."

"I'll share that with your father tonight, along with the rest of the news, unless you want to spend the night and tell him yourself."

"Just tell him that I love him, and I'll call him on Saturday. I have a funeral tomorrow, and a plane to catch this evening. I wanted to tell you face to face, Mom."

"I love you, Katie."

As they walked up the steps, Dr. McGinnis hugged her daughter, and whispered, "You are a rock with a heart of gold."

They stepped out onto the sidewalk and bright sunlight. Katie turned to her mother.

"Yours is the only opinion I have ever cared about all these years."

"I'm your mother, honey, I've been protecting you from heartache since you were a little girl. I want for you to be happy. Say hi to Doug from me. Book us a room in Key West."

Chapter Forty-Two

Leprechaun Slayers

School became a cruel experience for the six Big Bay High School football stars.

Coach Lenard had expelled all six from the varsity team, almost certainly guaranteeing a losing season, not to mention hopes of any college football opportunities.

While being comforted by his sweetheart, the quarterback let slip the fact that the boys had been high on something concocted during chemistry lab, that they thought they had been chasing a leprechaun. The young lady kept the secret for nine hours, and then shared it with the other cheerleaders. As the banished boys walked around school, they were taunted with jeers. The cheerleaders gave them the title of leprechaun slayers.

For the star wide receiver, injury was added to insult when he received a letter in the mail revoking his full ride scholarship from the University of Wisconsin. Ryan Hayden sat on his bed with the open letter beside him. He ripped it to shreds.

Screw coach Lenard for hanging me out to dry, his mind raced. He opened last year's Physics textbook, and removed a corked test tube from the hollowed center. *Coach said he'd go to bat for me. Screw him and the old man, big attorney, embarrassed. Tough shit if I can't get into law school now. Screw 'em. And screw that damn dog, and that damn preacher lady who talks about love all the time. I'll show her some love.* And he grabbed his groin. He tapped a little white powder from the test tube into his palm, and snorted it. *And screw that Mexican. He's first, damn runt.*

That evening Ryan Hayden walked down Grant Street and sat in a pile of leaves. Concealed in the darkness under a giant sycamore tree, he watched Timothy walk home at eleven-fifteen, and watched as Machete left five minutes later, walking back to his room at Poor Joe's. Ryan noted the time on his watch.

The following evening Ryan sat in the pile of leaves and watched the sequence repeat. Then he walked rapidly through the alleys, arriving at Poor Joe's before Machete.

Ryan snorted the white powder twice from his shaking hands the third evening before he walked to the Sycamore tree. He watched Timothy and Machete talk on the porch, then Machete walking up Grant towards the bar.

The high school Senior sprinted through the alleys and entered Poor Joe's through the rear door. Carefully, he walked down the wooden hallway and pushed the door open to the men's room. It was empty. He waited and listened.

Machete walked up the handicap ramp that led to the back entrance under the forty-watt bulb.

He was humming a song. The wood floor creaked as he passed the men's room.

Ryan pushed the restroom door open. Through the open door he pointed his father's 22-caliber target pistol.

He pulled the trigger without blinking.

The small caliber bullet struck Machete just behind his right ear. His legs buckled and he collapsed, bouncing on the old wooden floor once, before rolling over, looking up towards the ceiling with blind eyes.

Ryan threw the pistol towards the urinal and ran.

Malcolm ran past Machete, pausing only for a brief instant, and pushed the back door open with his nose. The dog ran into the darkness, in pursuit, his nose to the ground.

As Doug and Wendell knelt in the growing pool of blood, Machete whispered, "Maria...Maria...Maria," and then lapsed into silence.

Wendell pounded the hardwood floor with his fist, splattering blood on the wall. "Call an ambulance!" he shouted back towards the bar.

Doug groaned, and rested his forehead on the little Mexican's chest.

The rest of The Usual Suspects arrived in the hallway.

"Malcolm is chasing the shooter. Go get the bastard," Doug shouted. "Get that bastard and bring him back here."

The men ran in the darkness towards Malcolm's barking.

* * *

Stanley picked up the bedside phone.

"Stan, this is Lavern. Jack and I are in the E.R. Machete has been shot."

Stanley closed his eyes and opened them several times, hoping he would wake from a nightmare.

Danielle switched the bedside light on, and rolled over. Stanley reached back without looking and grasped her bare breast. His hand was trembling and cold. She crawled next to her husband and hugged him from behind.

"How bad, Lavern?"

"Serious. Small caliber, right occipital. No exit wound."

"I'll be right down. Do they have the shooter?"

"Not that we've heard. He was shot in Poor Joe's, Stan"

Stanley stood up and turned towards Danielle.

"Somebody shot Machete in the head. Lavern says it doesn't look good. I'm going in, honey."

Danielle walked to the dresser and returned with a framed picture of Chloe Norma. "Take this to Machete. It'll help."

Stanley dressed in silence. Daniele listened to his black Avanti start, the car he only drove on special occasions, the car he knew had special dispensation with the police. She could hear him downshift in the tight corners, and then accelerate away. *How bizarre is this*, he thought, downshifting and braking at the S curves, *that I care*. He accelerated and shifted into 4th. *I love that little guy...damn it.*

"Please keep Stan safe," Daniele whispered as she listened to her husband speed away, "And guide the hands of the guys working on Machete. If he dies, please welcome him home to be with his sister and mom."

Danielle plopped down on the bed. *I can't believe I'm praying for the guy who was going to kill my husband, the crazy little man who loves to hold my girl and wants to teach her Spanish.* "Lord, hold us close to you."

* * *

Malcolm had chased Ryan Hayden up a maple tree. He had bitten him in the right buttock while the young man struggled through the bottom braches, and again in the left calf, ripping the pant leg off.

From the street, Chief Strait focused his spotlight up in the direction the men were pointing. In the tree, peering down at the leaping German Shepherd was a tall young man, dripping blood. The men circled the tree. Ralph climbed through the branches towards the boy. Chief Strait radioed for an ambulance, and walked towards the tree.

"Don't hurt him, Ralph," the chief commanded.

He reached down and grabbed Malcolm's collar.

"Stay right there. Let's talk him down."

Ralph was within an arm's length of the boy, who climbed higher and then out on a branch to avoid being captured. Ralph stopped climbing.

* * *

Timothy and Dr. McCaferty met Stanley walking through the ER entrance. Dr. Smith walked out of ER Trauma room one with a Neurosurgeon.

They gathered in the nurse's station.

"I made a bone flap to relieve the pressure. X-rays show the bullet traveled through to the Frontal cortex; see the bleeding here." The surgeon pointed to a collapsed sinus on the x-ray viewer.

"I don't see any way this guy survives. I just talked to an old classmate at Cleveland Clinic who told me flying him down would be a waste of time. Any next of kin we can get in here?"

Doug and Wendell arrived and joined the group.

"He was an orphan. We're his family now," Doug answered from the back of the group. "Can we see him?"

The surgeon hesitated. Dr. McCaferty replied, "Yes, we may." And he led The Usual Suspects into Room One. *Geez, I'm one of the guys,* he thought .

Machete lay on the ER gurney with the side rails up. A ventilator made to and fro whooshing sounds as air was exchanged in a gurgling fashion. Dried blood encrusted both swollen eyes and around his nose. A nurse gently washed the blood from his face, and a respiratory therapist suctioned frothy mucus from the endotracheal tube. His swollen eyelids were taped closed. His tan complexion had faded to pale.

"We should let him go," Doug said firmly. "Let him be with his sister and mom." The time he walked down State Street with a pistol to the back of the little Mexican's head flashed through his mind. He felt like crying.

Kate McGinnis arrived. Stanley had called her.

"Oh no…no…no!" she cried.

"Kate, we need to take him off the ventilator."

The Usual Suspects formed a semi-circle around Machete, holding hands. They were joined by Dr. McCaferty and Dr. Smith.

Stanley laid the picture of his baby girl on Machete's chest.

Kate bowed her head. "Lord, here comes your servant Machete. You know the rough road he traveled to prove his love. Greet him with your love."

The respiratory therapist turned the ventilator off and removed it from the endotracheal tube.

Machete did not take a single breath for almost a minute. Then, through the endo-tube, came gurgling gasps. The respiratory therapist turned the suction machine on, and suctioned bloody frothy mucous. Machete began to breathe at 30 times a minute.

Stanley glanced at the cardiac monitor. It showed a sinus tachycardia of 120. Machete's blood pressure rose to 100/60, and his oxygen saturation was 93 percent.

"I think we should admit him to ICU," Stanley said to Dr. McCaferty.

"We stay right here," the surgeon retorted. "He can't maintain much longer; be a waste of an ICU bed."

Stanley glanced at Dr. Smith.

Stanley picked up the phone and called ICU.

"How many beds we have open?" he asked the Charge Nurse.

"We have 3 empty beds," Stanley said, looking at the three physicians.

The surgeon shook his head *no.*

"Jack, you know Machete. Lavern, you're the Chief of Staff."

"This one's on me," Dr. McCaferty said to the surgeon. "I'll admit him."

Dr. Smith nodded *yes.*

The surgeon glared at Stanley.

* * *

"Go to hell..." the young man near the top of the maple tree screamed.

Looking down, he watched a pack of little gnomes pointing up at him. They had circled his giant beanstalk. Ryan's body trembled everywhere at the sight of the giant gargoyle leaping at him. It had bitten him twice, and he remembered gargoyle bites were poisonous. The bright light from the mother ship blinded him, and he started crawling further out on the limb towards the light. When he reached the skinny portion, the branch bent precariously. The skinny branch crackled with rice-crispy sounds, and with a loud snap, broke away. Ralph lunged, briefly holding the young man by his shirt before it ripped away. Ryan Hayden fell 30 feet, landing on his belly in the tall weeds with a dull thud.

Blood oozed from his mouth and broken nose. The EMTs thrashed through the cocklebur and mare's tail, and carefully log rolled the young man to his back while supporting his neck. Ryan's pulse was absent, his pupils fixed.

"He's dead, Chief."

Chapter Forty-Three

A Father's Guilt

Ryan Hayden's family held a private funeral for their son at Johnson's funeral home, officiated by a pastor recommended by the Funeral Director.

Kate sat in the church office, thinking about the upcoming Sunday sermon when Ryan Hayden Sr. walked in. A powerful and successful Big Bay attorney, he also served on the pastor's finance committee at the Methodist Church.

"You wonder why I didn't ask you to preside at my son's funeral?"

"Never really spent any time on that one, Mr. Hayden."

"You're reputation is tainted by your association with those men, and your relationship with Doug."

"You're speaking of my fiancé."

"I'm going to file a lawsuit, several in fact: one against Doug and his dog, and the men who were responsible for my son's death, and one against Chief Strait and the City of Big Bay, holding him responsible for dereliction of duty and failure to protect a citizen, resulting in death."

Kate looked up from her desk with an expressionless face.

"You are by most accounts a good attorney, Mr. Hayden. You certainly can file lawsuits, if that's your way of handling guilt."

Kate paused.

"These men are my friends, and for that I don't apologize. They did absolutely nothing to contribute to your son's death, and I will not watch from a distance as you cause them misery."

"Yeah, right. Is that a threat?"

"I personally know the best Defense Attorney on the east coast, and he owes me. I'll give him a call."

"Who might that be?" Mr. Hayden replied with disdain.

"Garrison Dupree."

Attorney Hayden's head jerked to the side. He stared at Pastor McGinnis.

"And," Kate continued, "if I'm inclined to join the defense team for that trial, I'm even better than Garrison."

"You aren't even licensed here."

"Wrong already, counselor. And with your son's fingerprints all over the murder weapon, which happens to belong to you--by the way, how did a minor have access to the murder weapon, just for starters? Sure you want to pursue this?"

Ryan Hayden senior turned and walked out of Big Bay Methodist Church without saying another word.

Katherine Kennedy McGinnis had a slight smile on her face, watching

Chapter Forty-Four
Conflicted Love

Walking through the front door to tell Carla, Timothy's chest ached.

"Honey, Machete has been shot."

Carla looked up from the couch where she was reading, and looked at her husband, her pupils dilating.

"How bad?"

"Very bad, in the head. He's going to die."

Carla put the book on her lap, and held out her hand, beckoning Timothy to sit beside her.

"I don't think so. Machete is NOT going to die."

"The doctors are surprised he's still alive. They've taken him off the ventilator."

"I don't care...I don't care. They don't know everything, Timothy. Let's go to the hospital. I need to take care of him."

Timothy sat down and thought to himself, *Oh I really don't want her to see him this way.* "I'll talk to Stanley and see when a good time would be for you to visit."

"Right now! You call Stan and tell him Machete needs me right now! And tell him Machete is *not* going to die."

Timothy walked to the den and called.

"Hi, Stan. I just told Carla. She wants me to take her to the hospital, and to tell you that he's not going to die."

"Oh man. Well, Danielle is planning on staying with him a little while after work tomorrow, if he's still alive. Tell Carla that she'll drive over and pick her up at 4, and they can go together."

"She wants to go right now."

"Ok. Be right down. I can get her in for a quick visit."

Stanley and Danielle sat on the deck under the gas heaters. He put the phone down.

"Carla wants to see Machete right now. Guess I'll take her in. I'm not thinking this is such a good idea with his face all swollen."

"Machete needs her tonight. Drive her in Stan."

Stanley started to stand when Danielle grabbed his hand and pulled him down next to her.

"I'm so confused, honey. I feel heavy inside, feel sad deep down, like a family member is dying. How can I feel this way about a guy who came here to kill you and who kidnapped our Chloe? I feel this twisted knot in my stomach? All I want to do is bawl."

"I wish you could have heard Kate's prayer when we took him off the ventilator. She said, 'Lord here comes your servant Machete. You know the rough road he's traveled to prove his love.' Right then I knew why I felt so sad, standing there. He loves us. Machete came here with bad intentions and ended up loving us. I guess we love him, too."

"That must be it."

"I'll drive Carla over for a quick visit, and be right back. No sleep tonight."

"We've done it before. I'm going to take Chloe up to be with him tomorrow after work."

"I'm not sure that's a really good idea."

"I'm going to, and you're going to help me do it."

"We'll talk about it when I get back."

It was almost 4 a.m. when Stanley and Carla walked through the Emergency Room entrance, and took the elevator to the 2nd floor.

The ICU nurses looked up from the nurse's station with questioning expressions. Carla walked past them and directly into Machete's room. Stanley nodded and followed her.

Machete lay on a cooling blanket. His endotracheal tube was attached to humidified oxygen. Intravenous solutions ran in his left arm and through a subclavian line. His face appeared puffy, and both eyes were blackened.

Carla walked to the bed without hesitation. She reached over the side rail and held his cold hand.

Oh, he's so cold, she thought. She stared at his distorted face. Carla leaned over the side rail and put her lips next to his ear. She whispered for several seconds.

"We can go now," she announced, turning towards Stanley and two ICU nurses who had been watching from the doorway.

"I told him I would be back tomorrow."

The nurses looked at each other and shook their heads in disbelief.

* * *

"I wonder if we should postpone the wedding," Kate asked Doug, "until this is all sorted out."

NO...no shivered through Doug's mind. *No...no.* "It's not for six weeks. Let's not change anything until we know for sure. Just wait."

"I feel how hard this is for you, that's all."

"I close my eyes...I see that crazy little Mexican rocking Chloe in that vacant house, singing to her, and then Malcolm and me walking down State Street headed to the jail with my pistol against his head, and then we're playing poker together. He's grinning at me."

"He's a special part of our lives. I think we are all being tested by God."

"Looks like Machete lost."

"I don't think so, Doug."

* * *

Poor Joe's *Closed* sign stayed in the window all week. The ICU waiting room had standing room only much of the time. The Usual Suspects seldom left, often sleeping in the waiting room chairs, despite being asked to leave by hospital security. The nurses limited Machete's visitors to one at a time.

"We don't want him to be alone," Wendell said to Ramona, the Director of Nursing, when she walked into the waiting room and reminded the men there were rules and visiting hours.

"It's not right he should die all alone. We're his only friends, and we're not going to let that happen."

* * *

On the third day after the shooting, Danielle and Carla walked past the ICU nurse's station. Danielle carried Chloe. Several nurses pointed at the child. Danielle put a finger to her lips, and walked into Machete's room. Carla went to the head of the bed and whispered into Machete's ear. Danielle stood on the other side of the bed, holding Chloe. Then she gently placed the little girl next to him.

"Your sister is here to visit, Machete. Maria is here."

This visitation ritual occurred daily, at 3:30 p.m. Chloe was placed next to Machete and she touched his face while looking around at the array of medical devices making strange sounds. Occasionally, she reached up and pulled his ear.

Stanley and Dr. McCaferty stood in the nurses' station, reviewing Machete's chart.

"I really didn't think he would last this long, Stan."

"Me neither."

"We need to get the endo tube out before he develops necrosis. If we have to, we'll trach him."

"Let's do it."

The two friends quietly worked to remove the breathing tube.

Machete continued to breathe without difficulty.

On the twelfth day, Danielle placed Chloe next to Machete.

Carla was bending over the side rail, whispering.

"Maria......" The muffled sound came through the oxygen mask.

Everyone in the room froze in place and held their breath. The only sound came from the ventilator two rooms down the hall.

"Maria...Maria," Machete whispered.

Carla kissed him on his sweaty forehead.

Danielle squeezed his hand.

Machete squeezed back.

Chapter Forty-Five
From The Dark Side

The men gathered at Poor Joe's fourteen days after Machete's shooting. The blood stains outside the men's room, faded by bleach, remained a battle scar in the old bar, along with the old buckshot holes and faded dark blood stains embedded in the hardwood next to the kitchen area, the scars from historic battles.

"Stanley's going to stop after work, and fill us in on how Machete's doing," Timothy announced to the men sitting around the poker table. "Told me this morning that they were doing some preliminary tests today. The docs think he might survive after all."

Stanley arrived at 6:30, his face pale with fatigue, and little dark circles under both eyes. "I'll have one tall Basil's on the rocks," he said while pulling a chair towards the table.

The men sat silently, waiting.

Stanley took a large mouthful of the bourbon, swished it around like mouthwash before he swallowed. He took a second gulp.

"We think Machete's going to survive, providing he doesn't become septic, and there's no more swelling."

He took another large gulp, looked at Timothy and said, "I'll have another."

"I'll drive you up the hill tonight, Stan; have as many as you want, buddy."

"We had a Neurologist do some preliminary tests this afternoon. As of right now, and this is all subject to change as he heals, Machete is blind. It appears that he's lost his sense of smell, and has partial paralysis on the left side."

Timothy handed Stanley a replacement Basil's. Stanley took a sip and continued. "And, it seems he's lost his memory. When he was asked his name, he told the Neurologist, 'The angel calls me Machete.' He has no recollection of his childhood...nothing."

"Does he know you?" Wendell asked.

"He doesn't. I asked about the angel who called him Machete. He told me, 'Every day the angel whisper in the ear. She said many people love me. I need to stay. My baby sister needs me. Another angel brings my sister to me. Two angels come to me.'"

Stanley sighed. "He told me he can see with his heart, that he can see his baby sister in his heart. 'She comes to visit me, my baby sister and the angels visit every day.'"

"Is he going to get better?" Doug asked from the end of the table.

"Hard to say. Some of the damage is probably permanent. We'll have to wait for the swelling, the inflammation, to subside before we know. The Neurologist feels the blindness is permanent."

"But he's probably going to live, right?" asked Ralph.

"We think so."

"We'll empty the storage room under the stairs," Timothy said from behind the bar, "and turn it into a room for him. I'll build a storage shed next to the parking lot. Machete can have a room right down here."

"Us guys are going to take care of him, Stan. We'll take turns. He can live right here with us," Wayne said. All of The Usual Suspects nodded *yes*.

"He's our friend, Stan," Pete said.

"I know he is, Pete. You guys are really something."

Stanley finished the Basil's and motioned for Timothy to drive him home.

Timothy opened the front door. Stanley turned back towards the poker table. "...even though his intentions were to kill us and burn this place to the ground?"

"He's our friend now," Wendell replied. "We don't abandon friends."

"Yeah," Doug added from the end of the table. "He came over from the dark side."

Chapter Forty-Six

Reflection In The Mirror

"**T**imothy's going to convert that big storage room under the stairs to a room for Machete. The guys want to take care of him when he gets out," Stanley said as Danielle brushed her hair while preparing for bed.

"Think they can handle him?"

"We'll see. Probably after a stint in rehab. We'll see. Those guys are something else."

"I'll help them."

Stanley turned and looked at his wife's reflection in the mirror.

"What do you mean?"

"I'll take a leave of absence. I have connections you know. Take a leave, or maybe just quit for a while, and help the guys with him. I've been thinking about quitting until Chloe's in school anyway, being with her instead of taking her to daycare. We don't need the money, Stan. Chloe and I could go over and help the guys every day."

Stanley stared at the reflection of his wife in the mirror.

"Well?"

"I thought you missed the hospital, and that's why you went back."

"It was. Now I want to be with our daughter as she grows, and we can help with Machete together."

"I think I may be sleeping with an angel," Stanley said.

He walked to Danielle and hugged her.

"It's settled then, I'm going to! I'll write you a letter in the morning, boss man. And you're correct, you *are* sleeping with an angel," Danielle said.

She turned away from the mirror, and winked at her husband.

Chapter Forty-Seven
The Legend Of The Green Parrot

Miriam sat at a little round table under an umbrella in the courtyard of the Carmel Country Inn, waiting for her fiancé. She had spent the day on the telephone, mostly to Key West, making wedding arrangements while Jim made rounds at Monterey Community Hospital, and then saw patients at the Heart Institute.

She stood up from the table when his car drove into the parking lot.

Dr. James Roosevelt climbed out of the little roadster and watched Miriam walk towards him.

Then they were face to face. A sensation of breathlessness squeezed him and a pounding feeling in his chest. By reflex, he glanced down and felt his right radial pulse. When he looked up, his dark haired lover touched his lips with her lips, and they melted together in a tight embrace, so close they both could feel the pounding in their chests.

"Every time I look, I'm amazed by your beauty. Great to be with you again, honey."

Miriam snuggled in even tighter. "I can't wait until we're together every single day."

"Not much longer."

"I've made phone calls all day. This wedding is going to be awesome!"

"Let's drive up to Nepenthe for dinner; you can tell me all about it," he said.

He opened the passenger's door to the green MG and leaned in for another kiss.

* * *

Charter Captain Quinn O'Malley walked down Front Street, through the wrought iron gates and up the sidewalk to Harry Truman's Little White House.

"My name is O'Malley; have an appointment with Paul Hilson," he said to the lady in the reception area.

"He's upstairs in his office; I'll get him."

Paul walked down the stairs with a broad grin.

"Finally, the trifecta is complete!" he said. He shook Captain O'Malley's hand.

"Trifecta?"

"The modern day trilogy of Key West: Captain Tony Tarracino, Jimmy Buffett, and now I meet you. It is a pleasure to make your acquaintance Captain O'Malley."

"I'm not in that league." O'Malley laughed. "I'm simply a one boat charter service."

"And provider of fine cigars, truth be told Captain, and a legend at the Green Parrot."

"I do come across an occasional fine box," he said, handing a wooden box of Habana Bolivar cigars to Paul.

"I don't personally smoke, but thank you, Captain. How may I help you?"

"We both know not to believe most of what we hear in this town, Hilson."

"Fair enough."

"There are some friends of mine getting married here on the 15th. I'm in charge of security."

The men walked outside and sat on a bench on the west lawn. The

Events Director studied the captain's face.

"That's what I'm talking about; there you go being in charge of security. A simple one boat charter service in charge of security."

Quinn shrugged and stared back. "Well, I have a few other skills."

"We have our own private security here at the White House, Captain. The only time we don't get involved is during Presidential or dignitary visits…the Secret Service takes over."

The men stared at the White House.

"There's a security team I would like to hire for my friend's wedding, a team the Secret Service emulates. I would like very much for that team to be here during the wedding, in addition to your security, of course."

"What's going on here, Captain?"

"Let's say we may have a visiting dignitary, and leave it at that. I'd feel better with the extra shield around the place."

Paul Hilson smiled. "I've been around long enough to know when no more questions want asked."

* * *

The phone rang at the Big Bay Methodist parsonage at 11:12 p.m. Kate rolled over in bed and answered.

"Hi, Kate, it's Miriam!"

"Hi, Miriam, you ok?"

"Ooh…I'm sorry, it's after 11 there, I'm sorry."

Kate laughed. "I'm just lying here thinking about the wedding. You must be in California."

"Jim and I went out to dinner, and he just dropped me off. I made phone calls most of the day to Key West. I'm so excited."

"Me, too! After everything we've been through here, I'm realizing the big day is closing in. I'm getting the jitters. I do have all the invitations mailed."

"Not to worry, Kate; I heard about that awful shooting at Poor Joe's, and you were busy…got your back, girlfriend."

"Tell me about your day."

"I found us a wedding planner in Key West. Her name is Colleen Jansen… found her on-line and called …apologized for short notice and she just laughed and told me nobody would know and that we will have a beautiful wedding. She's delighted we are having the wedding at the Little White House… said it will be magical. It's her first double wedding and she seemed excited."

Miriam inhaled excitedly and continued, "And…she has a friend who is a renowned photographer…Angel Burke. Colleen said she has a studio in Key West…I hired Angel to take our pictures!"

"Whew, thanks Miriam, for doing all this…it's my first double wedding too," Kate laughed.

"And," Miriam continued, "Colleen said she knows the owner of a great catering service; she'll take care of that end of it, too. She'll send us a menu tomorrow to look over."

"I read about Truman's Key West White House last Saturday," Kate interjected. "Seven Presidents have stayed there…it's hard to believe our dinner is going to be served in the very room where world dignitaries have dined. What would I do without you?"

"Why… you and Doug would get married at the Justice's office." Miriam laughed. "This will be more fun, I bet!"

I spoke with the White House events director, Paul Hilson. We are limited to a total of forty in the wedding party; that's all they can seat in the dining area. That's no problem from my side, between Jim and I; we have eighteen flying down."

"I'll get my list together this week. I think I've gotten back most of the RSVP's. I'll call you," Kate replied.

"I've got one little problem…sorry I've waited this long to mention it."

"What, Miriam.?"

"I don't have a father to walk me down the aisle."

Silence ensued.

"Let's you and I walk together, side by side, Miriam. My parents and your mom can join us at the altar. That's what I want; you and I walking together, walking together and staring at the men we're going to spend eternity alongside."

"Thanks. Think it'll be ok?"

"It's Key West, Miriam."

* * *

"I talked with your mother today," Carla said to Timothy. He picked up his son from the crib and walked into the kitchen.

"Sabrina called you?"

"Nope, I called her. I got to thinking we haven't talked much since Charles was born, so I called her."

My wife is back, Timothy thought. "Well, lots has happened, honey, and since Dad died, she's got a social routine with the other service widows."

"I called her and we had a nice talk. We caught each other up on all the stuff in our lives, and then I told her we needed her to come to Big Bay, that we needed her help with Charles Dwight during the wedding and trip to Cuba."

Oh, wonder who hung up first. Timothy smiled at Carla. "Well, how'd that go over?"

Carla smiled a smile Timothy had not seen since Mackinac Island.

"She said, 'When do you need Grandma?' I told her we're flying to Key West on the 12th, and she wanted to know how the hell I expected her to get everything together and make it to Big Bay on such short notice. I told her not to worry, just pack enough for a couple of weeks."

Charles Dwight rubbed his daddy's right arm stump.

"And then I called your buddy Sammy, and hired him to fly over and pick her up on the 11th."

Timothy walked close to his wife, bent down and kissed her on the lips. "Welcome back," he said.

Richard Alan Hall

"I didn't like that place," Carla answered.

Chapter Forty-Eight

The True Believers

A black Chevy Suburban with several little antennas on the roof drove into the parking lot behind the A&B Lobster House next to the Key West Marina, and parked. Three young men in their late twenties exited. They were tall, all over six feet, and muscular. They strutted arrogantly past the Lobster House patrons dining on the porch.

Captain O'Malley sat on the Key West Dreamer moored at slip number eight, next to Conch Republic Seafood. His back faced the sidewalk as he read the latest edition of the Key West Citizen with the late afternoon sun shining over his shoulder.

"CAPTAIN O'MALLEY. CAPTAIN QUINN O'MALLEY!" shouted the tallest of the young men from the marina walkway.

Quinn twisted his head to the left and squinted up. He saw three young men dressed in dark blue militia type uniforms. They had Homeland Security Special Agent emblems affixed to their left shoulders. Each wore Douglass MacArthur style sunglasses, and holstered sidearms. Military type boots extended almost to their knees.

"Afternoon, young fellas... help you?"

"Come up here," demanded the young man who seemed to be in charge.

"Well, young fella, come on down here, commander," Captain O'Malley replied.

All three blue uniformed men produced gold shields and held them in the Captain's direction.

"Homeland Security," they said in unison.

"You don't say," Quinn replied. "You young fellas just fresh from the academy?" he quipped, glancing at his left wrist.

He pushed a button located on the side of his watch.

"I'm not telling you again. Get up here," the man who Quinn called commander said sternly.

"Am I under arrest or something?" Quinn asked with a wry smile.

"You need to come in for questioning. There are security concerns raised about the wedding at Truman's. I'm about to cancel the whole damn thing."

The smile froze on Quinn O'Malley's face.

"I repeat, am I under arrest?"

"That can be arranged. The guest list has been reviewed. Concerns are raised…something about visiting dignitaries requiring unauthorized security. I'm familiar with your history, O'Malley. Let's go."

The young agents stared with disdain down at the old Captain sitting on the mahogany deck of his 36-foot Taylorcraft, rubbing his Hemingway stubble. They were not aware of the six men coming towards them, three from behind, walking rapidly from the White Tarpon veranda, and three to their right, walking briskly around the corner from Conch Republic Seafood, all wearing a variety of colorful Caribbean Soul shirts, and little lions tattooed on the inside of their right forearms.

"So you're familiar with my history? Amazing. Probably an entire semester at the academy." Quinn grinned. "I think you would be well advised to join me for a little cruise." Then Quinn added, looking up into the sun at the men, "We can talk this out, to your satisfaction, and you can take notes, boys."

"Ok, that's it…you're under arrest for obstruction of a Homeland Security investigation."

The three Homeland officers moved to board the Key West Dreamer. The three men walking from the White Tarpon sprinted past them, jumping onboard with the captain.

The Homeland officers reached for their sidearms. Each felt a gun muzzle pressed hard into their lumbar spines as the men walking from the Conch Republic arrived from behind.

"Climb onboard, kiddo, 'cuz if I pull this trigger you'll live from the waist up, pissing your pants for the rest of your miserable life," the whiskered man said to the commander.

The Homeland Special Agents climbed onboard the Key West Dreamer. Captain O'Malley started first the starboard and then the port engine.

A young family with three preteen children watched from their table at the Conch Republic with excited wide eyes.

"They're rehearsing for a movie," the father said to his children, pointing towards the Key West Dreamer.

"Reminds me of that Hemingway book we read in 10th grade," the young mother said to her high school sweetheart. "What was it called?"

"*To Have and Have Not.* I wrote your paper for you."

"And you were rewarded, Peter," she replied. Her children watched their mom blush a little.

"I bet they're doing a remake of the Bogart movie," her husband exclaimed

* * *

"Now, was that so hard?" Quinn asked. "And for the time being, boys, let's put your sidearms in this duffel for safe keeping." Each agent handed his weapon to the man facing him, and only then was the muzzle pressure removed from their backs.

"YOU ARE FREAKING NUTS!" screamed the commander. "The Navy and Air Force will have your ass before you can get fifty miles. Can't wait to testify at your treason trial, old man."

Quinn nudged the throttles forward. The boat reached fifteen knots. From the corner of his eye, he watched the three Homeland men send hand signals to each other, discussing options for overpowering their captors.

"You take the helm, Andrew," Quinn said to the bearded man.

"I know that sign language, too," Quinn said. He formed several words with his hands. "Get this message?"

"What'd you mean, 'we'll enjoy our time in Cuba?' That's what you said. Who are you?" the shortest of the three agents exclaimed.

"I thought you college boys knew all the answers. I'm a charter boat captain."

"You'll never get away with this, O'Malley. See, here comes a chopper!"

Flying just above the waves, heading directly at the Key West Dreamer at 200 miles per hour from the direction of Cuba, charged a stealth helicopter. It circled the boat once and then hovered above them. Andrew pulled back on the throttles, slowing the boat to a crawl through the rolling waves.

A cable with a basket slowly descended from the black flying machine.

"You first," Quinn ordered the Homeland Security commander. "And you be sure to ask for the puerco asado; it's great with black beans and yellow rice. And flan for dessert."

"You're certifiable!" the young man screamed over the noise of the rotors.

Quinn leaned close to the young man's head. "Your mistake was threatening my friends. Never threaten my friends again, young fella... should you come back."

"WHAT?!"

"You, young man, are the guarantee there will be no further trouble. Say hi to Raul from me. He's a good friend."

The basket ascended to the black helicopter and returned empty for the next passenger, and then the next. When the side door was closed, the flying machine descended and hovered next to the boat. The pilot saluted crisply, and then his helicopter headed south rapidly.

The sun disappeared with a green flash just above the surface of the Gulf.

Looking up at the bulkhead in the helicopter, above the heads of six men dressed in black, the three Homeland Special Agents read the sign printed with large red letters...TRUE BELIEVERS.

* * *

A youthful band rocked on Schooner Wharf's outdoor stage as the Key West Dreamer maneuvered through the marina shortly before midnight. The percussion rolled over the warm salt water. Quinn smiled. "Oh, to be young again."

Maneuvering the Key West Dreamer towards slip 8, he watched the occasional glow from two cigars.

The men secured the lines. Quinn climbed off the boat and walked towards two men sitting in cane chairs.

The Key West Chief of Police and southeast Special Agent for the FBI sat smoking Cuban Bolivar cigars.

"Ron, Theodore, nice evening for a smoke."

"Hello, Quinn. Been fishing?"

"You know I get my fish from Fausto's, Ron."

"More to the point, Captain, we found a Suburban licensed to the Federal Government parked behind the steak house, and three missing Homeland guys....working out of my office, sent to interview you," the FBI agent said. He studied Quinn's face.

Quinn laughed. The six men on his boat stood on the deck and watched. The Chief of Police glanced at them nervously.

"Yes, Theodore, they were here, sure enough. Surprises me that Feds send boys to do a man's job. Those boys finished puberty coinciding with graduation from the academy, by the looks of their acne scars."

"Where are they, Quinn?" the chief asked.

"We took a little ride around Tank Island together, talked things over to everyone's satisfaction, and they took their leave right as the sun set. Beautiful sunset off Mallory Square...green flash, too."

"Where are they now?" the FBI agent asked.

"That's the thing about boys not yet reliable or trustworthy. You add raging testosterone, mojitos, and Cuban girls with skirts up to here, and their compasses start spinning. I'll bet they're lost in the Cuban section, having the time of their lives."

The Chief of Police smiled, a little.

"You remember those days, huh, Ron?"

"I married one of those girls…woke up three days later married to the most beautiful Cuban girl I'd ever seen…been married twenty three years."

"Quinn O'Malley, I should arrest you right now," retorted the FBI agent.

Quinn removed a Bolivar cigar from his pocket and lit it.

"I'm pretty sure they'll be back in a day or so, all hung over and sorry. Go easy on them Theodore. Got a wedding to attend to on Saturday, and then I'll check in with you down at the courthouse, providing the weather is beautiful for the wedding."

Theodore took a step towards Quinn.

"You and Mrs. Gunther should take a vacation together, Theodore…be good for your home life. I have contacts; set you up with a friend who owns a nice Caribbean Villa," Quinn said. He relit his cigar. "I could make arrangements."

"We'll discuss things soon. Nothing better happen to my men."

Quinn laughed. "They kinda remind me of the Hitler Youth. You think so too, Theodore?"

"Damn you, Quinn, I mean it."

The Chief and Special Agent walked away into the darkness.

* * *

The next morning Quinn entered the Truman White House, walked past the receptionist with only a nod, and up the stairs to Paul Hilson's office.

"Just saw the revised forecast for Saturday, Paul. The thunderstorms originally called for are gone. Looks like a sunny warm day now, perfect for a wedding."

Paul looked up from his desk.

"Sorry. They showed up, asking about the guest list and the visiting dignitary and I had no answers."

"You really want to know?"

"Absolutely not...I hate storms."

"It really doesn't matter. You'll be surprised," Quinn said. He walked down several steps, and turned back.

"I don't want you to feel badly over recent events," he said, looking at the White House Events Director.

Captain O'Malley smiled a sardonic smile. "This never was about the wedding, Paul."

Chapter Forty-Nine

He Can See The Other Side

Quinn O'Malley arrived in Big Bay on the 8:15 a.m. flight from Key West via Miami on December 12th. Stanley picked him up at the airport, and drove towards Poor Joe's.

"Had breakfast?"

"Handful of those little pretzels and two Biscoff cookies with awful coffee."

"How about a Dora special; going to be a long day."

"You buying?"

"Yes, sir."

"Good. Steak and eggs with a side of those little dollar pancakes she makes."

"You know that diet is going to kill you, right?"

"Steak and eggs are gonna have to wait in line for that honor, Stanley." And the captain laughed.

Stanley glanced at his passenger's face, and said nothing.

Timothy and Doug were sitting at the big table drinking coffee when Stanley and Quinn walked through the front door.

Timothy and Quinn hugged silently.

"How's Carla?"

"Been a miracle...absolutely a miracle, Quinn....no more nightmares. She goes out by herself, drives around; talking about going to Nashville and recording after the wedding. It's been since Machete woke up in that

212

hospital bed and called her an angel."

"Miracles are good. Take one any time you can get it, my friend. They never cease to amaze me," Quinn said.

He turned towards Dora in the kitchen area. "Speaking of miracles, how about steak and eggs and some of those dollar pancakes, Dora?" he said, and continued, "You still single?"

"Don't start sweet talking me, Captain. Medium rare on the steak and over easy on the eggs, right? I got your number, mister."

Quinn laughed. "Try calling me sometime when this place gets old, Dora. I'll show you a good time."

Dora chuckled. "I'm afraid of boats, Quinn."

Pete, Ralph, Wendell, and Wayne walked down the stairs.

"That smells good. I want the same," Ralph commented.

"We all do," Wayne suggested.

"And Stanley's buying," Quinn added.

"BIG tip for the cook, Quinn," Stanley retorted.

"You ready for the big day, Doug?" Quinn asked, pouring cream into a cup of coffee, diluting it by half.

"Never been so scared in my life really, Quinn."

Quinn laughed. "Well, take it from a guy who's done it several times, just do what you're told; it'll be fine. And practice saying, 'Yes dear.' Wish someone had given me that advice!"

"Yes dear...yes dear...yes dear," Doug muttered with a smile on his face. Then he looked at the men sitting at the table. "I really like being in love," the old vet said.

"I'm really happy for you, buddy," Stanley said. "That morning at the hospital, with you chasing the nurses around, swinging a wet mop, seems like a million years ago. It's great to see you happy."

"Thank you, Stanley...you and Doc McCaferty...I can't thank enough."

"Well, I can tell you they're excited at Truman's White House,"

Captain O'Malley said. "First double wedding there ever. Paul Hilson told me everything is falling into place beautifully. Hey, how's Machete?"

"He's in rehab; probably another month before discharge," Stanley said.

Timothy walked over and opened the door to the newly renovated room under the stairs, and switched the light on.

"We've made him a room, Quinn!"

"How wonderful. How nice," Quinn said, looking through the doorway into the room now equipped with everything a special needs patient could possibly require.

"Stanley helped us get all this stuff with the hospital discount," Timothy said.

"We're gonna make a little place in the corner so Malcolm can stay with him," Doug added.

Sammy Peck walked into Poor Joe's, dressed in his pilot's uniform.

"How do I look?" he asked.

"It still fits, buddy. Good for you," Timothy replied. "How long has it been since you flew the 2000?"

"Yesterday. Took her up for an hour. She still loves me. We leaving at 1400?"

"Yup," Timothy replied. "That's the plan."

"Good, we'll get to Key West while there's still sunlight. Makes landing easier."

Everyone stared at the gray haired Vietnam Vet in his dress pilot's uniform.

"Just kidding...a little pilot's humor."

"Let's drive over to the hospital," Captain O'Malley announced. "I want to say hi to Machete before we leave."

"Bonifacio flew in last night. I think he's over seeing Machete right now," Timothy said, reaching under the counter for his car keys. "They seem to be close friends."

Vincent Bonifacio was sitting in a chair next to Machete, who was sitting up in a reclining lounger with his feet elevated. Timothy and Quinn stopped at the door and observed the two friends talking.

"I'm sorry this happened, Machete...damn it my friend...very sorry."

Machete reached out and after several attempts put his hand on Vincent's hand, said, "I am fine; met the angels and now many friends. Es un mundo hermoso. Gracias a mi amigo."

Quinn and Timothy entered the room. Quinn shook Vincent's hand then bent close to Machete.

For several minutes Machete and Captain O'Malley conversed earnestly in Spanish. Then Quinn leaned down and kissed him on the forehead. "God bless you, my friend."

He turned towards Vincent. "We're taking off at 1400. Don't be late. The pilot wants sunlight when we land on that short runway."

"Maybe we should have Machete as his copilot."

Quinn chuckled as he and Timothy left the room. "That's not a bad idea Vincent."

As they traveled from the hospital, Timothy glanced at Quinn. "What was all the Spanish about?"

"He can see the other side, Timothy; he can see love."

They rode in silence the rest of the way back to Poor Joe's.

Timothy turned the old Buick's ignition off in Poor Joe's parking lot. The men sat in silence briefly. Quinn said, "He has no memory. It's as if his slate has been wiped clean. Kinda like being born anew...I'm jealous."

Chapter-Fifty

A Trip To Key West

The Saab 2000's twin Rolls Royce turboprop engines roared. The plane sped down the Big Bay runway and lifted off for Key West. All of The Usual Suspects and Dora were onboard. Timothy and Carla sat side by side, holding hands. Stanley and Danielle sat immediately behind them. Sabrina sat over the wings, with little Charles Dwight on one side and Chloe Norma on the other. Doug and Kate sat together across the aisle from Timothy and Carla. Vincent Bonifacio and Quinn O'Malley sat next to each other in the tail section.

Sammy Peck sat in the pilot's seat. Next to him, a young man who until two years ago had flown with the Blue Angels and was now the newest pilot employed with Big Bay Air, Samuel Andrew Peck, Jr.

Vincent and the captain reclined casually in their seats.

"Heard Homeland Security gave you some crap in Key West."

"Wasn't the kids' fault, simply doing as they were told. They're still vacationing, compliments of Raul...just to send a message."

"Also heard the message was received and the Director is mad as hell," Vincent said with a grin. "That was a little brazen, even for you."

"That man *does* hold a mean grudge."

"You stole his wife, Quinn. Adding insult to injury, you sided with Fidel during the Bay of Pigs."

"That was a long time ago, and I didn't steal anybody, Barbara ran from him quite willingly. He certainly doesn't miss an opportunity to remind me he's still alive."

"I think he'll quiet down, at least as long this administration is in office."

"How's that?"

"Had a conversation with the Chief of Staff; promised he would say something to the President on your behalf."

"Thanks."

"He appreciates the Montecristos and Bolivars."

"Understood."

"If you had to do it all over again, would you?" Vincent asked.

"Probably."

"Me, too."

Sabrina occupied Chloe and little Charles with magic tricks.

Kate grasped Doug's hand very tightly and bowed her head. Doug bowed his. His fiancé prayed out loud, "Lord, we are about to embark on the rest of our lives together. Please be with us, guide us and direct us, and protect us from evil. Help us live our lives together so those around us feel your love. Help us live our lives so we are pleasing to you." Kate looked up. Tears were dripping from Doug's chin and splashing on the airplane floor.

Doctor Lavern Smith and his wife Mary sat two rows ahead and across the aisle from Quinn and Vincent, Lavern reading neglected hospital reports while his wife read a newly published novel. The doctor smiled after listening to the conversation behind them.

Stanley and Danielle paged through vacation brochures Quinn had given them about Cayo Coco. "Almost two weeks. This is going to be fabulous," Danielle commented.

"I want us to check out old town while we're in Key West this time. I saw some places for sale on White Street; did a search on-line."

"You're kidding, right?"

"Nope. Let's look for a nice little get-a-way place instead of staying at the resorts."

David Chown arranged music sheets in the proper order for the wedding, and thought about his last trip to Key West, which ended up in Cuba.

Carla was sound asleep with her head resting on Timothy's shoulder. It reminded him of the time they were traveling back from The Woods Restaurant on Mackinac Island...and they were in a horse drawn taxi. He tried not to move so she would sleep on.

Chief of Police Strait and his wife Dawn read through travel brochures about Key West. Neither had been there. "Looks like an interesting place," Dawn said, looking at pictures from a Bahama Village Goombay Festival.

"Stanley loves Key West," Larry replied. He leaned close to his wife looking at the pictures.

Dr. McCaferty and his wife Kathy sat across the aisle from Sabrina. An hour into the flight, Chloe Norma climbed over Sabrina's lap, walked across the aisle and sat next to Kathy. Jack read *A Brief History of Time*, by Stephen Hawking.

Pete and Ralph played poker. Wayne and Morris slept. Wendell played solitaire and then watched out the window. When he spotted the Seven Mile Bridge, he proclaimed, "Almost there!"

The Saab circled Key West once and then descended rapidly, flying low over Mallory Square and then seemingly dropping like an elevator before touching gently on the tarmac. The reverse thrusters roared and the brakes squealed, stopping the plane. The runway had ended.

The pilot and copilot smiled at each other.

"Thanks, son."

Chapter Fifty-One

Janet Sue

The moon shown full on Thursday the thirteenth, two days before the wedding.

The Duval Inn had been exclusively reserved for the wedding party. The old building radiated growing excitement with each additional guest.

Rose Jackson and Jonathon arrived in the morning, shortly after Kate's parents.

Rose and Jonathon walked through the outdoor courtyard, hand in hand.

Holding her left hand high, she smiled. "I am Mrs. Jonathon Williams," she said through smiling lips.

Jonathon grinned at The Usual Suspects, just as Miriam and James Roosevelt, along with Miriam's mother Gladys, arrived by taxi.

Hugs, introductions and congratulations interrupted breakfast.

"Who are those guys walking on Angela Street?" Kate's father queried. "They look like Secret Service guys I saw when the President was at Fenway Park."

"And there's a bunch of them outside the Denny's two blocks up," Kate's mother added.

Quinn O'Malley laughed. He looked at Vincent Bonifacio with a questioning expression. "Any time the Truman White House has a special event like this, they put on extra security," he said with authority.

"What the hell is going on?" Quinn asked Vincent, walking through the alley, scattering several chicks trailing a hen.

Vincent retrieved a triangular shaped phone from his pants pocket, and punched a number sequence.

"Ron, this is Vincent; seems we have some unexpected help here, not that we're ungrateful." He stood still and listened before replying, "Thank the President for his consideration, and thank you, Ron." And he put the phone back in his pocket.

"The President ordered a special detail here; said he knows we have a dignitary guest arriving, and will be damned if anything happens on his watch, especially since they're so close on Guantanamo."

"Did you tell anyone?"

"No, and I know you didn't"

"What's this Guantanamo thing?"

"Damned if I know."

* * *

Colleen Janson and Angel Burke exited a taxi and joined the guests in the courtyard. Angel snapped impromptu pictures. Colleen clapped her hands for attention. "I want you to know how honored we are to be part of this," she said. "We'll have a little rehearsal tomorrow at noon. This evening the girls are going to celebrate at La Te Da starting at nine. You men are on your own. Tomorrow, breakfast at Blue Heaven at nine. Tomorrow evening the rehearsal dinner at Margaritaville at seven; we have the upstairs. Then Saturday we have a wedding at 1p.m.!"

Everyone clapped. Angel took more pictures. Miriam started to cry, just a little, and hugged Jim very hard. Angel snapped a picture.

"The men will be celebrating at El Siboney tonight," Quinn announced. "Taxis'll be here at seven thirty. Meet here in the courtyard."

* * *

The *Open* sign had not been turned on, and the parking lot had only one car, a large black Cadillac limousine.

"El Siboney, what's it mean?" asked Timothy.

"Doesn't translate well," Quinn answered. "The Siboney were the natives of the Caribbean."

Quinn glanced at the black Cadillac. He smiled and nodded at Vincent, who pointed to the men with sunglasses standing in the shadows.

Dr. James Roosevelt led the group through the front door with youthful excitement, and stopped abruptly. Fidel Castro stood up and walked towards him, extending his hand. "Congratulations, Doctor, I understand you are a very fortunate man," Fidel said. He looked directly into Jim's eyes. "It is an honor to be included in your celebrations. Please accept this evening as a gift from the people of Cuba."

The owner of El Siboney and his family nodded, eyes wide with delight.

Dr. Roosevelt turned towards The Usual Suspects, dazed, and then back to President Castro.

"If I wake in the morning and discover this was a dream, I'm going to be really pissed." And he shook Fidel's hand again.

"Someday I would like for you and your wife to visit. I will arrange for Miriam to have a concert at our Grand Opera House in Habana."

Fidel walked over to Doug. "I know you from your pictures, and reputation. I wish you and Katherine much happiness. I am honored to meet a man who has walked with the angels. How is Malcolm?"

"Thank you, Mr. President. Malcolm is staying with Machete in the hospital. Doc here saw to it." Doug nodded at Dr. McCaferty.

"I am very sad to hear that terrible thing. I admire that little man, thank you for saving his life, Doctor." He shook Jack McCaferty's hand.

"Oh I think I had very little to do with this miracle, Mr. President," Dr. McCaferty said, staring in almost disbelief at the bearded man dressed in a camelhair jacket.

Richard Alan Hall

"Miracles are good. I have known several in my time, Doctor…they are good."

The men moved around the table. Doug tried to have Fidel seated at the head, but he refused. "Tonight is a special night for James and Douglas; they are at either end, please. I'll be here next to my old friend, O'Malley. Actually, I'm not here; this place is on US soil, correct?"

Everyone laughed. Jim rubbed his face and thought, *Just wait until I tell Miriam who came to my party.*

Dr. McCaferty thought, *I hope we all don't get arrested tonight.*

Kate's father and Dr. Smith stared at each other in disbelief. *This feels like the twilight zone,* Lavern thought to himself.

Kate's father smiled. Now he knew why all the men with sunglasses had been lurking about.

Pitchers of house-made Sangria were replaced numerous times during the meal which consisted of medio pollo a la plancha (grilled garlic chicken), boliche asado (roast beef, dry rubbed with spices and marinated in orange and lime juice before being slow roasted overnight), and filete de cherna empanizada (breaded grouper filet), all served on large platters, family style, along with salad, yellow rice, black beans and buttered cuban bread.

"Take advice from an old man who has learned many a hard lesson," Fidel said, raising his glass of Sangria. "Listen to your women; they have a wisdom men cannot understand. They choose you for their husbands. Do not question their wisdom, young men."

Flan, mango cheesecake, and rice pudding came with pitchers of café con leche for dessert.

"I am an old man, and must take my leave. You young men have my best wishes for much happiness and much love in your lives. God bless you." And Fidel Castro walked towards the exit. Everyone stood.

Fidel turned and pointed in the direction of Quinn. "You are no spring chicken, either." And he was gone.

Jim looked at Doug.

"Can you believe who came to our bachelor party?"

Doug looked up from his second helping of flan. "Nothing surprises me with these guys, Jim. Welcome to a very exclusive club…just hang on."

"How the hell did he slip in the USA without being detected?" Ralph wondered out loud.

"Not so sure about the *not detected*," Timothy replied. Through the window he watched the black Cadillac leave the parking lot, followed closely by two black Suburbans.

"What a night; just wait until I tell Miriam," Jim repeated, this time out loud.

Kate's father poured another full glass of sangria, and mused in his Irish brogue, "My, my, my, Little Katie, you have just joined hands with a life of adventure, my, my, my. You take good care of her, Dougie."

"I promise," Doug answered. "Forever."

* * *

"I'm too old to go out and carry on; you ladies have fun. Besides, Chloe and Charles need me," Sabrina said while the ladies prepared for the bachelorette party.

"I'll stay with the little ones, too," Miriam's mother added.

After opening the doors to the stretch Cadillac, the limo driver handed each of the ladies a card with his cell phone number. Miriam noticed a small tattoo of a lion on the inside of the driver's right forearm. *What a strange little tattoo*, she thought.

"If any of you ladies have any concerns, call me…call that number," the driver said through the window before he slid it shut.

"Here we are!" announced Colleen Janson. The limo pulled to the curb and stopped at the La Te Da. "Stay together, ladies. Have fun!"

The cosmopolitans and platters of spicy royal red shrimp aided the festive atmosphere.

"You should have seen Doug's face the first time I walked into Poor Joe's. To make matters worse, I was crashing the men's night poker game. He stared at me like I was a ghost or something. The first words out of his mouth were, 'Are you married?' I wanted to go over and hug him right then, but settled for pulling up a chair and winning the next three hands."

"Tell us the story about how you met Jim," Carla said. "I don't think everybody knows."

Miriam laughed.

Angel snapped pictures from artistic angles.

"Doug was in the hospital. I wandered down the hallways looking for his room, and when I turned a corner I ran smack-dab into this resident reading a chart. We really hit hard...broke my guitar and his glasses. He offered to have a friend fix the guitar, and we went out to dinner at Benjamin's. Then he moved to Carmel and I thought that would be the end of it...till he called, almost every day!"

The ladies listened to a band while they relished the French onion soup.

"Hey!" Danielle exclaimed, "Let's go down to Irish Kevin's; it's a wild and crazy place." She pulled out the card and called the limo driver.

Colleen shook her head, thinking, *Oh boy, here we go.*

The ladies walked through the open front doors. Irish Kevin stopped playing his guitar. From the stage he shouted, "The bride and bridesmaids are here, ladies and gentlemen. Come on up here and give Kevin a kiss!"

Danielle shot back, "Not in your wildest dreams."

"Oh, we have some live ones here...up you come!" he shouted back. "Sing us a song and your drinks are on me."

Miriam and Carla huddled briefly, shared something with the group, then climbed the steps to the stage.

Miriam asked Kevin for his guitar.

"You better watch out
You better not cry
Better not pout
I'm telling you why - Santa Claus is coming to town

He's making a list
And checking it twice,
He's gonna find out
Who's naughty and nice…"

The standing room only crowd and the tourists on the street applauded enthusiastically. Irish Kevin clapped and demanded, "Just one more, ladies. You could have a future in music. Just one more."

Miriam started and Katie joined her. With their arms around each other they sang a Beatles song,

"Love…love…love
There's nothing you can do that's not been done
Nothing you can sing that can't be sung.
There's nothing you can make that can't be made.
No one you can save that can't be saved.
Nothing you can do but you can learn how to be you
In time. It's easy
All you need is love, all you need is love."

Kate's mother wept.

The ladies sat at a big round table which Irish Kevin had cleared, shooing the patrons away, telling them it was time for them to go to Sloppy Joe's.

A tall man with a military style haircut, and dimples when he smiled, approached their table.

"May I buy you ladies a drink?" he inquired, smiling.

"You could if we were paying, but we're not, so thank you," Kate's mother replied.

"Well, at least allow me the honor of bringing the next round. Looks like you ladies are all drinking cosmos."

"I'll have a French martini!" Carla said. She waved her empty glass high.

The man walked to the bar and conversed with the lady bartender, using first names. He slid a fifty-dollar bill towards her. She took it.

Before he lifted the tray loaded with cosmopolitans and one French martini, he deftly poured clear liquid from a little vial, concealed in his palm, into the French martini.

"Enjoy, ladies!" he proclaimed. He set the tray on their table and distributed the drinks. Then the man retreated to the bar area and watched, chatting and laughing with the bartender.

"One more stop before we head back. Let's walk over to Captain Tony's," Danielle suggested.

As the ladies waved goodbye towards Irish Kevin and walked out onto Duval Street, the man with the dimples got up.

Carla glanced back in front of Sloppy Joe's and spotted the man following.

He winked at her.

"Oooh... hessh a cute one!" she slurred. She slowed her gait.

The man walked faster.

...and then she swooped in from the place where she had been watching, and was on the sidewalk, bumping into the man following Carla.

"Oh! Excuse me, sailor, beg your pardon. What's your name, good looking?"

The man took a step back and smiled his dimpled smile.

"Well hello, beautiful. Wayne's the name; how 'bout yours?

"Janet Sue. And I'm thirsty."

"You new in town?"

"I've been around, sailor."

The angel gently guided the serial rapist by the hand into Sloppy Joe's, and pushed him to a barstool. He sat down. She leaned into him, kissing him on the forehead.

One of the bartenders thought he saw little sparks of blue electricity arc silently from her lips.

Shivering convulsions twitched from the top of his head and traveled through his body to the ends of his toes. He gasped, and slumped a little against the bar, as urine appeared on the bar stool and dripped to the floor. The right side of his face drooped, and his left arm hung, useless.

She turned, walked out of Poor Joe's, using the Green Street exit, and faced left.

The ladies had stopped walking and turned around, watching Carla looking back at Sloppy Joe's. Colleen went back a few yards. "Let's skip Sloppy's tonight." And she guided Carla, rejoining the group. Kate stopped at the intersection when a homeless man sitting on the curb in the gentle rain falling from the dark sky held out a Bird of Paradise woven from bamboo.

She leaned over and kissed his wet head, and shoved a twenty-dollar bill into his filthy shirt pocket.

Built in 1851, the two story wooden structure appeared on their left, painted yellow. They hesitated and peered into the dimly illuminated smoke-filled room through the wide open doors, staring at the various undergarments stapled to the low ceiling, and the thousands of business cards.

"Truman Capote and JFK drank here, so did Hemingway when it was called Sloppy Joe's," Colleen Janson said. The ladies hesitated, looking at the crowded bar. "Jimmy Buffett started here, playing for tips!"

A wrinkled old man with a cigarette hanging from the left side of his mouth stood up from a bar stool and greeted them.

"Come on in...there is always room for beautiful ladies in my bar!"

"Captain Tony, meet the girls from Big Bay, here for a wedding," Colleen replied.

"Welcome ladies, drinks are on me tonight." And he led the ladies through the crowd.

"Thank you, Captain," Colleen said, kissing the old man on the cheek.

"Anytime for you," he replied, and he patted her on the butt twice before she grabbed his hand.

...and then she stood alongside the young blond bartender with a ponytail, in Captain Tony's Bar, watching the ladies from her unseen dimension as they celebrated life, and she protected them.

Richard Alan Hall

"I feel awful," Carla mentioned to Timothy the following morning, preparing to join the wedding party for breakfast at Blue Heaven.

"Little too much last night, honey?"

"I think so… can't remember a thing."

Chapter Fifty-Two
The Catholic Priest's Son

Marco González's father had been a Catholic priest at Our Lady of Assumption in Santiago de Cuba. In 1947 a shy petite nun from the convent next door gave birth to a baby boy. Father Gonzalez became a daddy on February 2nd.

In shame, the young couple took their baby son and moved to Havana. Both soon had work at the Partagas cigar factory. Six weeks later an Episcopal priest married them.

Marco found school quite boring. The schoolmaster and his teachers discussed the boy's behavior, the master contending Marco was a slow learner, and should be sent to a trade school. One teacher protested. She had recently graduated from Universidad de La Habana. She insisted her young student be tested. Her beautiful smile won the schoolmaster over, and Marco spent a weekend being tested in the school library, all alone except for the teacher.

Marco Gonzalez's IQ measured 148.

He was immediately promoted from the 7th grade to the 10th grade. He graduated from high school at age 13. He entered Universidad de La Habana and the study of Biology. Marco earned a Master's Degree at age 17. Then he entered Medical School.

He was working as an Emergency Room Physician in 1973 when his life changed forever.

He looked up while washing his hands. The entrance doors for the

Richard Alan Hall

Emergency Room had slammed open wide. Two men dressed in green fatigues burst through the doors with pistols in their hands, followed by two men supporting a man between them.

Fidel Castro's green shirt had a dark bloodstain on the left shoulder.

"Assassination attempt!" one of the men holding a weapon said.

Fidel looked up from the stretcher at the young Emergency Room physician.

"Are you good at this?" he asked.

"I am the best, and getting better, Mr. President."

"Good answer. Fix this, please."

Quickly and quietly Dr. Gonzalez and a nurse cut away the bloody shirt. The nurse bathed the wound with iodine as Marco injected Xylocaine. With slender long tipped forceps, the doctor probed the wound. He retrieved a small lead bullet. "Small caliber, probably a 22."

"Yes," said Fidel with a wincing smile from the stretcher. "I have a weakness for beautiful ladies, and this one shot me with a tiny pistol she had hidden in her purse." He paused. "Her father was Fulgencio Batista's Chief of Staff. She holds a grudge." And he laughed.

"This should completely heal in four to six weeks. Let us know if you develop fever or drainage, or if the pain worsens, Mr. President."

Fidel Castro sat up, and then stood up. Marco's head came to Castro's shoulder.

"You are now my personal physician," he said, looking down at Dr. González.

"I will take this up with your administrator next week. I am your only concern, Doctor. Is that acceptable with you?"

"Yes, sir, I am honored."

"Today never happened."

"I understand."

Now there he sat, in the front seat of a U.S. Secret Service Suburban. The President of Cuba was in Key West for a summit with the President of the United States.

* * *

A Black Chevrolet Suburban with tinted windows drove down Angela Street and stopped in the Duval Inn parking area outside the courtyard. Paul Hilson opened the driver's side passenger door, and climbed out.

Stanley and The Usual Suspects were standing next to the bar area under the giant rubber tree, drinking breakfast mojitos. Paul motioned towards Stanley to join him. They walked back to the Suburban and climbed in. It drove off in the direction of Truman Avenue.

"You didn't tell me that you're friends with Fidel Castro," Paul said.

"You never asked," Stanley replied. "Actually, I've only met him twice."

Paul shook his head.

"He's requested that you and his personal physician be his medical detail while he's in the U.S."

"What!?"

"He'll be here Monday for a summit meeting with the President and Secretary of State."

Stanley took a deep breath. "Oh." *He doesn't know he's here already.* "A summit meeting at Truman's White House?"

"The place is already crawling with Secret Service."

"I've seen them around town."

"This is Dr. Gonzalez," Paul said, nodding to the front seat. "He's Castro's personal physician."

Dr. Gonzalez twisted and reached his hand between the bucket seats.

Stanley and the doctor shook hands.

"President Castro insists you and I work together while he is in your country. His friend, and mine, Dr. Blue, spoke many praises about you over the years. President Castro will have it no other way, Mr. McMillen."

"I am honored and I accept, Doctor."

"Gracias. This will be a historic time. I have little details. They are going to discuss Guantanamo."

Paul smiled. "Good thing we planned the wedding when we did. The summit is scheduled to begin Monday. I was afraid they'd cancel everything and secure the grounds tomorrow, but the Chief of Staff said, 'Just go ahead, the Secret Service will work around the wedding.'" He shook his head again. "How do you know Castro?"

"Long story, Paul. You might ask Quinn O'Malley some time."

"Oh…say no more."

"We must keep this among ourselves," Dr. Gonzalez said.

"I need to tell Danielle," Stanley answered.

"Why?" asked Paul.

"She's my wife."

"I know that, Stanley. Why does she need to know now?"

"We have plans to vacation on Cayo Coco next week."

"Oh …got it. She going to be ok with this?"

"She'll be thrilled for me."

Doctor Gonzalez turned towards the back seat again. "Your wife and daughter will receive invitations to dine with the Cuban delegation."

"We'll find a sitter." Stanley laughed.

"President Castro loves little children. Chloe will be invited."

The doctor paused.

Stanley thought, *These guys don't miss a trick; he even knows Chloe's name.*

"We have been given the use of an ambulance--a traveling E.R; I will show you--that will never be further than one block from the President at all times. You and I are to be no further than one room away while he is at the summit."

"Twenty four hours a day?" Stanley asked.

"Yes, until he returns to Cuba."

"Well, for certain I better discuss this with my wife."

The doctor smiled.

"You and your family will not regret your service, amigo."

The Suburban stopped in front of the Duval Inn.

"See you at the rehearsal," Paul said.

"We will talk on Sunday," the doctor added.

* * *

"What was that about?" Ralph asked when Stanley walked past the pond into the courtyard.

"We were beginning to worry... a little," Wayne said.

"If I told you, they would kill me," Stanley said.

"He's probably not kidding," Quinn said, and then he laughed.

So did everyone at the bar.

Stanley sprinted up the stairs, hoping Danielle was in their room. He was too late.

The ladies had all left for the rehearsal.

Chapter Fifty-Three

At Last!

S aturday morning and the large wrought-iron Presidential gates at the intersection of Whitehead and Caroline Streets stood wide open with Marines in dress uniform standing at attention.

The men walked past the Marines and up the sidewalk towards the Little White House for the wedding.

"Last time I remember those gates open," Quinn said to Stanley, "was when Jimmy Carter visited."

Stanley shivered. Quivers and prickly tingles of excitement spread over his back and arms, all the way to his fingertips.

The ladies had arrived at the White House at nine-thirty. Colleen Janson had arranged for two master stylists to be there. Paul Hilson made available the upstairs dressing rooms in the Presidential Suites, and provided a brunch, including mimosas.

Angel Burke snapped picture after picture of the precious moments.

Miriam and Katherine stood on the balcony overlooking the east lawn, watching their guests arrive, waiting for the nail polish to dry.

"This is a fairytale day," Miriam said, looking down over the ledge.

Kate's eyes started to tear a little. "Damn!" she exclaimed. "I'm going to look a sight if my makeup runs."

Miriam hugged Kate very tightly.

"We're standing on the same balcony that Presidents and First Ladies have stood. This day is beyond my wildest teenage dreams," Kate continued. She dabbed at her eyes. "And our today will be as magnificent as any occasion ever held here, Miriam. Today, love is radiating from this old place like never before." And she dabbed at her eyes again.

Miriam hugged Kate again. "I love you."

Paul Hilson knocked on the door to the suite.

"Ladies…everyone decent?" he asked through the closed door.

Danielle opened the door with the retort, "Depends on your definition of decent, Paul."

Paul laughed and hesitated. "We have a special guest requesting a brief minute with you ladies. He would like to personally give his best wishes."

The seven ladies looked at each other.

"He apologizes that he is unable to climb the stairs. He's in the living room."

Miriam led the ladies down the narrow stairs and around the corner to the living room.

Fidel Castro stood up from the chair next to Truman's piano when the ladies entered.

Miriam stopped with a puzzled look in her sparkling eyes, and then extended her hand.

He spoke to her in Spanish for several minutes. And she answered in Spanish.

"I have enjoyed your recordings," Castro continued in English. "Someday you and your husband must visit Habana and share your amazing voice in the Grand Opera House."

Miriam blushed.

Fidel turned slightly and held his hand in Katherine's direction.

"I don't know Spanish," Kate said with a smile.

"Douglas told me of you last evening. I have never in all my travels met an Irish Catholic attorney, Methodist preacher with a black belt in karate. Douglas is a most fortunate man; he not only has met the angels, he is about to marry one."

Kate stood in the Key West White House living room, speechless, looking at the elderly bearded man with soft eyes.

"Thank you, Mr. President," she said softly.

He turned and faced Danielle and shook her hand "It is an honor to meet the wife of Stanley. Doctor Blue told me of you, and that you and your husband are the best nurses he has ever known. Stanley thinks you are a saint…smart husband."

President Castro approached Carla, and took her right hand with both his hands. They stood staring for several seconds before she said, "Timothy told me about how you helped him. He is alive now because of the meeting you hosted. Thank you, Mr. President."

Several more seconds passed before Castro spoke.

"We are all here to help each other. We meet at the appointed times. I am alive today because Timothy's friend O'Malley saved me in the 50's. O'Malley is Timothy's friend because Stanley and Danielle met the Captain in the bar. Today I meet the love of Timothy's life and the one who saved him…Timothy told me this, dear one…you saved him…and I am honored to meet you."

He turned and shook hands with Miriam's mother. "Gladys Munoz! Es un honor conocer a la madre de la novia." He smiled, and continued in English, "Your soon son-in-law is very proud of the work you do with charities in your country. He said this is a better world because you are here with us."

"Gracias, Senior Presidente," she answered.

He turned to Katherine McGinnis's mother, and extended his hand.

"I don't speak Spanish, either," she stated with a smile.

"You would learn quickly, Doctor. I hear of your wonderful work with the children in Boston. I will consider it a personal honor if sometime soon you come to Habana as a visiting professor and lecture to our medical students."

"Thank you very much."

"Your daughter is honeymooning in my country, you know."

Kate's mother shot a look at her daughter. "I did not, but then, why should that surprise me?" And she laughed. "I'll be honored to lecture in Havana."

Lastly, he approached Sabrina. "Your son is a reflection of you,

Sabrina Fife. He has your courage and loyalty. Like you, he dares to be honest. It is an honor to meet the mother of Timothy.

"I have taken too much time on your appointed day already," President Castro said, looking at the brides.

An aide handed him two envelopes.

The President of Cuba handed Miriam Pico and Katherine McGinnis each a small white envelope with a Presidential seal.

"You each have my best wishes for much happiness and much love in your lives."

He turned to leave and walked towards the side door. He stopped, looked back and said with a smile, "The summit is a good excuse to meet you on this special occasion. Thank you. Perhaps someday soon you will be my guests."

And he left.

The ladies looked at each other, bewildered.

"How did he know us?" Sabrina asked.

* * *

Stanley stood at the podium under the giant gumbo limbo tree on the east lawn of the Truman White House, and looked west. The twenty wooden folding chairs on either side of the grass aisle were occupied. Doug and his best man, Timothy, as well as Jim and his best man, stood to his left.

Carla and Danielle stood to his right.

Glancing up, Stanley watched four men wearing sunglasses, holding sniper rifles with silencers, taking positions at the four corners of the White House balcony.

David Chown played several songs on an electronic keyboard, watching for the brides to appear on the sidewalk.

Stanley smiled when he spotted, in the very back row to his left, a rare sight. There, together, sat Captain Quinn O'Malley, President Fidel Castro,

Richard Alan Hall

Vincent Bonifacio, Dr. Jack McCaferty, and his wife Kathy, and Dr. Lavern Smith with his wife, Mary. *That row has changed my life*, he thought. He reached into his jacket pocket, searching for the wedding notes.

And then they were present, bride-by-bride, side-by-side, arm in arm, walking down the sidewalk from the White House towards the grass aisle between the wooden chairs.

David Chown began to play *Fly Me to the Moon*.

Carla moved to the podium and took the mike from the stand.

She sang. Everyone stood.

> "Fly me to the moon
> Let me play among the stars
> Let me see what spring is like
> On Jupiter and Mars
> In other words, hold my hand
> In other words, baby, kiss me
> Fill my heart with song
> Let me sing for ever more
> You are all I long for
> All I worship and adore
> In other words, please be true
> In other words, in other words
> I love you."

Doug cried, watching his bride walk closer and closer. Timothy squeezed his hand and whispered, "You can do this, soldier."

Dr. James Roosevelt swallowed hard, especially after glancing at Doug. He could feel the pounding in his chest again.

For an instant, Doug thought he saw three ladies walking. From the second row, Wendell did see three. He smiled, watching Janet Sue ascending to the balcony. She sat on the railing next to one of the guards, her arms crossed. She winked down at him.

I'm not saying a word, he thought. *Wonder what the pictures will show*, he said to himself.

Jim took Miriam's hand. Doug's trembling hand squeezed Kate's.

Stanley took a deep breath and spoke.

Danielle stared at him confidently.

"There is not a more wonderful feeling on this earth than to hold the hand of the one you love, and to see the love dancing in the eyes of your lover saying, 'I am with you now and will be forever.' By its very nature, love is an unconditional commitment. The ancient Greeks had a specific word for this love, agape, which is an unconditional, self-sacrificing and thoughtful love. The novelist C.S. Lewis used agape in his writings as the highest level of love we are capable of achieving, a selfless love, a love that is committed to the well being of your lover. Paulo Coelho, in his book, *The Pilgrimage*, called agape 'the love that consumes the highest and purest form of love that surpasses all other types of affection.'

"A wonderful thing occurs when two people love each other in this selfless fashion, putting their partner first; they both end up number one in their special union... and that is a union which cannot be broken.

"Love is our most precious gift to give. It is a miracle really, and the only catalyst that when shared, will merge two souls into one.

"Miriam and James, Katherine and Douglas, it thrills our hearts that together you have found this love. May your lives as husband and wife be filled with much success and happiness... and much love.

"Miriam, do you take James to be your husband?"

"I do."

"James, do you take Miriam to be your wife?"

"I do."

"Katherine, do you take Douglas to be your husband?"

"I do."

"Doug, do you take Katherine as your wife"

"Sure do!"

James slipped a ring on Miriam's finger. She pushed a ring on his.

Doug slipped a simple gold band on Kate's ring finger. Kate placed a similar ring on his finger.

"We love you, guys. By the power vested to me by the state of Florida, I hereby pronounce you man and wife."

Stanley recited most of this from memory. The tears blurred the words on his folded pages.

Jim and Miriam kissed.

Doug and Katherine kissed.

"Ladies and gentlemen, I am delighted to present Dr. and Miriam Roosevelt, Douglass and Katherine Cronkite."

David Chown played Tupelo Honey. The four newlyweds walked towards the White House and the reception on the west lawn, followed by dinner in the Truman dining room.

Stanley glanced to the back row. President Castro, Vincent Bonifacio and Captain Quinn O'Malley were gone.

The west lawn, arrayed with yellow, pink, and red hibiscus bushes, bustled with the commotion and excitement of the reception. Wait staff circulated through the guests, offering a selection of delectable little treats. Two bartenders stood behind a portable bar, shaking adult beverages with enthusiasm.

David accompanied Carla while she sang love songs. Jonathon retrieved his trumpet and joined them.

A table situated between two park benches painted white displayed boxes of Bolivar and Montecristo cigars. The labels of origin were Habana, Cuba.

The festivities continued for several hours, people laughing, snacking, and sipping. Carla even tried a Bolivar cigar. After a few puffs, she handed it to Timothy with a pale grin. The newly wedded couples were driven to Mallory Square and the Southernmost Point for wedding photos.

Dinner began at seven p.m. in the Truman dining room. Dr.

Roosevelt and Doug insisted that Stanley sit at the head of the table, with Danielle at his right, and that he say a prayer before the meal.

"Lord, thank you for this glorious occasion of love shared among friends. Be with our newly married friends; guide them, direct them and hold them close to you throughout their lives."

Stanley lifted his head and looked directly at a picture on the wall over Danielle's head of President Harry S. Truman in the exact chair at the head of the table.

He shivered, and leaned close to Danielle.

"This is surreal."

"What this is…is perfect," she replied. "This couldn't be more perfect."

Dancing followed dinner in the Truman living room. David Chown smiled while he tickled the ivories on Harry Truman's personal piano. Carla stood next to the piano and sang.

Happy people in love hugged and danced until Paul Hilson turned the lights off at ten p.m.

Chapter Fifty-Four

A Puppet On A String

The French restaurant, Croissants de France, served Sunday morning brunch for the wedding party in the garden area at the Duval Inn.

"You guys are going to have a ball; just go with Quinn tomorrow like we originally planned. This summit hopefully will not take too long, and then Danielle and I will catch up," Stanley said.

"Any idea what it's about?" Timothy asked.

"Rumor has it they're negotiating the return of the Guantanamo Bay Naval Base."

"Not everybody is going to be fond of that," Timothy interjected.

"Not everybody is ever going to be in favor of everything," Quinn bantered.

"What?" Pete queried.

"It'll be nice to have our two countries separated by ninety miles of water back on friendly terms," Dr. McCaferty said, munching on a pastry. "Fidel is a friendly fellow."

"He's a communist," Wayne said with irritation.

Pete snickered, "Look at all us, all living at Poor Joe's, kinda like communists."

"That's a little deep for you," Chief Strait said with a grin.

"Way over your pay grade," Wendell added.

Quinn sighed. "I'll tell you a little about my friend on our trip tomorrow. Fidel is no different than any of us. Did what needed doing in order to survive, and sometimes, often in fact, to our regret. He is changed. Everyone here has changed from when we started. The Pope's visit to Cuba seemed to change him even faster."

"He did say, 'God bless you,' at El Siboney's Thursday night," Ralph commented.

"Wait until you hear why he did what he's done," Quinn said. He stood up. "I've gotta get back to the marina. See you tomorrow at 8 a.m....sharp!" And he winked at Danielle.

"I'll be back for you two Thursday."

* * *

The Key West Dreamer idled away from slip number 8 at eight thirty under a warm morning sun.

Captain O'Malley had purchased seven large Styrofoam cups of café con leche at the Cuban Coffee Queen. The ladies took their coffee below. The men carried the luggage down and stowed it, then rejoined Quinn in the pilothouse.

They rounded Tank Island and headed in the direction of Cayo Coco at twelve knots.

Dr. Roosevelt sipped at the hot Cuban brew. "What about Castro, Captain? You mentioned you'd tell us the rest of the story."

Quinn stared straight ahead.

"You'll not read this in a history book, Jim, but here is the truth. Castro asked the U.S. government for aide and assistance at the very beginning of the rebellion. Batista was a generally despised despot; did have the support of our government, and certainly the mafia."

Quinn took a sip of coffee.

"He asked for help and was rejected. Not to miss an opportunity, Nikita Khrushchev offered to finance the rebellion and supply weapons."

Quinn took another sip. "Fidel agreed. He told me after they were victorious, he felt like a puppet on strings."

"You believe him?"

"Jim, we were roommates for two years. We were classmates at the University of Havana."

Timothy and Doug smiled.

"What'd you study?"

"Law. We studied law, Jim. He's helped me several times over the years, and I've helped him. We have never tried to mislead each other. He's a good friend."

Timothy interrupted, "Jim, we were at a meeting a while back where Castro and Quinn presided; I can tell you from watching them together, they're friends."

"Oh," Jim exclaimed, "who are you guys...really?"

A soft pinging sound emitted from the navigation station. The sound became progressively louder, followed by an alarm bell ringing.

Quinn glanced at the screen and then to the starboard.

"What?" asked Doug.

"Is that a fish finder?" Jim asked.

"Sort of...sonar," Quinn answered. He pulled back on the throttles to eight knots.

One hundred yards to the Key West Dreamer's starboard, a periscope peaked through the surface and followed, looking at the boat.

Then the submarine surfaced.

Jim looked aghast. His complexion faded to pale. He had a sudden memory of sitting in the Bijou Theater with his parents and sister, watching *The Hunt for Red October*.

Doug and Timothy watched Quinn's face.

The captain reached into a drawer and retrieved a large handheld radio. He had a conversation in Spanish for several minutes, before putting the radio back in the drawer.

The submarine sank below the surface. The pinging sounds from the navigation station became softer and stopped seven minutes later.

"What was that about?" Dr. Roosevelt asked, still pale.

"Just some friends with a message. They dropped off a few Homeland

Security guys at Fort Jefferson on the Dry Tortugas."

"Why do we need Homeland Security at a Civil War fort?"

"Good question, Doctor."

Chapter Fifty-Five

I Love This Life

Stanley approached the third security checkpoint while walking towards the Key West Truman White House with a smile. He held out the lanyard draped around his neck, showing Cuban credentials provided by Dr. Gonzalez. Three Secret Service agents and a metal detector guarded the Front Street entrance.

"State your business," demanded the agent blocking the metal detector.

Two men wearing sunglasses stood on either side of the metal detector, holding submachine guns.

Stanley noticed armed agents spaced evenly around the perimeter fence line surrounding the building.

"Medical detail for President Castro," Stanley replied. *This should be interesting*, he thought, *watching the expression on the agent's face.*

The agent studied the lanyard, then Stanley's face.

"Where did you get this?"

"Dr. Gonzalez."

"Who?"

"President Castro's personal physician."

"Are you a Cuban citizen or an American citizen?"

"American."

"Let me see your driver's license."

The agent walked away while discussing something on a portable radio.

The two men with submachine guns stared at him without expression.

Stanley heard, "Yes sir, right away, sir," and the agent walked back to the entrance with a sort of smile. "Sorry for the inconvenience, sir. Doctor Gonzalez is waiting for you in Mr. Hilson's office."

While walking up the sidewalk, Stanley noticed two familiar figures standing on the balcony where Miriam and Katherine had stood Saturday afternoon. The President of the United States and the President of Cuba stood facing each other, talking earnestly.

President Castro spotted Stanley walking towards the White House, and waved, while commenting to the U.S. President, who turned and waved.

Stanley waved back as he walked into the white wooden building.

"Things are progressing quickly," the doctor said, greeting Stanley.

"How do you mean?"

"The under-secretaries worked out most of the details, our Presidents seem to enjoy each other's company, and there are no problems. They may sign the agreement this afternoon following lunch."

Doctor Gonzalez paused. "Just between us medical people, I saw the agreements last night when I took the President's blood pressure. He handed the papers to me and said, 'What do you think?' The agreement calls for normal trade relations, a return of Guantanamo Bay, free travel between our countries, and Cuba apologizes for the missile crisis. I told the President I believed it was about time."

"Wonderful," Stanley said.

"If the agreement is signed after lunch, President Castro will fly back to Habana today. The invitation for you and your family to join the Cuban delegation for dinner this evening still stands."

"We will be honored, Doctor."

"At the old Cuban Consulate on Eaton; you know the building?"

"I do. What time?"

"Nine."

The Five 6's pink taxi stopped at Eton and Grinnell. Stanley and Danielle, carrying Chloe, exited, walked up the steps unto the covered porch, and into the two story white wooden Consulate building.

A long rectangular dark oak dining room table had an elaborate sparkling chandelier suspended over it. Twelve chairs sat on either side of the table, except for one highchair.

Applause erupted when the American family entered the room.

The Cuban Vice President Council of State stood up.

"It is an honor to greet the first United States guests," she said, "to our newly reopened Consulate. We are honored that you can join us. President Castro extends his apologies; he has returned to Cuba. He hopes to see you again soon."

They were seated next to Dr. Gonzalez on one side, and the Vice President of State on the other, next to Chloe.

"I am a grandmother now," she said to Danielle. "I love being Abuela!"

This reminds me of sitting around the big table at Poor Joe's, Stanley thought, watching the laughter and celebrating. *I can't believe we're even here.*

"What a week, huh?" Stanley said to Danielle.

"Well, I certainly was right!" she replied.

"What're you talking about?"

"Remember that first time on the Key West Dreamer when we were both a little scared and I told you my life would be an adventure if I married you? I was right. You make my heart smile, honey. I love this life."

Stanley reached under the table and patted his wife's leg, and squeezed it once.

Dr. Gonzalez pushed his dinner plate aside and leaned forward so he could see Stanley and Danielle.

"We are presently constructing another Critical Care wing at Habana Hospital, and would be honored if you both help with planning and teaching. President Castro would very much like for you to join us."

Danielle leaned forward to look directly at the doctor.

"Stanley and I have discussed working in Cuba; it is an honor to be asked. We have a friend in our hometown who is recovering from a grave injury. He needs our help right now. When the time is right, we will join you."

Doctor Gonzalez smiled. "Fidel knows this," he replied.

He glanced at Stanley. "It is wonderful to make your acquaintance. I hope we do work together soon."

Looking over his glasses at Stanley, Danielle, and Chloe, who was climbing out of the highchair and onto the Vice President's lap, he said softly, "God bless you."

Stanley reached under the table and squeezed Danielle's leg again.

She winked at her lover.

Seldom As They Seem

Epilogue

"I never exactly made a book. It's rather like taking dictation. I was given things to say."

— C.S. Lewis

To be continued…

Richard Alan Hall
lives in Traverse City, Michigan
with his wife Debra Jean
and their three dogs: Basil, Hayden,
and a red haired hussy named Lucy.